The Rebel from Shepherd Mountain

Robert Bewell
8-27-02

The Rebel from Shepherd Mountain

Evault Boswell

Authors Choice Press

San Jose New York Lincoln Shanghai

The Rebel from Shepherd Mountain

Authors Choice Press
an imprint of iUniverse.com, Inc.

For information address:
iUniverse.com, Inc.
5220 S 16th, Ste. 200
Lincoln, NE 68512
www.iuniverse.com

ISBN: 0-595-13831-4

Printed in the United States of America

CHAPTER I

Summer was a special time in his life. The purple stain of blackberry juice on fingers pricked by the thorny bushes. Even his mother's admonishment to quit eating more berries than he put in his bucket.

Piles of corn on the cob, steaming as the pure churned butter melted over the golden kernels. Warm milk squeezed from the cow's udder directly into his open mouth.

And there were the picnics at nearby Elephant Rocks, a natural formation of granite boulders arranged on top of hill as though ancient god giants had been interrupted playing a game of marbles. Leaping from rock to rock was fun while the adults screamed at you to come down and the girls giggled at your daring.

The hay ride, stuffing the sticky itchy hay down the girl's back while they pretended to be upset.

Summer was the warm soil of the corn field oozing up through his toes, or the squish of the dark mud at the edge of the pond as he sank in up to his ankles. Or just laying on his back in the pasture and watching the clouds change shape as they floated over the canvas of blue.

One of the joys of summer was not wearing shoes except on Sunday and a trip to Ironton to buy a new pair was a sure sign that summer was almost over.

Aaron Bloom leaned on the hoe and looked down the dirt road that curled around the side of Shepherd Mountain toward his home.

Through the shimmering waves of heat he could see a distant pall of dust rising into the August afternoon.

He squinted into the sun and shaded his eyes with his hand to watch as riders crossed the ford of Stout Creek. They were hardly visible through the brown fog of dust from the road.

He could only tell that they were Union Blue and a ball of fear, or hate rose in his throat and stuck there.

So far, the Bloom family had been able to avoid involvement in the Civil War that was ripping the state, families, and friends apart.

It had not been easy for his Paw, for Willard always spoke his mind.

"Ah ain't never owned no slaves," he had said,"But that don't give a bunch of Yankee Dutchmen the right to tell me I can't if I want to."

But for the most part, the Bloom family had stayed secluded on their small farm in the foothills of the Ozarks and out of trouble, except that every Saturday Willard came home, his sun reddened face turned crimson after listening to the old geezers at the feed store arguing about the war.

They led a simple life, raising almost all of their own needs on the one-hundred and eighty acre farm in spite of the rocky soil.

There were wild persimmons, so sour when not ripe they made your tongue feel fuzzy, but juicy and sweet when they had reached maturity.

Aaron felt the fear boil up in the pit of his stomach as the riders, their saddles creaking, turned in the gate and headed up toward the house.

The leader was a fat, dumpy Sergeant who rode an old work horse, its back swayed under his weight until the toes of his dirty boots seemed to almost touch the ground. He had small eyes that peeked out from under enormously bushy eyebrows. His nose was flat and flared. Tobacco stained his ragged growth of beard.

The huge hooves of the horse stuck to the dust of the road before letting go reluctantly.

The Sergeant only glanced at the teenage boy standing in the potato field with a hoe in his hand as they rode up the hill toward the farmhouse.

Aaron saw his Maw come out on the porch, wiping her hands on her gingham apron, but he could not hear what was being said.

He knew the soldiers were from Camp Blood, located in the valley between Shepherd Mountain and Pilot Knob, or Bogey Mountain, as it was called by the locals.

Camp Blood was little more than a hole in the ground, an earthen works that offered little protection should an army decide to mount cannon on Shepherd Mountain and lob shells into it.

But it was all that stood between St. Louis and the Confederate army. Its real purpose was to protect the iron ore being taken from Pilot Knob, a six hundred foot high volcanic cone of sixty per cent pure iron, and to guard the end of the line of the Iron Mountain Railroad.

The fort had a small garrison of Federal troops, a large portion of them Dutch. Their drunken brawls in nearby Ironton and their raids on farms in the area to confiscate food and supplies and to steal horses from anyone who might be even vaguely connected with the Southern cause had everyone scared.

Aaron watched as most of the soldiers headed around to the barn.

His Paw came out of the house and stood beside his Maw. The Sergeant sat on the overloaded horse in the front yard.

Then Aaron saw his Paw go back into the house and in a few moments, come back again. He had the old sixteen gauge shotgun in his hands.

The fear in his stomach became a scream as he watched his Paw point the gun at the Sergeant. Still he stood frozen as he watched his Maw take his Paw by the arm and his Paw lowered the shotgun.

Aaron saw the flash and then the sound of the shot rang down the hillside and bounced off Shepherd Mountain.

It was as though the Sergeant's right hand had exploded. Aaron saw the puff of smoke hanging in the air as he watched his Paw crumple to the porch.

Then he heard the scream.

✳   ✳   ✳

Sam Hildebrand was a contented man. Living in his little log cabin on the bluffs of Big River, tending his crops, hunting and fishing whenever he wanted, and loving his wife, Margaret and their five children, was all he wanted out of life.

Of course, it was not always serene. His happiness had been interrupted on a number of occasions with squabbles with his neighbors.

It was the custom in the area of Big River Mills area of southeast Missouri to release the young shoats in the woods and let them fatten up on the profusion of acorns.

It was sometimes difficult to tell one pig from another and when it was butchering time in the fall the Hildebrand boys seemed to harvest more pigs than they had released, or so the neighbors said.

On several occasions, usually after a few snorts of "bursthead", the disagreements had become more ominous confrontations, including a few fist fights, and even landed Sam and his brother Frank in a law suit at the St. Francois county courthouse in Farmington.

Sam was a big man, well over six feet tall, with broad shoulders and a barrel chest. He and Frank usually won the fights that didn't take place in a courtroom.

And now their enemies had found a new excuse to get revenge on the Hildebrand family.

The nation was in the early stages of the Civil War and the Vigilantes, led by Firman McIlvaine, one of the Hildebrand's oldest foes in the pig wars, were using their assumed authority to chase down not only anyone who leaned toward the Southern cause, but those they just didn't like, which of course, included the Hildebrand boys.

Sam decided it was time to find out which side of this war he was on so he went to see Judge Franklin Murphy.

"I ain't never had no slaves," he told the Judge, " And I can't see fighting for something I never had."

Judge Murphy was a tall, thin old man with sharp features, sunken cheeks, and a predominant nose that ended in a point. He had been caught several times in the middle of the pig wars between the Hildebrands and the McIlvaines.

He reached up and scratched the bridge of his nose with his right forefinger before he answered Sam.

"Best thing for you to do, Sam," he said, "Is put in your crops, tend your pigs, and keep your mouth shut."

"That's what I want to do," said Sam, "But them vigilantes keep riding by my place, whooping and hollerin' like they's gonna make trouble."

The Judge scratched his nose again. "You just make sure that if there is trouble, you ain't the one that starts it."

Sam looked at the Judge for a moment and spat a brown stream into the dust.

"I ain't gonna start anything," he said, "But I promise you I'll be the one to finish it."

*   *   *

Aaron ran up the hill, his hands clasped around the hoe handle so tight his knuckles were white. Hot tears streamed down his cheeks and he could hear himself breathing, a rasping spasmodic sound that came from somewhere deep within him.

Before he had time to think about what he was going to do, he was in the yard, standing not more than ten feet from the Sergeant's horse.

The splash of red on his Paw's white shirt told him it was bad. His Maw was sobbing softly now as she cradled Willard's head in her lap. She swayed to and fro as his blood blended with the pattern in her apron.

Aaron turned to face the Sergeant.

"You kilt him!" he said, his voice coarse and hollow.

"Put down the hoe," the Sergeant said. The slightly built, bare footed, cotton-headed youngster seemed to pose little threat to him, but he didn't intend to take any chances.

The 1860 model army Colt revolver was still in his hand.

"You kilt Paw!" Aaron shouted, and this time his words were clear and rang with anger.

He lifted the hoe as high as he could and lunged toward the Sergeant. He swung it as hard as he could but the Sergeant fended it off with his left arm.

Aaron lifted it again to swing but the Sergeant caught the handle and with a sudden yank, pulled it toward him.

Aaron's head smashed into the edge of the saddle and for a moment, he was stunned.

He looked up to see the Colt coming down in a wide arc and tried to duck but the hammer of the gun caught him on the cheek just below the right eye and tore a gaping slash, almost to the chin.

For what seemed an eternity, Aaron hung to the pommel of the saddle and stared at the Sergeant. It was a face he would never forget. Then the world began to turn red.

Then it turned black.

He fell to the ground just in front of the work horse. The Sergeant reined back and the horse reared up just a little, then brought a massive hoof down on Aaron's left leg.

The sudden snap told everyone the leg was shattered and as Alma Bloom left her husband to run to the aid of her son, the soldiers rode back toward the road, carrying or leading all of the Bloom's live stock.

Alma took off her apron and tried to stem the flow of blood from her son's face.

Fear gripped her as she heard the wagon coming up the road.

CHAPTER 2

Sam Hildebrand had only gone to school for two days, where he learned two letters, one shaped like the gable end of a house, and the other like an ox yoke on end.

When his father, George, gave him a choice of working on the farm or going to school, it was an easy decision for Sam to make.

He was too fond of hunting and fishing to be cooped up all day in a classroom. His school would be the majestic bluffs that overlooked Big River.

Sometimes he would spend weeks up on those bluffs hunting, or down on the river bank fishing and just enjoying and learning all he could about nature. Living off the land, dining on persimmons and sipping sassafras tea, with freshly picked blue berries for dessert was a way of life he was born to live. Soon he became an expert woodsman, a talent he was to put to good use later.

His parents, George and Rebecca, had settled in St. Francois County in 1832 and in the fertile bottom land of the Big River, they raised their crops and ten children. Sam was the fifth born.

Digging up tree stumps by hand and hauling rocks was hard work for a young boy, but Sam had preferred it to school.

George's legacy to his family was the two story stone home he had built with the help of his sons. It was, beyond a doubt, the finest home in the Big River Mills area.

When Sam married Margaret, the daughter of a prominent businessman, he built their log cabin only a two hundred yards from the stone house.

In 1850, George Hildebrand passed away and the Hildebrand brothers continued to work the home place and raise their hogs.

But more Dutchmen had moved into the area and soon "fist and skull" fighting was a common way of settling wild hog claims.

And now night riders came in the darkness of midnight to curse the Hildebrand's. Flaming torches were tossed not only at the stone house George and his sons had built, but also at the log cabin Sam had built for his wife, Margaret, and his five children.

With Margaret and the young ones huddled in the rear of the cabin, Sam knelt below the front window, his rifle in hand.

Suddenly a stone smashed through the window and Sam could take no more. He only fired once over the heads of the Vigilantes, then immediately was forced to the floor by a volley of shots that plunked into the logs of the cabin.

"Cease firing!" he heard a voice that sounded like Firman McIlvaine holler, and then it was very quiet.

Again he heard McIlaine's voice. "We'll be back for you, Hildebrand, when your wife and children are not there for you to hide behind."

Sam fired a shot in the direction of the voice, but only heard the sound of hooves as the riders rode away.

He could hear the baby crying and Margaret's words of comfort and knew they were all right. Then he collapsed in the corner of the cabin.

"Frank and I will have to take to the woods," he said, "They won't bother you or Momma if the men folk ain't here."

Then in the darkness he felt the soft hand of his mate on his shoulder. With the baby in her arms, she sat beside him and shared his fear and sensed the heaving of his chest as the rage built inside him.

There in that dark corner, Sam made a decision that would change his life forever. He only knew one way to overcome fear, and that was to turn it into hate and revenge.

*   *   *

He had been a man waiting for a war. Working in the leather store, not getting along with his brothers, or even his own father, and living with the memory of what had happened in California, had become a very unsatisfactory lifestyle and Sam Grant was determined to change it. The bottle he had sought to comfort his inward pain had ceased to do so a long time ago.

Then came the Civil War. Grant, at the end of his ropes and finances, had left Julia and the four children in Galena and went to visit his father in Covington, Kentucky.

Crossing over to Cincinnati, he had gone to see his old friend from Mexico, General McClellan. As a matter of fact, he had gone to see him several times, but the diminutive dandy of a General had always seemed to be busy or away when Grant came to visit.

Finally, Governor Yates of Illinois appointed Sam Colonel of the 21st Illinois, a rowdy bunch of farm boys that Grant soon settled down and turned into soldiers.

In June of 1861, the 21st was ordered to Ironton, Missouri, with Grant in command. It was he knew, the redemption of his career.

He had been promoted to Brigadier General in early August, primarily because of the efforts of Elihu B. Washburne, who headed the Illinois congressional delegation. The fact that Sam's home town of Galena was in the Congressman's district, of course had helped.

But the newly appointed General was dressed in civilian clothes and a private's coat as he took the crumpled pieces of paper he had been given by his old friend in Ironton, John Emerson, from his pocket and studied them.

"What about these reports of our men killing innocent civilians?" he asked.

"There has been a lot of looting and taking of private property, but only from southern sympathizers," Emerson said.

"This report says a man was killed yesterday," said Grant, handing the piece of paper to Emerson.

Emerson glanced at but didn't have to read it. "Yes, there was a farmer up on Shepherd Mountain killed when he resisted some of our men."

"Was he a Confederate?" asked Grant.

"I do not know."

"Since you are a civilian," said Grant, "I would appreciate it if you would visit the family and see if they have any needs and see to it that those needs are met."

"All right, Sam," Emerson said, "But this could cause a lot of problems for you, for the men have been given a free rein to confiscate supplies and horses from the local citizens who seem to favor the South."

"As of right now," Grant stormed, "That practice will cease!" He turned to one of his junior officers. "See that it is done."

"Yes sir," the officer replied.

Sam chomped down on the butt of his unlit cigar. "Now let's get back to the real war and review these plans on how to defend Ironton from the thousands of Rebel soldiers under the command of General Hardee headed this way."

Emerson could feel the sarcasm in Grant's statement.

"Those plans are for the defense of Ironton, the railroad, and Camp Blood," said an officer, "Unless we stop the Rebels here, they could very well march on St. Louis."

"Hardee will need a defense plan before I do," said Grant as he ignored the officer and spoke to Emerson, "I plan to take the offensive."

"But three-quarters of your men have only been in camp and training for five days," argued Emerson, "How do you plan to make offensive moves against a large army?"

"For one thing," Grant said, "The army is not as large as has been reported. Sure, you got Hardee down near Greenville somewhere, but its that rascal Jeff Thompson that keeps running all over the country with his calvary that has fooled our scouts into believing there is a large army. All he's got is a bunch of irregulars and bushwhackers who ride fast and strike hard."

He paused and looked around at his officers. There was complete silence.

"Stop the swamp rats and southeast Missouri will be secure," he said, "Bring me a new plan for hunting down Thompson."

*   *   *

When Aaron woke up, he was in his bed. It was dark except for the flickering glow of the coal oil lamp creeping through the slightly ajar door to the kitchen.

He moved his head and the pain jammed him back into the pillow. He lay still, not daring to move again. Then the pain in his leg hit him.

"Yeh, it looks like he's gonna have an ugly scar, " he heard a voice in the kitchen say.

It was old Doc Hawn from Ironton.

"I set the leg as best I could," he continued, "But we'll just have to wait and see if he'll ever walk right agin."

"Thank you for doing the best you could," Alma said.

"Well, if old Henry hadn't heered that shot and come and got me, the boy mighta bled to death," said Doc, "Henry nearly kilt his mule driving that wagon to Ironton and back to fetch me."

"What about his face?" asked Aaron's Maw.

"It'll heal all right, but they's gonna be a scar, like I said," said Doc, "Caint be helped. But the jaw wasn't busted and he didn't lose no teeth. Just the skin tore something awful."

Even in his pain, it occurred to Aaron that he had never seen Doc Hawn sober. He hoped that this time was the exception.

In a few moments, Aaron heard the screen door close gently and footsteps going down the porch steps.

He lay quietly, trying to remember what had happened. Then he wished he hadn't.

The door opened about half way and from the corner of his eye, he saw his Maw come into the room. She came to the bed and touched his forehead softly, like she had done when he was sick.

Then she turned and stared through the lace curtains into the ebony night.

They were both silent for a very long time.

"Is he," Aaron started and then didn't finish. He couldn't bring himself to ask the question, but he had to know.

"Paw's dead, ain't he?"

His Maw buried her face in the curtain and wept.

When she had finished crying, she turned from the window and touched lightly the bandaged face of her teenage son.

"Someday I'll kill him," he said, "Some day I'll kill him."

✳   ✳   ✳

Two days later, Aaron heard a rapping on the screen door. He saw his Maw walk toward the door, wiping her hands on her apron as she had done the day his Paw was killed.

Fear for her rose up into his throat and in spite of the pain from his face and the broken leg, he pulled himself up in the bed and stained to listen.

"Mrs. Bloom?" he heard a voice ask.

"Yes," his Maw replied quietly.

"Mrs. Bloom, my name is John Emerson. I am a friend of the new commanding officer in Ironton, General Ulysses S. Grant, may I come in?"

"No you may not," Alma said, "Yankees are no longer welcome in this home."

"I understand how you must feel," began Emerson.

"No you don't," Aaron heard his Maw say, "You can never know how I feel and I must ask you to leave."

"I am not a soldier," pleaded Emerson, "And have only come to bring you General Grant's condolences and regrets."

"I do not want anything from this General…whatever his name is," said Alma.

"Very well, " said Emerson, "But perhaps you would like to know that your husband's death was not in vain, for Grant has rescinded the rights of Union soldiers to take personal property from civilians."

"I am sure my crippled and scarred teenage son will be glad to hear that," said Alma.

"He did hear it," said Aaron from the bedroom doorway.

Emerson looked at him in shock as Alma turned to see her son leaning against the door frame, the shotgun cradled in his arms, aimed at Emerson's midsection.

"And if you don't leave right now," he continued, "You will be the first Yankee I kill."

Emerson walked backward across the porch, turned and ran down the steps, and mounting his horse, was soon out of sight.

Alma hurried to help her son, who had collapsed on the floor, back into bed.

CHAPTER 3

Frank and Sam had not been too uncomfortable living in the woods for over two months. It was a life style they both knew and loved but being separated from their family was beginning to tell.

But then the blue norther had blown in and freezing temperatures had made life more than just a little uncomfortable.

Sam and Frank could not remember a winter when it had turned so cold so early.

"Ah can't stand it anymore," Sam said, more to himself than to Frank, "Ah'm going to the house."

Frank only grunted and tried once more to tuck the corners of his blanket in so the northwest wind could not penetrate.

It would have helped if they could build a fire, but with the foliage gone from the trees, even a little smoke could be seen from a distance.

Of course, Sam knew how to build a smokeless fire by using dry wood cut from the center of dead limbs, but even the smell of burning wood might give their hiding place away. There was not enough room in "Hildebrand cave" for the both of them and besides, with the frozen and slick ground, getting into the cave would have been a problem, for it hung over a hundred foot cliff with only a couple of footholds making entry possible. From the top of the bluff, the cave was invisible.

Sam picked up his rifle and started toward the house. He walked through the woods without making a sound. It was if he knew where every dead limb and rock was. He loved the woods, especially in the dark. Without even thinking about it, he moved among the trees to minimize being silhouetted in the soft moonlight.

He had heard no movement in the woods or on the road all day, but still he approached the cabin with caution. As he neared the clearing, he paused and surveyed the scene, scanning with his eyes in a semi-circle. He would have seen a single shadow that did not belong.

Only then did he step out of the woods and walk toward the house.

There was no light, but since he reckoned it must be about an hour before midnight, this did not concern him. Margaret would have the young ones tucked away, but she would not be asleep in anticipation of his coming.

Creeping up to the door, he whispered, "Margaret".

There were a few moments of silence and then he heard her shuffling across the floor and the door cracked open just enough for him to slip inside.

Margaret lit a small candle and began to prepare Sam a meal of corn pone, beans, and salt pork. Cold, of course, for they did not dare risk a fire since she told him the Vigilantes had been in the area all day.

Sam was not one to speak much and Margaret had learned not to ask too many questions. What little conversation they had was in whispers.

She had learned not to expect any overt showing of affection from her husband but never doubted his love and concern for her and the children.

Sam never ceased to be amazed at the strength of this woman he had married. Brave and gentle were words that came to his mind.

Margaret was almost a foot shorter than Sam, and her frame was robust, but not obese. Only in her twenties, she had already had five children and her auburn hair already had a few strands of grey, although she hid them by wearing her hair in a bun, and tucking the wayward ones inside.

Just as he was sitting down to eat, they heard a sound in the yard. Their eyes met as they both realized it was a top rail falling off the split-log fence.

Sam did not say a word, but picked up his rifle, stuffed a piece of corn pone in his coat pocket, and slipped silently to the door.

Stepping cautiously out into the dark, he was careful not to leave the shadows of the cabin. He took a moment for his eyes to adjust to the lack of light. Standing up against the side of the house he once again roamed his eyes over the clearing.

This time there were shadows that didn't belong, shadows of men moving across the field toward the cabin. Sam detected an opening in their line and made a dash for the woods.

The shouting of angry men and the crash of gun fire filled the night! Taking cover for a final run for the woods, Sam heard several bullets slam into his hiding place.

He squatted and pressed his body up against his cover for a few moments.

Then he felt a liquid oozing slowly down his forehead.

"I've been hit!" he said out loud as he put his hand to his forehead. It was sticky, very sticky. It didn't feel like blood. It didn't smell like blood.

He stuck his finger to his tongue and tasted.

It was molasses, very slow molasses.

*   *   *

Aaron wiggled his toes in the almost freezing water. He poked a finger through the hole in the bottom of his shoe.

It had been four days since he had started out in spite of the bitter cold, heading south, or at least he hoped he was going in that direction.

Leaving his Maw alone had not been easy, but it had to be done and he knew her brother Henry would see that she wanted for nothing.

It had been almost three months since his Paw was killed. Three months of pain as his mother tended to the wound on his face and his broken leg.

The wound had gotten infected and old Doc Hawn had very little to give a boy to ease the pain. If he had been a few years older, Doc would have shared his bottle with him.

But his Maw's cool hand and soothing voice had brought him through the sleepless nights when only exhaustion brought relief.

Many times he had awaken to find his Maw asleep beside his bed in the rocking chair.

The wound had finally healed, slowed by the infection, and the scar was ugly. Perhaps if Doc Hawn had been sober when he sewed it up.

His leg only hurt when he walked on it. But the pain was nothing compared to the embarrassment of the bad limp that made him feel like a cripple. "Well, I guess I am a cripple," he finally decided.

The scar would fade some, the pain would ease, and the limp was only slight, exaggerated in his mind. But the hate in his heart remained intense.

It had been after midnight when he had eased into his Maw's room and pinned the note to her pillow.

"Gone south to fight the Yankees," it had said, "I love you."

He had tried hard to think of something else to say, but decided she knew and it was just to difficult to put into works, especially on paper.

Slipping down the road that wrapped around Shepherd Mountain, he had crossed Stout Creek and left the road in order to avoid patrols from Camp Blood, whose name had been changed to Fort Davidson since his Paw was killed.

He had heard the Sergeant had been transferred but it did not matter, he would find him sooner or later. Word had also come to them that General Grant had been relieved of his position at Ironton and since his departure, the raiding of civilians had started up again.

The corn bread and dried meat he had packed for the trip had run out and now he sat on a sand bar on what he figured was the St. Francis River in southeast Missouri with an empty belly and a hole in his shoe.

In the distance he heard the rumble of heavy wagons, the hoof beats of many horses, and the occasional crack of rifle fire.

He pulled his shoes on, grabbed his bedroll, and scrambled up the embankment, hiding in the washed out roots of a huge oak tree that clung precariously to the side of the river bed.

The sounds grew to a crescendo as a cloud of dust and riders burst into sight down the road. They were followed by two heavy wagons pulled by the biggest horses Aaron had ever seen. There was a wild look on the faces of the horses as they were whipped fanatically by their drivers.

Aaron had never seen a Confederate uniform, but at least they weren't blue. As a matter of fact, each rider seemed to be dressed in a hodge-podge of clothing, hardly what you could call uniforms.

He stepped out into the open, feeling an excitement he had never known before.

A lanky rider on a magnificent stallion reined up in front of him. His face was almost hidden by his ragged, dust laden beard and handlebar moustache. His beady eyes flashed with excitement.

"Are you crazy, boy?" he hollered at Aaron, "You could get killed out here!"

He glanced back into the cloud of dust behind the wagons as though he saw something Aaron could not see.

"I came to join the Confederate army," Aaron shouted. It occurred to him as he spoke that perhaps this was not a good time to do so.

"I reckon you just did," the rider said, stretching out a long arm, "Come on up."

       ★   ★   ★

Sam laughed when he realized he had taken cover behind the molasses mill that stood in the yard. Even in the cold, the bullet hole had been large enough for the sweet liquid to seep out.

The men closing in on him stopped. Stalking a trapped Sam Hildebrand had made them nervous enough, but to hear him laugh as they neared his hiding place, was altogether unnerving.

Sam leaped to his feet firing once in the air and made a final run for the edge of the woods. He turned once and started to fire at his enemies, but realized the flash of his rifle would give away his position, and there were simply too many guns out there in the dark.

Once he had reached the tree line he paused, knowing that even the Vigilantes would be smarter than to follow a Hildebrand into the woods.

He lay in the dark, listening, and heard Firman McIlvaine's name called several times. He even thought he recognized the stocky leader of the mob and raised his rifle to fire, but decided against it.

Firman and Sam had been raised in the same community and though they had their differences, it seemed impossible that the young man was so intent on killing Sam.

He figured McIlvaine had been influenced by the members of the committee, who under the guise of protecting the families of Big River Mills, were only advancing their own greedy purposes.

How could Sam have known that the horse he had traded for with his cousin Allen Roan had been stolen from John Dunwoody, a member of the committee.

Sam didn't believe, as the Vigilantes contended, that Allen had killed Ming, either. But apparently being the cousin of an alleged horse thief and murderer was all the committee needed to hunt down the Hildebrand brothers. It was apparent to Sam that the committee was only interested in forcing people out of their homes so they could buy them cheap when they went on the auction block in Farmington when the taxes were not paid.

An ironic part of the episode was that the horse he got from Allen wouldn't work in harness, and Sam had traded it off the next day.

Soon the Vigilantes grew tired and left, but still Sam waited in his hiding place. When he was certain they had really left, he headed for a place in the woods only Margaret would know.

In a short time, she joined him with the children, all dressed and ready to travel. She returned to the house and in the darkness packed a mule with all the necessities she could and by early morning light, they met five miles from their home and spent the day.

When darkness came, they headed south.

CHAPTER 4

Frank Hildebrand had taken all he could stand. The Missouri winter of 1861 was unusually harsh. By the middle of November, he decided that to die by the hand of the Vigilantes would be better than freezing in the woods.

He had heard nothing of Sam since he left him almost a month ago. Frank knew that Sam was capable of taking care of himself and although he had heard shots the night Sam went to the house, he was certain that if something bad had happened, his mother would have sent little brother Henry to find him.

Making his way carefully into Big River Mills at night, he went directly to the home of Judge Franklin Murphy.

The Judge answered Frank's knock on the door himself. He had a flannel night shirt hanging on his lank frame, and carried a lantern.

"Frank Hildebrand!" he said as if he had never expected to see a Hildebrand brother again, "Come on in."

As Frank slipped in the partially opened door, the Judge glanced up and down the road and then gently closed the door.

In a few minutes, Frank learned of Sam's fight with the Vigilantes, but the Judge had not heard anything from him since.

"What should I do?" ask Frank.

The Judge scratched the bridge of his nose with his forefinger for a moment.

"I think the best thing you can do," he said, "Is to go to Potosi and join the home guards."

Frank stared at him in disbelief. "Join the Guard?"

"Look, the Judge continued, "You need to prove your loyalty to the Union. You already have one brother who has enlisted in the Federal army, and the Vigilantes would not dare attack one of their own. I will give you a note of recommendation to Captain Cassleman."

Sam and Frank had been very upset when older brother William had enlisted in the Union army, but since they did now know if they were Federalists or secessionist themselves, it had not split the family apart.

They had always respected and trusted the good Judge and Frank saw no reason to change that practice now. Besides, the alternatives were to go back to the woods or face the local Vigilantes.

The Judge gave Frank a cold supper, an extra blanket, and a place to sleep in the barn, but the Judge insisted he leave for Potosi, some fifteen miles away, before sunup.

By mid-morning, Frank was in Potosi, in Washington County, waiting for an audience with Cassleman.

As a matter of fact, he was kept waiting for several hours and was beginning to get a little nervous about the whole affair.

Suddenly the door burst open and Firman McIlvaine entered, along with several others of the Vigilantes from Big River Mills.

Frank jumped to his feet, but there was no exit not covered by the Vigilantes or Cassleman's men.

"In the name of the Committee and the United States of America," said Firman, " I arrest you for the stealing of Carney's mare and the abduction of Mrs. Carney, aiding your cousin in the murder of Ringer, abetting your brother in his escape from justice, and treason against the United States of America."

Frank looked around at the group. There was James Craig, John House, Joe McGahan, John Dunwoody, and William Patton. All the men the Hildebrands had met with fists or in court in the past.

Outside, his hands were tied behind his back and he was placed on a horse.

"Where are you taking me?" he asked.

"Back to Big River Mills," Firman said, "You are to be arraigned before Judge Murphy and made to pay for your crimes."

               ✶   ✶   ✶

Aaron partially jumped and crawled while the rider pulled and almost at once he was on the back of the stallion and again it was running at a gallop after the wagons, crossing the river at a ford just downstream.

The rider kept looking over his shoulder as they choked on the dust from the wagons. Aaron was holding on as best he could. At least he was glad the gunfire had stopped.

Still they kept up the pace for about thirty minutes, finally stopping at a pond to water the horses, who were covered with foam, but still prancing from the excitement of the chase.

A couple of riders headed slowly back down the road.

Aaron slipped from the horse and almost fell to the ground as he landed on his bad leg.

His new found companion dismounted and led the stallion to the pond. He pulled some dead grass and began to rub the horse down.

"General Jeff Thompson," he said, sticking his hand out to Aaron, "Confederate States of America. What's your name, boy?"

Aaron was still looking back down the road.

"Don't worry, boy," said Thompson, "They never chase us past the St. Francis. Too many rebs down here for the Feds to tangle with. Besides, we are about to enter Mingo Swamp, and they don't call me the Swamp Fox for nothing."

"My name's Aaron Bloom," said Aaron as he wondered if he was supposed to be in awe of the Swamp Fox.

He didn't know much about the army, but he had a feeling you didn't ride with a General when you had been a soldier for less than an hour.

"Those wagons are loaded with lead for rebel minie balls," Thompson said. "They almost got us for sure this time. Had to burn the bridge over the Big River near Potosi, but they found a ford and kept coming. That rascal down at Cairo, Grant, must have got wind of what we were doing."

"You've done this before?" asked Aaron.

"Several times, Thompson said, "But this time was close."

"Where are we going?" asked Aaron, who assumed that he was now a Confederate soldier who would be taken to headquarters somewhere to be sworn in and given a proper uniform.

"Greene County, Arkansas," Thompson answered, "Crowley's Ridge, to be exact. You'll find a lot of your fellow Missourians down there."

He looked closely at the boy and Aaron got that funny feeling he felt when someone saw his scar for the first time. But the General didn't ask any questions about that or his limp.

"How old are you, boy?"

"Nineteen," Aaron lied and knew at once that Thompson didn't believe him.

"Look more like sixteen," he said, "But it don't matter. The South needs everyone who can carry a weapon.

He turned as his two scouts returned and one of them tipped his hat. "Let's get headed south," Thompson yelled, "This lead will fill a lot of blue-bellies."

    *   *   *

At the name of Judge Franklin, Frank's hopes lifted a little. The Judge was known as a fair man and was not going to be forced by the mob to do something he did not see as just.

"How'd you know where I was?" asked Frank.

"Why that was simple," Firman grinned, "Captain Cassleman is a close personal friend of mine and he sent word to me as soon as you got to Potosi."

Frank's hopes faded as he pondered the fact that Judge Murphy had sent him to Cassleman. It seemed unlikely to him that the judge would not know of the friendship of McIlvaine and Cassleman.

By mid-afternoon, Frank stood once again before Justice of the Peace Franklin Murphy.

Firman had scribbled the charges against Frank on a piece of paper and read them to the Judge. Then he handed the paper to Murphy and stepped back to await the decision.

Judge Murphy scowled at the paper and scratched his forehead with one finger. He looked up finally at Frank. There was little compassion in his eyes, only fear, Frank concluded.

"I'm just a justice of the Peace," he said to Firman while his eyes continued to be riveted on Frank. "The only authority I have is to hold him over for trial, assuming these charges can be substantiated."

Firman's face reddened.

"The charges are true!" he snapped, "Just sign an order and we will take care of this horse thief and murderer in short order."

"I cannot in good conscience do that," the Judge said.

"Then, by god, we will find a judge who has the courage to do so," said Firman.

He motioned and a couple of Vigilantes grabbed Frank by the arms and forced him out the door.

"Let's take him to Justice Cole down at Ste. Genevieve County," said Firman, "He'll give this Hildebrand his due."

✷   ✷   ✷

Traveling only at night, Sam led his little family through the woods, with one hand on his rifle and one of the children on his hip. Margaret walked behind him, carrying the baby.

As the moon shone through the clouds, Sam was overwhelmed by the courage of Margaret. Her pale face glowed with an inner peace. Sam thought she even looked cheerful, and he thought he heard her titter once when he got tangled in a bush.

The second morning found them on Wolf Creek, a few miles south of Farmington. They stopped and cooked breakfast and feeling secure that no one had followed them, continued during the day to an area known as Flat Woods, about eight miles south of the little town of Farmington.

Sam rented a log cabin from a Mr. Griffin and when his family was safely housed, he left to return to Big River Mills, hopefully to bring more of their belongings back with him.

Again traveling under the cover of darkness, he arrived at his home at about dawn.

He immediately knew something was wrong as he surveyed the area from cover and noticed the front door of his cabin was hanging by one hinge.

He ran quickly across the open area and entered the house.

All of their things were gone, from what they had left of the cooking utensils in the fireplace, to the rest of their clothing.

Sam stomped around the empty room, cursing the Vigilantes in general and Firman McIlvaine in particular. He determined to head for town and kill as many of his enemies as he could.

But he knew such an attack would probably result in his own death, a possibility he was willing to accept, but then, there was Margaret and the children.

Reluctantly, he started back toward Flat Woods. The events of the past few weeks kept running through his mind. It was obvious the Vigilantes were determined to destroy him, but he couldn't really figure out why, unless it was all about them pigs.

He didn't have any slaves. He was a simple man who had not involved himself in politics or other people's business. All the wanted from life was to raise his family in peace, do a little hunting and fishing, and tend his farm.

It must be the pigs. The reports about the Hildebrands loving pork a little too much were common gossip in the county. But Sam considered himself to be an honest man and couldn't help it if out in the woods, all pigs pretty much looked alike.

Eating the wrong pig seemed hardly a reason to kill a man and run his family out of their home, anyway.

Maybe it was the war. But again, Sam had not spoken out for or against either side. And he had taken Judge Murphy's advice, putting in his crops and minding his own business.

All the way back south, Sam pondered on these things, trying to make sense of it all.

Margaret knew something was wrong when she saw his eyes, which normally showed what was inside the man, for Sam was not one to express emotions outwardly except on occasions when he was really riled.

"It's gone," he told her, waving his hands in a distraught manner, "It's all gone, they took everything."

Margaret stood silent for a few moments. His eyes told her that he blamed himself for their misfortune.

"We'll make do," she said and picked up a broom and began to sweep the dirt floor of the cabin, "We'll make do."

*   *   *

Before dusk they had crossed the county line to the small community of Punjaub and once again, Frank Hildebrand heard the charges against him read to R. M. Cole.

Cole, not being anxious to offend the mob or get involved in the business of another county, took a long time looking at the paper on which the charges were written.

He was a pompous little man to be such a small time politician. His balding head still clung to long stands of dirty grey hair that hung over his ears and down the nape of his neck.

His paunch was ample, especially since he was just over five feet tall and stood on tiny feet.

He had survived by not getting involved in other people's business and by scrounging what little graft he could out of the people of the county. He did not wish to cross Franklin Murphy, for he might need a favor from St. Francois County sometime.

He was also well aware of the Hildebrand boys reputation and decided he did not want to get involved with them, either.

"Why don't you take him to Judge Murphy?" he asked.

"We did," Firman said.

"And what did he say?"

"He claimed he did not have the authority to sentence horse thieves and murderers and would have to hold him over for trail."

Cole's eyes lit up.

"Well, gentlemen," he said, folding the piece of paper, "I'm just a humble Justice of the Peace myself and besides, this man's alleged crimes took place out of my jurisdiction. I'm afraid there is nothing I can do."

"Look," Firman pushed, "Frank was not only involved in the murder of Ringer in St. Francois County, but he and Sam Anderson went to the Carney farm at night intent on stealing a mare. They even took Mrs. Carney, against her will and in night clothes, all the way to the Beckett farm to look for the mare. I believe part of that farm is in Ste. Genevieve County. Is that not true?" His face was red again.

Cole frowned. "I really wish I could help, but there is nothing more I can do without more evidence."

"Sir, we intend to do this thing legally, but we do intend to obtain justice for this man's victims." Firman's voice had become high pitched and emotional.

"I'm sorry," said Cole, "But there is nothing I can do."

"Let's go men," said Firman, " I have evidence that he stole a mule in Jefferson County and we will take him to a judge up there who has the courage to enforce the law."

Frank had been before two judges and as they loaded him on the horse to begin the trip to Jefferson County and a third judge, it occurred to him that no one had inquired as to his innocence or guilt nor had he been given an opportunity to speak in his own behalf.

Then the cold fear settled into his bowels as he realized that these men intended to kill him, legally or illegally.

They had ridden about five miles from Punjaub when Firman held up his hand and called for a stop. There had been whispering among the Vigilantes during the ride.

Firman nodded and a rope was produced. A large oak tree stood beside the road and in a few moments, a thirteen loop noose had been fashioned and thrown over a lower limb.

No one spoke, but Frank's horse was led under the tree and the noose was placed around his neck and tightened against the side of his head.

When everything was in place, Firman did not hesitate, but slapped the horse on the rump and Frank dangled in space.

The man who had tied the noose had done a poor job, for the knot failed to break Frank's neck when it slammed against it.

Frank danced from the end of the rope, his body jerking spasmodically as he struggled for breath but in a few moments he hung motionless at the end of the rope.

The mob sat on their horse, just looking at him for a while

"Gonna be a fuss when folks hear about this," one said.

"Only fuss there's gonna be is folks treating us like heros," Firman said softly.

"What about his brother Sam?" asked another.

"I ain't afraid of Sam Hildebrand," Firman almost screamed, "Let him come and he'll get the same treatment."

Frank's body moved slightly in the breeze, turning in a silent dance of death.

"Cut him down and carry him back to that sink hole we passed a while ago," said Firman, "He's about to disappear and no one will know what happened if we all keep our mouths shut."

It was the twentieth of November, 1861, when Frank's body was dropped into the thirty foot deep sink hole.

On the twenty-first, Firman McIlvaine was back at Big River Mills, bragging about how he had run off one Hildebrand and given the order to hang another.

CHAPTER 5

The driver's seat of one of the two huge wagons was a lot more comfortable than riding double on the General's horse. As they headed south, Aaron thought of his Maw and wished he was home.

General Thompson rode along side of the wagon and for the first time, Aaron took a good look at his new commander. He was tall and muscular, with a full beard and a handlebar mustache that turned down at the ends instead of up. He had small eyes, and once when he took his felt hat with the black feather stuck in the band off to wipe the sweat from his brow, Aaron could see that he had a high forehead.

The wagon driver noticed that Aaron was looking at Thompson.

"He used to be the mayor of St. Joe," he said as he spit a stream of tobacco juice that just missed Aaron, "Gave up a pretty soft life to fight for the Confederacy, Now he's known as the Swamp Fox and we are all Swamp Rats". He laughed and the almost black juice ran down his chin. He wiped it off with his sleeve.

Merriwether Jefferson Thompson had indeed sacrificed to fight for the South. But he had always longed to be a soldier and after being turned down by West Point and the Lexington Military Academy, he worked as a clerk, fur trapper, railroad surveyor, organized a gas company, and dabbled in real estate.

"We ain't sure if he's a real General or not," the driver continued, " But they ain't nobody askin'."

Crowley's Ridge turned out to be less than Aaron had hoped for. The country was almost flat as you approached from the north but you could see a low rise of ridge on the horizon through the blue haze.

Aaron already missed the Ozark foothills.

The camp, or town, or whatever you called it, was a totally disorganized clutter of log cabins, shacks, and even some tents.

He could see women hanging out wash while clusters of men stood or squatted around campfires.

A cheer went up as they saw General Thompson and the wagons. Several men ran to meet them, waving their hats and shouting.

Aaron got lost in the excitement. He took his bed roll from the wagon and began walking down what passed for a street between the shacks and tents.

"Just get into camp?" someone asked.

Aaron turned to face a gentle looking man who wore funny little glasses that sat out on the end of his nose. A corncob pipe was in his hand, and he took a long draw on it.

"Yes sir," Aaron answered.

"When's the last time you et?"

"I had some beef jerky the wagon driver gave me", Aaron said, "But I sure don't know where my next meal is comin' from."

"Well, I do," the stranger said, "Come on in and I'll ask Anna to fix up some grub. What part of Missouri you from?"

"Our farm is up against Shepherd Mountain," Aaron said,

" Not far from Ironton."

"I know the area well," the man said as he put his hand on Aaron's shoulder and guided him toward a small log cabin. "Me and Anna lived in Sedalia all our lives before the war. My name is William Lemley, but folks just call me Bill."

They stepped into the semi-darkness of the cabin. The floor was dirt and although mud had been chinked in the cracks between the logs, you could still see daylight in spots.

A coal oil lamp hung from the low ceiling, but gave off very little light. The cabin had the smell of burnt wood, mixed with the pungent odor of the coal oil lamp, but there was also the lingering odor of home cooked food.

Aaron could hardly see a thing for a few minutes but as his eyes grew accustomed to the dark, he realized there were other people in the room.

"This is my wife, Anna," Bill Lemley said, "And over here is our daughter, Mary Lee."

Aaron stuttered a hello to Anna but stared at Mary Lee until it became embarrassing. He had always had a hard time talking to girls and this was the prettiest one he had ever seen.

Her raven black hair surrounded her face in curls. Her dark eyes were big and round and flashed when she smiled and said "Hello."

"Howdy," Aaron managed to say after taking a deep breath. Then he realized he must sound like a country hick.

"I'll get some vittles on," said Anna, "You come and help, Mary Lee, whilst the men talk."

*   *   *

If it had not been for worrying about his family, the quietness of his home on Wolf Creek in south St. Francois County would have been pleasant. It has been a harsh Missouri winter, with snow deeper than normal and the northwest wind drifted the snow over the split-rail fence that surrounded their little cabin in Flat Woods.

There were times when Sam could even enjoy his family, playing with the children and sitting quietly as Margaret read to them as they huddled around the fireplace in the evening for warmth. Sam wished that he had learned to read and write, but it was too late now.

He could read the woods. He knew the tracks and dropping of every critter in the forest, and could tell how long it had been since they passed. His ears were attune to nature, sensing danger, or the lack of it, from the birds.

Not only the animals were his allies, but the trees and fauna of the woodlands spoke to him, whispering with their leaves a song of compassion for this man who loved them.

Every root, every plant was a source of food, shelter, or medicine to him. Sam did not think of living in the woods as survival, but as a way of life to be savored.

And that is why the cabin confined him. He could relax for moments and help Margaret heat the stones on the hearth to wrap in blankets and place on the children's feet at bedtime. He could feel at peace for a short time when he and Margaret crawled between the comforts, ragged though they may be, and embrace in silence in the early hours of the evening.

But soon Sam would be up, sitting in front of the dying embers in the fireplace, staring into the smoldering ashes as he boiled inside with hate.

It was April of 1862 when Sam borrowed the old single blade plow from Mr. Griffin, hitched his emaciated horse to it, and began to break ground for a garden.

There was still the danger of a late spring freeze, but Sam and Margaret both needed the activity, and the children's diet during the cold winter of mostly parched corn, hickory nuts, and soup made from a cache of potatoes and cabbage the last tenant of the little cabin had made, expecting to be there themselves in the winter. Mr. Griffin had told Sam where to look for them, but Sam had already seen the signs where a shallow circular trench had been dug on a sloping plot of ground. The small drainage ditch for the surface water was a dead giveaway. Placed in the trench were the cabbages roots covered by the head of one another.

The potatoes, Sam knew, would be deeper, about a foot or two below the frost line, packed in straw, covered with dirt, and topped with a piece of tin.

But the warmth of spring brought a hunger for fresh vegetables to go with the abundant supply of rabbits and squirrels Sam could shoot in the woods.

After plowing up the plot, Sam returned to the cabin with an armload of firewood for the yet chilly nights and of course, for cooking. He had just laid the wood down and dipped a drink from the water bucket when he heard the sound of galloping horses, shots, and angry voices.

He pulled Margaret's dish towel curtain aside and looked out to see a large group of Federal blue troops, charging toward the cabin, already within rifle range.

"They found us," he said softly to Margaret. Their eyes met in an embrace and Margaret began stuffing children under beds. Sam grabbed his rifle, and ran out the door. He knew getting as far away as possible from his family was the best thing he could do for them, that even the Dutch Yankees would not harm a mother with her children.

He ran through his newly plowed garden plot and hurdled the split-rail fence as the bullets began to whiz by him and kick up dirt at his feet.

The firing was intense, but the mounted soldiers had to stop and tear down the fence to continue the chase.

He had just reached the edge of the woods, only a few feet from cover and safety, when the ball slammed into his leg, just below the knee. Sam knew at once that the bone had been broken, but he clung to the brush and hopped on one leg deeper into the woods.

He went directly to a shallow gully he had noted on his hunting expeditions, crawled into it and pulled dead leaves over him, making certain that he left no unnatural looking movement of the leaves, his face being the last thing to disappear in the shallow ditch that could be his grave. The pain in his leg was tremendous but he could not utter a sound, not even a groan.

The Federals stopped just short of his hiding place and crept forward. Even this far south, they had heard of the Hildebrand cunningness in the woods and moved with extreme caution.

"He's got to be around here close," he heard one say.

"I know I hit him," said a young excited voice, "But he didn't go down."

They searched for a brief time and walked around Sam's hiding place. One even jumped over the gully. Perhaps their search was abbreviated because of Sam's reputation, or perhaps they had another agenda, but the woods soon became very quiet.

Sam lay still until he was certain that they were gone, his ears attune to the forest sounds, or the lack thereof.

Finally he poked his head out of his hiding place and with as little movement as possible, surveyed the area.

His nose told him something was wrong before his eyes focused through the trees where the cabin and his family were.

It was on fire!

In that gully, his leg shattered, his family standing outside the burning cabin while the soldiers in blue stayed to be sure nothing was taken out, Sam Hildebrand declared war on the United States of America.

It was all he could do to constrain himself, rise from his grave, and at least end the life of one or two of his tormentors. But a larger plan was brewing in Sam's mind.

"Have I the mark of Cain?" he asked himself, "That the hands of men should be turned against me?"

Sam declared aloud to an unhearing and uncaring god that he was, for the sake of revenge, a Rebel.

CHAPTER 6

Aaron could not decide which was more pleasant, the aroma of the salt pork sizzling in the skillet, or stealing glances of Mary Lee as she and her mother prepared the meal.

Aaron thought about his Maw and for a second didn't hear when Bill asked him a question.

"I said, how old are you, son," he asked.

Aaron withdrew his attention from the blackened pots on the hearth and the lovely black hair of Mary Lee.

"Sixteen," he said, "But I told General Thompson I was nineteen." For some reason, he found he could not lie to Mr. Lemley.

"Why did you leave your home?" Bill asked.

Aaron began to tell his story, but when he got to the part about his Paw being killed, he choked and could not speak for several minutes. Bill Lemley just waited, while Mrs. Lemley and Mary Lee pretended to be busy with the pots.

When he regained his composure, he continued with the story and when he came to his vow of vengeance, his voice rose and was clear.

Bill Lemley recoiled from the obvious hate that exploded from the lips of this teenager with the disfigured face and gimpy leg. The sounds from the hearth ceased as the women stood stunned by the outburst.

Aaron sunk back into his chair, his chest heaving and his reddened cheeks tear stained. He felt no embarrassment, however, for his tirade had come from the hate in his heart.

Bill sat silently, pulling gently on his pipe, which had gone out. When Aaron's rage had calmed, Bill leaned forward.

"Everybody down here has a story similar to yours," he said, "This war has got us all hating each other." His voice got low and Aaron could hardly hear him. "Sometimes within our own families."

Soon Anna and Mary Lee were serving up heaping tin plates with boiled new potatoes, poke salad, and a slab of salt pork, Aaron bit into a slice of hot bread and for a few moments he even forgot how pretty Mary Lee was.

"I'm sorry about the tin plates, " Anna said, "In Sedalia we had real china and tableware.

Aaron was still chewing on the bread when Bill reached out and took him by the hand.

"Let's ask the Lord to bless the food," he said.

They joined hands around the small table. Mary Lee was on the opposite side from Aaron and he was glad, for he did not think he could stand to hold her hand just now.

"Lord," Bill prayed, "We thank thee for your many blessings and for keeping us safe in this troubled time. We ask you to watch over our friends and relatives back in Missouri, even those who seem to hate so much. We thank you for this new found friend, Aaron, and ask you to protect him in the days ahead. Now, Lord we ask you to bless this food of which we are about to partake, amen."

Anna and Mary Lee said amen too, and Aaron felt a rush of embarrassment for having eaten some bread before they had prayed. His Maw would not be proud of that.

But embarrassment soon turned into enjoyment as he dug into the first decent meal he had eaten since leaving home. By the time Anna sat a bowl of hot apple cobbler, dipped from a cast iron Dutch oven in front of him, Aaron decided he was going to enjoy being a Rebel if they ate like this all the time.

Aaron sat in the Lemley home after supper while Bill puffed on his pipe and talked of Sedalia before the war. They had a small, but comfortable home and were very active in the Methodist Church. Bill had his own business, making harnesses and traces, and on occasion, some very decorative saddles.

"The saddles were more like a hobby," he told Aaron. "You could work for a month on one and hardly get your money back for it."

He talked about the troubles that came long before the war started, as even the members of their church were divided about the slavery issue.

"Even members of my own family…" he started but never finished and Aaron didn't ask.

Aaron suddenly realized he had no place to sleep that night and as though he could read his mind Bill said, "Reckon you can sleep out back in the wood shed tonight." Aaron thanked Anna for the meal, muttered a goodnight to Mary Lee, and stepped out into the darkness of the Arkansas night.

The shed wasn't much. Just a lean-to on the back of the cabin and not high enough to stand up straight in. Aaron moved a few sticks of fire wood and finally settled down in the blanket Anna had given him, but sleep did not come easily.

As he had done so many nights before, the scene of his Paw's death rattled around in his mind. The face of the Federal Sergeant chased him into the depths of the blanket.

"You killed Paw!" he screamed, sitting up suddenly and banging his head on the beam of the low roofed shed. He was sweating profusely and could only hope he hadn't disturbed the Lemleys.

Morning came only after an eternity of tossing, turning and even some tears. The chill of dawn crept through the cracks of the shed and he pulled the blanket tight around him. He lay quietly in the grayness of the day, trying to remember where he was. Then he remembered Mary Lee and Anna's cobbler.

Dust flew from the ceiling as Bill Lemley banged on the door to the shed. "Come on in for breakfast," he said, "And bring an armload of firewood with you."

Aaron slowly opened the door and the early morning dampness caressed him and sent a chill up his back. He tried as best he could to plaster down his unruly mop of hair. His mother would be angry if she could see it.

He stumbled around and picked up several sticks of firewood and hurried to the front of the cabin.

Inside the smell of bacon frying filled the air, crowding the memory of the cobbler from his mind. Mary Lee knelt before the fireplace and looked up from the crackling bacon she was frying and smiled at him.

He could only imagine what he looked like, and worst yet, what he smelled like. His clothes had not been off his back since he left home except once when he had stripped and tried to bath in the chilly waters of the St. Francis River.

"I 'spect you better get down and see the old Swamp Fox this morning," Bill said, "Since he's the one who brought you to camp and he will probably leave soon to go to his headquarters up in the swamp."

"Yessir," said Aaron, as Anna handed him a plate of bacon, fried eggs with soft yokes, and a sourdough biscuit.

He ate the food slowly, looking up to catch a glimpse of Mary Lee and then dropping his head quickly as their eyes met.

Was she always smiling?

There still was no sun as he stepped out of the cabin and followed the trail Bill had told him to take to find the General's cabin.

"What chew want, boy?" the man squatting by the door asked.

He was getting tired of being called boy. "I want to see the General," he said.

"Yeh?" the soldier said, leaning over and spitting out a stream of tobacco juice that just missed Aaron's foot. "What makes you think the old Swamp Fox wants to see you?"

"Well, he brought me to camp," Aaron answered, "And I'd like to find out what he wants me to do."

"I want you to come in," a voice from the doorway said.

The soldier jumped to his feet and brushed off the seat of his pants.

"Come on in, boy," General Thompson said, perhaps a little annoyed, Aaron thought.

The cabin was clean and still smelled of breakfast and stale tobacco. In the center of the room was a small table and two chairs.

"Sit down," Thompson said, motioning toward one of the chairs. He lifted a blackened coffee pot from the pot-bellied stove and poured a tin cup full. "You want some coffee, boy?"

"No sir," said Aaron.

"I understand you stayed with the Lemley's last night." It was a statement, not a question, and Aaron suspected the General knew just about everything that went on at Crowley's Ridge.

"Yessir."

"About a half mile behind their cabin is a small hut you can use. Consider any belongings you find in it your own, for the man who lived there will not be needing them again."

"Yessir."

The General took a small piece of paper from the table and began writing on it. "Take this note to Captain Bolin. The soldier outside will take you to him."

"Yessir."

"You are now a private in the Confederate Army," Thompson said, "Bushwhacker Division."

"Yessir", Aaron said as he took the note and headed for the door.

When he stepped outside, the soldier said, "Come on, boy, I'll take you to Bolin."

Aaron wondered if he had been listening in.

They walked in silence through the woods until they came to a clearing that held a number of small shanties and tents. The wood smoke hung heavy over the camp. There seemed to be only men about. Several of them were washing clothes in a huge kettle over an open fire.

They turned to look at him as he passed. Aaron heard someone curse softly.

The soldier knocked gently on the post outside one of the larger tents. "Got a new recruit for you, Captain," he said, pulling the tent flap back and motioning for Aaron to go in.

Captain Bolin sat on the edge of a cot pulling his boots on. Aaron waited in silence until finally the officer spoke.

"You got a gun, boy?" Bolin asked.

"Nosir."

"You got a horse, boy?"

"Nosir."

"How you expect to be a soldier without a gun or a horse?"

"I don't know, sir."

"I'm gittin' tired of hearing you say sir," Bolin tamped his foot into the second boot and looked directly at Aaron.

"Well, sir," Aaron said, "I'm getting tired of being called boy."

Bolin chuckled. "Reckon you'll do. I'll have Corporal Haile get you a weapon and a horse. We ride north at daybreak tomorrow."

*   *   *

When Margaret was certain the soldiers had left, she went into the woods to search for Sam. She had seen him get hit and knew he could not have gotten far. She also knew that no city soldier boy could find Sam in the woods if he did not want to be found.

Soon she located him, still in the gully.

"Go on back and take care of the children," Sam said, "I ain't hurt bad."

Realizing that she could not move him alone, Margaret went in search of help and found a neighbor, Jesse Pigg, who came and helped her move Sam to his home, where they tended the wound.

Jesse Pigg straddled Sam's leg to hold it down.

"This is gonna hurt a mite," he said, "Do you want a shot of burst-head?"

Sam nodded no and the only sound he made when the hot iron touched his flesh and the smoke rose was a slight sucking noise. Pigg put a splint of sorts on the leg.

"The ball musta hit right on the bone," he said, "Should heal nice and straight, ifen you stay off it awhile."

For two weeks, the Hildebrand clan stayed at the Pigg home, and since Jesse's wife was gone and his children had left home, there was plenty of room and he was certainly enjoying Margaret's cooking.

"Captain Bolin is in the area on a recruiting trip," he told Sam one day. "And through the Knights of the Golden Circle, I have sent word to him that you need help."

The next day, an officer in butternut uniform arrived at the Pigg home after dark.

"Captain Bolin of the Confederate army has sent me to check on you," he told Sam, "Tell me what happened."

With Margaret at his bedside, and her calloused hand clutched in his giant fist, Sam told the story, right from being driven from their home at Big River, to the fire, and to his declaration of war on the Union. His big hand squeezed Margaret's so hard she felt pain, but didn't flinch.

When he finished, the soldier asked Sam many questions, so many that Sam began to get a little irritated.

Finally the man rose. "All right, rest easy," he said, and started to walk out of the room. "Mr. Hildebrand, I am sorry to be the one to have to tell you, but Mr. Pigg has informed me you have not heard that your brother Frank was hung by the Vigilantes last November and his body thrown in a sink hole in Ste. Genevieve County. You have my sympathies."

He put on his hat and left the room.

Sam was so taken aback that he could not speak at first. Then he looked at Margaret in astonishment.

"What does he mean, rest easy?" he said, "We ain't got no home or clothing or food. Our children are suffering and if we stay here, the Federals may return and burn the Pigg home, too. And now he tells me Frank, a dear boy who never harmed a soul, has been murdered!"

It was about as many words as Margaret had ever heard Sam speak at one time. He rarely showed emotion, but now his head fell against her breasts and he sobbed for a long time.

"It'll work out, Sam," she said through her own tears.

The next night a detachment of Bolin's men arrived with a springboard wagon. There were hurried goodbyes as Sam hugged each of the five children. They told him his family would be taken to a save place in Bloomfield in southeast Missouri until he could join them again.

Once again he looked into the eyes of his mate, wondering if he would ever see her and the children again, for he knew inside that it was kill or be killed now.

The wagon, besides Sam, was loaded with medical supplies.

Jesse Pigg came to the side of the wagon just before they pulled out. Sam tried to thank him for his kindness, but couldn't speak.

"It was George Conecious that told them where you were," Jesse said.

A pain ran down Sam's leg as the wagon started. He lay flat on his back, looked up at the stars and vowed not to forget that name.

He thought of his mother and the grief she must be suffering with one of her sons dead and another she knew not where.

＊＊＊＊＊＊

It was not a pleasant trip for Sam. The jolting of the springboard wagon over the narrow road and through the woods had not been easy on his still healing leg.

There was also the constant reminder that he was separated from his wife and children and might never see them again. And if that wasn't enough, the death of his innocent brother cried out for vengeance from the sink hole on the Ste. Genevieve plank road.

Traveling down the western side of the St. Francis River, the little caravan pitched camp near the Madison County line and prepared breakfast. With the wagon still, Sam dosed off, but was awakened by the sound of riders coming into camp.

Beneath the canvas wagon cover, he wrapped his hands around his rifle, loosened the old navy Colt pistol that stuck in his belt, and listened.

"Well, boys," one of the riders said to the wagon driver, "What have you in the wagon?"

"Drugs and medicines for Captain Bolin's camp," was the reply.

The riders dismounted and after pouring themselves a cup of coffee, squatted around the fire and began a lively conversation. One fellow could be heard above the rest, a jovial young man, judging from his voice, who soon had the others laughing, although as near as Sam could tell, he had not said anything really funny. Or perhaps Sam was just not in the mood for humor.

He peeked through a hole in the side of the wagon, but the young man heard the noise of Sam's movement and sprang to his feet, his hand on one of his pistols.

"Who in thunderation have you in the wagon?"

The wagon driver spat on the fire. "Some fellow from St. Francois County, wounded and driven out of his home by the Federals."

"The devil you say, that's my home county, let's have a look at him."

He came to the wagon and carefully peeked in, only to have his nose meet the barrel of Sam's pistol. For a moment he froze, then smiled a broad grin.

"As I live and breath," he almost shouted, "If it ain't old Sam Hildebrand hisself. How are you doing, you old rapscallion?"

"Not too well, Tom," said Sam as he pulled himself up to a sitting position and carefully released the hammer on the pistol, "And what is Tom Haile, the dare devil of the woods, doing down here?"

"Well, I ain't trying to pass myself off as medicine roots, like some folks I know," and he laughed and turned toward the others to be sure they had heard him. "Did you bring any good horses with you Sam?"

Obviously Haile was referring to the Roan episode, but Sam failed to see any humor in it.

"Well, we got to get some horses by hook or crook for the Swamp rats to ride, and I imagine it will be by crook, for those blue bellies have seemed reluctant to give them to us."

Haile stepped into the stirrup of his horse and swung into the saddle.

"If you are on your way to join up with Thompson, you might as well meet some of your fellow rebs," he said to Sam. "The ugly one on the roan is John Burlap, that tall skinny one over there is James Cato, and the kid on the work horse is a new recruit, Aaron Bloom, from over in Iron County."

Sam tipped his hat to all three and they nodded in recognition.

Aaron looked at the bulky man closely. They was a sparkle in his eyes that belied his circumstances. Perhaps fire would be a better word for it, but Aaron had no way of knowing how the flame had been fanned by hate.

"Come on, let's ride, boys," said Haile, "Get rid of the rest of that coffee and into the saddle, Cato."

Cato put his foot into the stirrup and started to swing up. Suddenly there was a loud clanging noise and he was nearly dashed to the ground as his horse reared.

Someone had tied a tin cup to Cato's spur.

"It's a shame someone would do that to a man," said Tom Haile. Then he dashed through a puddle of muddy water, over a rocky point, and disappeared into the brush, but they could still hear him laughing.

*   *   *

The little medicine wagon resumed its journey after breakfast, for they had crossed the St. Francis river and could travel by day since the Yankees had been reluctant to venture south of the river.

In two days, they arrived at Crowley's Ridge where Sam's wound was attended to and he was made as comfortable as possible.

Captain Bolin and his men had not come back from the horse procurement raid as yet and General Thompson had established his headquarters north, across the swampy country east of the St. Francis in Mingo Swamp, which he knew and loved so much.

Sam got cabin fever after a couple of weeks, and although the leg was not back to normal, he felt he could travel. Obtaining a horse, he headed north, along with several other newcomers.

M. Jeff Thompson was a Virginian who loved weapons and dreamed of glory on the battle field. He had been defeated in the election of 1861 in his bid to be elected secretary of the legislative arm of the Missouri government, an election that saw Sterling Price elected presiding officer. The fates of war were destined to draw them together in a different struggle.

It was at Moreau Creek near Jefferson City that Thompson first displayed his flamboyant style of leadership and courage. when Colonel Shanks, commander of the Iron Brigade was killed, Thompson rallied the men and led them in a charge that sent the Yankees running.

And now the lanky and mechanically minded Thompson greeted his latest recruit, an unlearned, simple minded man who only wanted revenge and his family and life style restored.

Sam was rather surprised as to how he was received by the General. Not only did Thompson seem to be sincerely interested in Sam's physical condition, but asked about his family and requested that Sam take time to tell his story.

And so Sam did. Thompson listened intently as he related the story, from his intent to avoid the war, to the killing of his brother, and the attack on his home in Flat Woods.

When Sam finished, Thompson drew a sheet of paper out of his desk drawer, dipped the quill into the ink well, and scratched on the paper with it.

Rising, he handed the paper to Sam.

"You are now commissioned as a Major in the Confederate army, Bushwhacker Division. Enlist what men you can, fight on your own hook, and report to me every six months."

Outside, Sam looked at the paper he could not read, wrinkling his brow as he did so.

"Well, if that's what the General says it says," he mumbled to himself, "I guess that's what it says, but I'll be durn if I ask anyone to read it to me."

Back at Crowley's Ridge, he presented himself to Captain Bolin, who had finally returned from the raid.

"I presume," said Bolin, "That you have been to see the old Swamp Fox?"

"Yes, I have."

"What did he do for you?"

Sam handed him the paper after trying to straighten out the wrinkles it had gotten from being in his pocket.

Bolin glanced at it. "Well, Major Hildebrand…"

"Sam, if you please."

"Very well, then, what do you propose to do?"

"I propose to fight."

"But Major…."

"Sam, if you please."

"All right, Sam," said Bolin, "I see you have a commission of a Major."

Sam was not aware that he outranked the Captain.

"Well Captain," he said, "I can explain that matter. He formed me into an independent company of my own, to pick a few men if I can get them, go where I please, when I please, and when I go up against my old personal enemies up in Missouri, I am expected to do a "major" part of the fighting myself."

Bolin laughed and produced a black bottle and Sam's commission was duly toasted and saluted.

"Well sir," said Bolin, "I obtained one of the same kind. I have one hundred and twenty-five men, and we are what is denominated "Bushwhackers". We carry on a war against our enemies by shooting them. My men are from all parts of the state, and each one has a grievance to address back home."

He poured another half glass from the bottle and offered Sam another, which he took, although he was not used to drinking real whiskey, but figured if he could handle home made "bursthead" he could keep up with the Captain.

"In order to enable our men to do their job effectively, we give him all the aid he may require. After he sets things to right in his section of the county, he promptly comes back to help others in return. We thus swap work like the farmers usually do in harvest time. If you wish to have an interest in this joint stock mode of fighting you can unite your destiny with ours, and be entitled to all our privileges."

Sam wasn't sure what privileges were but he lifted his glass toward Bolin and they downed the rest of the brown brew.

*   *   *

After their encounter with Sam in the medicine wagon, Aaron, Cato, Burlap and Haile spent most of the next two weeks riding all over southeast Missouri, dodging Federal patrols, sleeping in barns and riding through downpours.

Aaron had about decided the army was not as exciting as he had hoped it would be. Sleeping on the ground or in a barn was not his idea of comfort, but he would daydream that he was home and his Maw was cooking ham and beans, with apple dumplings for desert. Most of the food had been jerky and corn pone, because they could not build a fire.

But a couple of times they did dine well at the home of a Confederate supporter.

The trip was an educational one, he surmised, for on future adventures it was going to be very important to know who and where your friends were and how to communicate with them.

"Most of the people who help us are members of the Knights of the Golden Circle," Tom told him, "You got to memorize their names and locations and the secret signs we use to identify each other with."

"What is the Knights of the Golden Circle?" asked Aaron.

"Boy, you have been raised out in the hills, hain't you?" Tom laughed, "The Knights are a secret fraternal order whose purpose is to preserve the Southern way of life."

"What's them secret signs?"

"You give the wrong sign and you might be dead. You give the right sign and don't get the right answer, get out of there as fast as you can."

"You gonna teach me?"

"Sure am," Tom said, "Along with where and how to sleep safe, where to get food, how to steal horses, and if you behave right, I'll even take you to our favorite swimming hole just south of Farmington."

"That ain't far from my home," Aaron said, "Maybe I could go see my Maw."

"No way, this trip," answered Tom, "If we get the horses I'm thinking are in a little barn just outside Fredericktown, we'll be hightailing it back to Crowley's Ridge, with no time for family visits."

As they rode along, Tom explained to Aaron that if he passed his finger across the right side of his nose, and the sign was answered with a finger crossing the left side, he would know he had a friend.

Another signal was to shake hands and extend the forefinger to press the wrist of the other man and if he responded the same way, you knew he was a member of the Knights. It was a sign that could be given right in front of an enemy, and they couldn't see it.

It was after midnight when the four rode up to the little farm house just outside Fredericktown. There was no light in the clapboard structure, and not even a dog barked as they headed around back to the barn.

"Walk your horse soft," Tom whispered,"Don't bump into anything. Not a sound, you hear?"

Aaron nodded but in the darkness doubted that Tom could see it.

Tom dismounted and walked slowly to the barn door, then gently lifted the bar that held the door closed. It squeaked just a mite and Tom stopped, while Aaron, Burlap and Cato held their breaths. The only sound was the muffled movement of the horses inside the barn.

After a few seconds that seemed like hours, Tom eased the bar out of the brackets that held it and laid it on the ground.

With Burlap on one side and Cato on the other, the doors swung open.

The shotgun blast caught them all off guard. Aaron's horse reared and he nearly fell off. Tom flattened out on the ground and Burlap jumped behind the door. Cato, unfortunately, took refuge in the barn lot, where plenty of fresh cow manure had been deposited.

"You ain't gittin' no more of my stock," a voice hollered from the dark abyss of the barn.

"Old man," yelled Tom, "They's eight of us and only one of you. You ready to die for them scraggly horses?"

The only answer was another blast from the shotgun, as Tom rolled to one side and evaded the buckshot.

Aaron heard the crack and saw the flash from Tom's pistol, aimed at the point of flash from the muzzle of the shotgun.

A light had been lit in the house, and someone was running toward the barn. Aaron drew his pistol and prepared to shoot when he noticed it was an older woman, dressed in a flannel nightgown, and wearing one of those puffy little night caps.

She only glanced at the dark shadowed men as she went directly into the barn door and disappeared into the darkness within.

Then Aaron heard the scream.

He was in the corn field. The throbbing sun pressed him down as he gripped the hoe and ran up the hill. He stumbled on a clod and fell, skinning his elbow. He could see the glint of the sun on the barrel of the pistol. The blue uniforms filled his front yard. His paw stood on the front porch, his white shirt covered with blood.

Then he heard the scream.

"You kilt him," she cried, "You kilt him!"

Burlap and Cato went into the barn and emerged leading two fine looking mares and in a few minutes the foursome were mounted and headed south, the mares in tow.

That night, Aaron lay on the ground somewhere south of the St. Francis but couldn't sleep.

It was strange how much that woman's scream sounded just like his Maw's.

CHAPTER 7

Traveling only at night, Sam worked his way up the eastern side of the St. Francis, avoiding the normally traveled trails and the few roads that pierced the wilderness.

He skirted the swamp, although before he left Greene County, he had squatted around enough campfires and drank enough strong black coffee to learn every trail and hiding place in Mingo.

He also carried in his head a list of those along the route who could be depended on to help him if he needed it, and had been taught the necessary Knights of the Golden Circle signs to get out of trouble if need be.

On June 12 he arrived at Flat Woods and rode silently by the burned out cabin that had been his and Margaret's temporary home for such a short time.

Jesse Pigg had told Sam that George Cornecious was the informer who had led the Federals to Sam and his family.

Finding George Cornecious was not easy. Perhaps he knew that Sam knew, or maybe he had informed on others, but Mr. Cornecious was a hard man to locate.

But Sam's patience was as strong as his hatred, and on the third day, he found Cornecious and his victim only saw the flash of fire from the muzzle of Kill-Devil in the bushes before the ball slammed into his chest and he tumbled from his horse.

Sam carved a notch in the stock of "Killdevil" and headed to Flat River, and remained in hiding for several days on the little stream, that had no right to be called a river.

Finally, he took a pone of bread, the gift from a Southern supporter, and walked to Firman McIlvaine's farm at Big River Mills.

Apparently Firman was not as concerned about Sam's possible return as Cornecious had been, for he was working with his negroes in the field, located on top of one of the bluffs that had been Sam's playground as a boy.

Sam hid in the corner of the fence and waited.

Firman was working in a part of the field out of the range of Killdevil. Sam worked his way around the base of the bluff and came up the other side, only to find Firman had moved.

"Jest stay in one place," he said to himself.

He went back down to the river and stretched out on a large rock to rest and think.

Upstream, he saw movement and grabbing Killdevil, he leaped for cover behind a huge hickory nut tree.

It was Firman! Watering his horse, and not more than fifty yards away!

Sam propped Killdevil across a limb and sighted, but no matter how he moved, he could not get a clean shot because of the trees and brush and he did not want to miss and send his target into hiding.

That night, he slept under an overhanging protrusion of rock and at dawn ascended the bluff and placed himself in clear view of where Firman and his men had stopped cradling the day before.

Soon the negroes showed up and began to cradle the rye. Sam looked across the field and saw Firman shocking what had been cut the day before.

The day passed without a chance to hit his enemy. That evening he returned to the watering hole, but Firman did not show up.

Again he slept under the rock ledge, this time a fretful sleep as he was beginning to believe it was not meant for him to avenge the death of his brother and the persecution of his family.

On the third day, no one showed up to work and crossing the river on a fish dam, Sam found them working in another field.

For several hours, Sam watched his foe cut away at the rye until he got to within one hundred yards.

When Firman McIlvaine stopped to whet his scythe, Sam raised Killdevil and fired.

McIlvaine fell instantly and Killdevil got another notch.

        *   *   *

The cabin General Thompson had told Aaron he could use was little more than a lean-to, small and dirty, but after Mary Lee and her mother had helped him clean it up and furnished him with fresh blankets for the single cot, he found he could sleep at night and besides, Mary Lee's cabin was just down the road and he seemed to be welcome anytime.

As a matter of fact, as soon as the little troop got back from Missouri, Aaron unsaddled his horse, rubbed her down good, made sure there was hay and water, and headed for the Lemley's.

Once again he was welcomed in and invited to stay for supper. Poke salad, with wild onions, dandelion greens, and other wild plants Mrs. Lemley had gathered from the forest, with hot bacon grease poured over it, tasted almost of as good as his Maw's wilted lettuce.

Of course, when you were at the same table with Mary Lee, everything tasted good.

After supper, Mary Lee volunteered to walk him home and together they strolled up the trail toward his cabin, walking as slow as they could so the trip would last longer. It had rained hard all day and the trees were dripping, the trail muddy and slippery. Aaron was glad, for several times he had to take hold of her arm because she slipped. Or did she?

He told her about his trip and how he had learned a lot from Tom Haile. He didn't tell about the farmer that was killed.

"You learned from that scalawag?" she asked, "I didn't think he had a brain in his head."

"Well, when you are operating in the field of combat," Aaron said like the veteran he now considered himself to be, "You learn to live by your wits or your head may soon be gone."

A vision of the farmer's wife running toward the barn in her nightgown and cap flashed though his mind.

"There has already been so much hate and killing," Mary Lee said, "I just wish the war would end and we could all go home."

"Well, I guess I do to," said Aaron, "But I got a job to do, even if the war ended tomorrow."

"You mean the Sergeant?"

Aaron nodded and they walked on in silence for a few minutes.

"Hey crip," someone said from the woods, "What are you doing with a pretty girl like that?"

Aaron and Mary Lee stopped as the three dirtiest young men they had ever seen came out of the woods and approached them.

"You hear me crip?" ask the largest of the three, "I bet that girl would rather be with a real man like me, don't you?"

"We ain't looking for trouble," Aaron said as Mary Lee drew close to him and they started on up the trail.

"Well, I ain't looking for trouble, neither," the stranger said, "I'm looking for a woman, and it looks like I just found me one, ain't that right, crip?"

Mary Lee was squeezing Aaron's arm as they tried to walk on but the bully blocked the trail.

"Take him, fellers," he said.

Aaron fought as hard as he could but before he could do anything, he was pinned up against a tree and the leader had grabbed Mary Lee by the arm.

"Come on, honey," he said, "Let me show you what a real man can do." He smiled through teeth stained brown by tobacco and yanked her toward him.

"Let her alone," cried Aaron, "You got no cause to hurt her."

"O, I ain't tendin to hurt her," the bully smiled, "I'm gonna make her feel real good."

He pulled Mary Lee down to the ground and fell on top of her.

"Come on, honey, let's start with a little kiss."

Aaron struggled to get free but the two were larger than him and he could not break their holds, even though their attention was fixed on Mary Lee.

Mary Lee squirmed and tried to scream but the bully put his hand over her mouth.

And then there was someone else there. The figure had stepped out of the woods as though he had materialized from nothing. A big man in a Federal blue coat and butternut pants.

He grabbed the bully by the nap of the neck and the seat of his pants and seemingly effortless, tossed him sprawling into a nearby gully. Then he turned to the two who held Aaron.

They released their grip on him and began to back slowly away from the newcomer.

Once free of their grasp, Aaron picked up a tree limb and dove into the gully in a rage and straddled the bully, who yelled for help but looked up just in time to see his friends high tailing it down the trail.

Aaron raised the limb and was about to bash in the head of his adversary when a huge hand wrapped around his wrist, stopping him in mid-swing.

"No call to kill him, boy," the intruder said, "They's enough Yankees to be kilt without us starting on each other."

Aaron looked up into the face of their rescuer. It was the man in the medicine wagon.

"Let him go," Sam said.

Aaron got off the bully and as soon as he was clear the trouble maker jumped up and ran off in the direction his friends had gone.

Sam and Aaron turned their thoughts to Mary Lee, whose dress was torn and covered with mud. She stood against a tree, sobbing softly.

"Where does she live?" asked Sam.

"The Lemley's," Aaron managed to say. His breath was coming in short deep gasps and his knees were trembling. He pointed in the direction of the Lemley cabin.

"Take her there," said Sam, and he walked off into the woods, disappearing as mysteriously as he had come.

Mary Lee's mother took her daughter in her arms and into the bedroom. Sitting on the side of the bed, she held her tight and rocked back and forth until finally, the crying subsided.

Bill Lemley had taken the rifle down and was loading it when there was a rap on the door.

Aaron opened it and there stood Sam.

Sam looked at Bill and the gun. "No need for that, although I know how feel. I have children of my own."

Bill started for the door, but Sam's huge body blocked it. His vivid blue eyes danced in the flickering light from the fire place.

"Them boys have decided they don't want to be Rebels anymore anyway, and right now are packing their horses and riding out of camp. Said they probably wouldn't stop 'til they got to Texas."

Bill slumped a little and his grip on the gun relaxed.

"Is the girl all right?" Sam asked.

"Yes, I think she will be fine, thanks to you. Aaron has told me what you did. I thank you."

"No need," said Sam. He turned to Aaron. "Boy, you look like a scrapper to be so small and you got enough hate in you to kill a lot of Federals. I'm leaving on a raid in the morning, you want to go along?"

Aaron looked at Bill, turned his head to glance toward the bedroom and then met Sam's gaze directly.

"I sure do," he said.

"Fine, I'll see you at the corrals at daybreak and I intend to get you a new horse. You can't keep up with Sam Hildebrand riding that work horse you had the first time we met."

*   *   *

Rebecca Hildebrand sat in the comfort and safety of the stone house in Big River Mills that had been her home since George had built it with the help of his sons.

Now Frank was dead and Sam was gone. William was also gone but in a different direction as he had enlisted in the Union Army. Washington had taken no part in the war, but continued to mine lead while her youngest son, Henry, a mere lad of thirteen, stayed at home with his mother. One daughter, Mary, had died just after her betrothal to a fine local boy named Landusky.

But now Rebecca sat alone, her Bible open on her lap as she rocked gently in her chair and prayed for her sons.

Her prayers were interrupted by the arrival of a great many horsemen in the front yard.

Peeking out the window, she saw they were Union soldiers, along with members of the Vigilantes.

She opened the door and stepped out on the front stoop.

"Madam," a Federal officer said in a deep French accent, "I am Captain Flanche of the United States Army."

He pause and glanced around as though to draw support from his comrades. Captain Esroger from North Big River Bridge rose in his stirrups and Captain Adolph, commanding a Dutch Company stationed at Cadet, coughed nervously.

Captain Flanche continued. "You are hereby ordered to leave this place at once, taking nothing with you except immediate personal needs."

"Leave my home?" asked the stunned Rebecca.

"Da," piped in Captain Escroger, "Because of the acts of treason by your sons we have been ordered to confiscate this property in the name of the United States of America."

Rebecca's knees crumpled under her. For a moment she swayed and almost fell, but the lad Henry had joined her and supported his mother.

"You may take one bed from the house," said Adolph, "But nothing more."

"May I keep my Bible?" she asked and held it up for them to see.

The brave Captains looked at each other rather sheepishly.

"Oui," said Flanche, "You may keep your Bible, Mrs. Hildebrand."

Rebecca swung her eyes over the group of men and was surprised to see Judge Franklin Murphy there. He dismounted and approached her.

"I will have someone see to the moving of your bed," he said, "Where should we take it?"

Rebecca could not think. Finally she stammered, "To my brother's home on Dry Creek, up in Jefferson Country, I guess."

The Judge nodded and a couple of the Vigilantes went into the house.

Rebecca wrapped her arms around her Bible and walked out the gate of her yard, probably never to return, she thought. And burst into tears.

*   *   *

Aaron did not sleep much that night. At dawn, he was at the corrals with his newly acquired Enfield rifle which he did not know how to use and an old pistol he doubted would work, even if he did know how to use it.

Sam was already there, his horse saddled, and after a few minutes, two more of the little expedition showed up. Aaron was glad to see John Burlap and James Cato, and was not unhappy that Tom Haile was not going.

Not that he disliked Tom, but it seemed to him that killing Yankees was serious business and killing innocent farmers who are defending their homes was not part of the war effort.

Besides, he was getting tired of Tom's practical jokes.

"Try this one for size," Sam said.

Aaron had his back to Sam and as he turned around, he saw one of the prettiest horses, if a horse could be called pretty, he had ever seen.

She was not a large horse, and was golden with a flaxen mane and tail.

He put his arm around her neck for a minute and then swung up into the saddle Sam had already put on.

"She'll do fine, Mr. Hildebrand. Thanks a lot."

"Let's get one rule straight," Sam said, "My name is Sam, not Mr. Hildebrand or Major Hildebrand."

"Yes, sir, Sam."

"Now git down offin that horse and come into the stables, I got something for all you boys."

Cato, Burlap, and Aaron followed Sam into the stable. He handed them each a pile of clothing.

"Put these on."

They looked at each other in amazement.

"Them are Federal uniforms," Burlap gasped.

"Yep, and where we are going, they will probably keep your necks from stretchin," Sam said, "Now git into them."

Aaron's uniform was too big and Cato's had a bullet hole in the back, but none of them wanted to ask any questions of Sam.

And so, on the hot summer morning of July 13, 1862, Sam and his little army worked their way up the east bank of the St. Francis.

It had rained hard the day before, and the river was bank full. The boys hesitated to enter the swollen stream but Sam plunged in and the three followed.

Cato was scratched pretty bad by a floating tree limb and for a moment, Aaron thought their army life was going to come to a premature end.

Drifting with the current, the horses struggled through the muddy water and struck the opposite shore about a half mile downstream from where they had entered and scampered up the low embankment.

Soon Sam had a fire going so they could dry out and pulled a black bottle from his bag and after taking a big snort, passed it to Burlap.

John looked at the bottle for a moment and turned it up, then handed it to Cato as he wiped his mouth on his sleeve.

After he had taken a swig, James gave the bottle to Aaron.

Aaron had never had a drink in his life. Well, except for the apple cider his Paw had made that had fermented by accident. Or at least that was what Paw had told his Maw.

He took a deep breath and turned the bottle up.

The other three laughed as he spit most of the burst-head out, coughing and gagging.

"Didn't you like the taste?" Burlap asked, "Ain't you never drunk burst-head before?"

"I ain't never drank coal oil before, either," said Aaron, "but it sure can't taste any worse than that stuff."

The next morning, they headed for Bloomfield in Stoddard County.

"My wife and family are there," Sam told them, "but I got to be careful not to let anyone know who she is."

Just outside of Bloomfield, they met a man on the road walking who seemed to be elated to see them.

"Glad to see you Feds," he said excitedly, "There are some Rebels in Bloomfield. Best you not go in alone."

"How many are there?" asked Sam.

"Hard to tell," the man answered, "I been with some of them all morning, pretending I wanted to enlist in the Confederate Army, but they wasn't standing still long enough to count."

"I see," said Sam, "Did you learn anything we might be able to use?"

"I shore did, I got the names of a lot of Rebels in Greenville and Fredericktown."

"Come ride with us," Sam said, "Our commanding officer is in Greenville and you can relate your information to him."

"You bet," the man said as he crawled up on the back of Sam's horse.

Aaron and Cato and Burlap looked at each other in disbelief. Sam was as calm as could be and almost convinced them he was a Fed.

But two miles up the road, Sam halted.

"My name," he said to his rider, "Is Sam Hildebrand and I sir, am a Rebel and you are a dead man."

He knocked the man off the horse and raised Killdevil.

The blast at close range and the suddenness of the killing startled Aaron. The man's face seemed to explode in a crimson flood and he fell backward, twitching in the dirt road for several minutes before his body finally stilled.

Sam sat side-saddle, took out his knife, and cut a notch in the stock of Killdevil.

"You can learn a lot when you are a Yankee," he said without smiling. "I got a feeling there is one spy who will fail to report."

*   *   *

July 6th, 1862 was a bright sunny Sunday, and Washington Hildebrand and Mary's betrothed, Landusky, were working alone in a drift underground when a company of cavalry under Captain Flance rode up.

The men were ordered to come out of the mine, which they did, never suspecting the reason for this visit.

No questions were asked. Flanche ordered them both to walk off toward a nearby tree and gave the order to fire.

Both men fell immediately, their bodies torn by the multiple rifle shots.

Four days later, Captain Esroger and his troops rode up to the home of John Roan, about three miles from the Hildebrand home.

The old man came out on his porch bare footed, his white locks blowing in the wind.

"John Roan, you vos one tam prisoner," Esroger said.

He detailed six men to march behind Roan.

They march about a mile from the house when they halted and Esroger ordered John to walk another six paces.

The old man realized what was about to happen. He raised his hands in prayer.

The last word he heard on earth was: "Fire".

                                    *   *   *

Traveling only at night, Sam and his squad reached the home of Landusky, about ten miles from the Hildebrand home. The black crepe on the door told him all was not well.

Mrs. Landusky, dressed in mourning black, threw her arms around Sam and told him of the murder of her son, along with his brother. "They killed old John Roan, too," she said between sobs.

"Where is my mother?" Sam asked.

"Thrown out of her home," said Mrs. Sandusky, "I'm told she went to her brother's farm up in Jefferson County."

Sam did not flinch, but Aaron could see the muscles in his jaw contracting and releasing while the veins in his neck stood out like blueish rivers ready to flood.

Aaron spoke first. "What we gonna do?" he asked Sam.

"First, I am going to see my mother," he answered, "And then I plan to kill every member of the Vigilante Committee and every Federal soldier I see."

There was no emotion in his words. It was simply a statement.

"You boys can head on back to Arkansas if you want, this is going to get messy and it is my problem, not yours."

Aaron looked at Cato and Burlap.

"I came to ride with Sam Hildebrand," he said, "And I reckon that's what I'll do."

The other two nodded and that night, they started for Dry Creek. There were many Federal troops in the area and they had to take a circular route and morning caught them short of their goal.

"Follow me," said Sam.

He rode up the side of a small hill and circled it more than half way up, not completing the circle, but stopping at a spot where they could see where they had started up the hill.

Sam told the boys to sleep, he would take the first watch but before they had time to doze off, he spotted a group of Federal tracking them up the hill and around the semi-circle trail they had left.

Mounting and riding to another hill before the group had time to get to their camping place, Sam and the boys again rode up the hill in a circular pattern.

When the Federal tracked them to that hill, they apparently decided the trail was too warm, and headed off in another direction, pretending to see trail signs that weren't there.

The next night found Sam and his little army in the vicinity of Dry Creek and leaving the boys in the woods, Sam went to his uncle's house.

Creeping up to the home, he could hear voices and climbed up on a bee-gum to look in a window.

There were two men in the room he did not recognize.

One of them moved toward the window and Sam ducked out of view as the bee-gum collapsed under him and he tumbled to the ground.

"What's that?" he heard someone inside yell, and soon the door opened and his uncle appeared with a light and a double barreled shotgun.

Sam had already cleared the picket fence and crouched on the other side.

His uncle cursed the damage to his bee-gum and the thief who had turned it over, and told the strangers and his family to go back in and he would guard against further intruders.

He stationed himself by the fence, the shotgun cradled in his arms.

Sam did not know if his Uncle suspected who had turned over the bee-gum, but he determined he had better be careful, or he might get peppered with buckshot.

Slipping through a hole in the picket fence, Sam crept to within two sections of the rail fence his Uncle was leaning against and dared not speak his name.

But his Uncle had heard the movement. "Is that you, Sam?" he whispered.

"Yes," said Sam, "It's me."

"Stay where you are," his uncle said, "Till I get rid of these neighbors. Half the blue bellies in the county is looking for you."

An hour must have passed before the strangers left and Sam was given the sign to come in.

Rebecca almost collapsed when she saw her son. Stumbling into his arms, she began to weep bitterly, and even Sam felt the tears welling up in his eyes.

"Oh, my dear son!" she sobbed, "Have you indeed come to see your mother? I thought I would never see you again on earth."

After a while, Sam went out and got the boys and brought them in for a fine supper at two o'clock in the morning while Sam's Uncle kidded him about trying to steal his bee-gum.

"Yeah," said Sam,"Them Federal may never get me, but a couple of bee-gums have come close."

Rebecca was tranquil when Sam left. She knew he had to go. With two sons already dead and the other in the Union army, she could only pray that somehow they could be a family again.

*   *   *

The younger brother, Henry, had stayed at the old home place since his mother was cast out, along with an orphan boy who had been living with them.

Now, once again, the lad heard the clopping of hooves and squeaking of saddles as the front yard was filled with soldiers.

Henry stood in fear and astonishment as the soldiers began to tear down the fence and throw the pickets into the house. When it was piled up just inside the front door, a fire was lit and soon the home was in flames. The barn received the same treatment.

Captain Esroger was there and he ordered Henry to leave at once. "This is the end of the Hildebrand family of Big River Mills!" he shouted at the lad.

Once again, to Henry's surprise, Judge Murphy was there.

"Best you go, boy" he said, scratching the bridge of his nose, "Best you go."

Henry mounted his horse and had ridden about two hundred yards when he was shot in the back.

And now there were only two Hildebrand brothers left. One wore the blue of the union, and the other wore blue, but fought for the butternut.

*   *   *

Before daylight had fully bloomed, Sam and his small army rode back down the trail they had come, entered a small creek and stayed in it for three miles, then boldly rode on a public road for six miles or more.

Leaving the road, they again semi-circled a hill, and hid themselves near the top of a bluff, where in the distance, they could see the Hildebrand home.

Sam lay on a rock outcropping and peered at his home place. Just out of sight, he knew, was the cabin where he and Margaret had been so content.

Finally, the exhaustion from lack of sleep and being in the saddle so long overcame him and he slept.

Aaron shook him awake.

"Sam!" he cried,"Look!"

Sam rolled over and shook his eyes clear of sleep and looked toward his home.

Then he leapt to his feet! There were Federal soldiers there!

A wisp of smoke came from the front of the house and soon blossomed into a red flame.

The soldiers watched their handiwork as a single small rider left the scene as fast as his horse could carry him.

Sam's chest began to heave and he strained to see.

Among the soldiers in the front yard of the Hildebrand home, which was now engulfed in flames, stood a tall, humped back man in civilian clothes and as Sam watched, he reached up and scratched the bridge of his nose with one finger.

Sam said not a word, but ran to his horse and would have mounted and rode to his death had not Cato and Burlap caught him and pulled him down. It took both of them to hold him on the ground.

"Let me go," Sam cried, "Let me die and take as many of them with me as I can before I die!"

With the other boys holding him, Aaron straddled Sam's chest.

"You go down there now," he said, getting right in Sam's face, "And you might kill six or seven of them. Wait your time, and you can kill a hundred."

Sam stopped struggling. He could see the logic in that, but the hate of the present wanted very much not to accept the logical.

He crawled out on the outcropping and watched the flames consume his home. A great yellow tongue shot up as the roof George Hildebrand had said would stand for a century collapsed.

If Sam could have seen two hundred yards beyond the burning house, he would have seen his baby brother being shot in the back.

Chapter 8

Aaron was glad to be back in Arkansas. He had tasted burst-head for the first time, and had seen another man killed. It was good to be back to the relative serenity of Crowley's Ridge, and of course, Mary Lee.

He was glad to see that she was her old self, that the attack by the bully had not changed her, except perhaps she did seem a little quieter than in the past.

They walked through the woods but were careful to stay within sight of the Lemley cabin.

He shared his adventures on the raid with Sam and when he told her about the spy being killed, her eyes flooded.

"O Aaron," she said, "So many people are suffering because of this war."

"Well, the Federal started it," he answered, "But we Rebs are bound to finish it. Everyone knows one Reb can whup twenty Yanks."

"I don't believe there are winners or losers, only a lot of innocent people being hurt and families being split up."

"Your dad had trouble with someone in his family, didn't he?"

Mary Lee took a deep breath.

"Yes, his brother," she said, "They just couldn't agree and there was a terrible fight at home in Sedalia. Pa's brother vowed he would meet him on the field of combat someday, and would not hesitate to shoot him. Then he went off and joined the Union Army."

"The Federal troops came and took everything we had and burned the house," she continued, "And Pa is certain his own brother told them he was a Rebel."

"Sam has a brother fighting for the North," Aaron said, "It would be a terrible thing to look down the barrel of your gun and see your brother in the sights."

"It's just so meaningless," Mary Lee said,"A preacher came into camp the other day and he had some St. Louis newspapers and Aaron, most of the war is being fought in the east. These killings in Missouri will have no effect on the outcome of the war, they are purely for vengeance."

Aaron was silent for several minutes.

"What about my Paw?"

"Killing the Sergeant will not bring him back and I'm afraid it will not bring you any peace, either."

"But he's got away with killing Paw!" Aaron felt his face begin to flush.

"The Bible says that vengeance is the Lord's"

"I don't believe that stuff any more. If there was a God he wouldn't let any of this have happened in the first place."

Mary Lee looked directly into his eyes. "There is a God and one day we will all have to face him," she said, "Please don't have blood on your hands when that happens, Aaron."

Aaron looked down at the ground and was silent.

"Aaron," said Mary Lee softly, "I love you."

He looked up into her face and tears welled up in his eyes.

"I love you, too," he managed to say through the lump in his throat.

It suddenly occurred to him that he did not know how to kiss a girl, but the thought lasted for only a moment or two as Mary Lee stood on her toes and touched her lips gently to his.

Her arms encircled his neck and he clumsily put his around her tiny waist.

"Mary Lee!" her mother called from the cabin door, "I have some chores for you."

Aaron blushed a deep pink. Had she been watching?

Mary Lee stepped back from his embrace and headed for the cabin. About half way, she turned and looked back and she was smiling.

     *   *   *

That evening, Aaron went down near the corrals. Knots of men gathered around small fires, smoking pipes, poking sticks in the fire, drinking coffee or burst-head, and working themselves into a frenzy as they reviewed how they had been treated by the Federals or some vigilante group.

These sessions, he knew, usually ended up with a renewed determination to return to Missouri and kill some of their old enemies. Tonight was to be no exception.

Aaron squatted at a fire with Sam and Tom Haile. The usually jovial Tom was silent and somber, poking a stick in the fire and staring into the flames.

Aaron looked at Sam.

"He just learned today they have killed his father," Sam said.

He was in the front yard of his home. On the porch, his Maw cradled his Paw's head in her lap, while the dark crimson flow crept down the front of this white shirt. His knuckles were white on the handle of the hoe.

Aaron groaned audibly as his mind came back to the present.

"You all right, boy?" Sam asked.

Aaron nodded and stared at the fire with Tom. He searched for words of comfort but could find none.

Finally, Sam spoke. "I'm riding north in the morning, you two want to go?"

Tom and Aaron continued to stare at the fire, but both nodded yes.

"Sunup," said Sam, as he got up and brushed the dirt off the seat of his pants and started walking away.

He stopped and looked back at the boys. "Don't forget to bring your Federal uniforms."

When darkness became full, Aaron got up and headed back to his hut, but stopped at the Lemley's to let Mary Lee know he was going in the morning.

"Oh, Aaron," she said, "You just got back. Can't you rest a while and let it be?"

"Tom's father was kilt," he said.

Mary Lee wanted to argue with him but could tell his mind was set. She sensed the closeness he felt with Tom because of his own father.

Their hands touched for a moment as he stepped out the door into the black Arkansas night and he struggled with an urge to tell Sam he couldn't go.

"It won't be long," he said, "I'll be back before you know it."

Her eyes were brimming and her throat filled with so much emotion she did not speak. She could only pray silently as their fingers parted and then he was gone.

As Sam, Tom and Aaron rode out of camp the next morning, Tom seemed to have some of his spirit back, but was not the dervish Tom they knew so well. Aaron wondered if even revenge would restore it.

They traveled the usual route, passing through Stoddard County and into Wayne County.

Just before sunset, Sam called a halt.

"Got word of a man named Stokes, who lives just up the way, has been bragging about how he was going to help the Federal catch me," he said. "I think we will pay Mr. Stokes a little visit. You boys put on your blue uniforms."

Just after dark, Sam rode up to the Stokes house and knocked on the door.

The door opened almost at once and a thin, bushy haired man stuck his head through the opening.

"Well, Mr. Hildebrand," Stokes said as a smile flashed on his bony face. Do come in, I see you are well and still smarter than the Feds."

"Are there any blue-bellies in Greenville?" Sam asked.

"None sir, " Stokes said, "None at all. I was there today and the place is entirely free of the scamps. By the way, are you alone this trip, Mr. Hildebrand?"

"Yes, I am taking this trip by myself."

"Glad to assist you in anyway I can," said Stokes, "You are welcome to spend the night in my home. Would be glad to have you stay longer, if you wish."

"Well, thank you," said Sam, "But I am going down the road to the Camden house, I'll spend the night there."

Sam mounted and rode off in the direction of the Camden farm and Stokes slowly closed the door.

He was excited, although his legs felt like pure molasses on a July afternoon. It was the chance of a lifetime! He knew there were Federal troops in Greenville and he finally determined the best thing to do was to ride into town tonight and turn Sam in.

But as he was pulling on his boots, there was another knock on his door.

Opening it again, he found two Federal soldiers standing in his front yard. In the darkness, he failed to see how young they were.

"Well, sir," said one, "We are hot on the trail of Sam Hildebrand. He robbed a man on the Greenville road, not five miles from here just before sunset and he came in this direction. Have you seen anything of him?"

Stokes was ecstatic. "I reckon I have, by George, he was here not more than an thirty minutes ago. I tried to detain him but he said he was going to stay at the Camden place tonight. Hold on a minute, I'll get my gun and go with you, we've got him this time!"

"There's really no need for you to go," said the soldier, "Just give us directions to the Camden farm."

"Oh, no, I will go with you," said Stokes, "You would have a hard time finding it in the dark. And besides, I have waited a long time for this."

"All right, the soldier said, "Come along, we are always glad to have the help of a citizen of your stripes."

Stokes walked into the woods with the two soldiers and there they were joined by another on the dark trail.

"How many men do you have with you?" Stokes asked.

"Twelve."

"This is going to be grand," Stokes said, "I have been planning for months for Sam Hildebrand's capture, and tonight we have him for sure."

He continued to brag about the times he had almost caught Sam on previous occasions as they walked in the direction of the Camden farm.

Finally, the soldier who had met them on the trail stepped in front of Stokes.

"I am Sam Hildebrand myself."

Stokes had no time to refute his boasts, for Sam emptied Killdevil in his belly.

Tom and Aaron watched in silence as Sam cut another notch in Killdevil.

*   *   *

Dr. Melclair Mercer arrived at Crowley's Ridge in the heat of summer and decided this was a good place to have a revival, and considering all the black bottles that were being passed around, he was probably right.

It was unclear where Dr. Melclair had received his doctorate in religion, or even what denominational lines he espoused, but it soon became clear that he could yell loud and sweat a lot.

Most of the men who were making raids north to kill their old enemies under the guise of fighting a war, did not particularly desire to have a preacher in camp telling them they were sinners. Most of them already were aware of that.

But those families who had fled oppression and had left behind their churches missed not only the spiritual aspects of religion, but the social need the church had filled in their communities and lives.

And so, not too many questions were asked of the good pastor as plans were made for a revival meeting.

The Lemley family, of course, were among the leaders in promoting the meetings and Mary Lee looked forward to what she hoped would be a return to at least a form of civilization as they had known before the was in Sedalia.

With Bill Lemley's help, along with some of the other family men, the good reverend selected a site in the woods to hold the meetings.

The trees and undergrowth were cleared and seats were made from split logs and stumps. A rough hewed pulpit was erected at the front and on each side of it, forked sticks were driven into the ground and long poles placed on them.

"They'll have to do for mourner's benches," Dr. Mercer said, "Soon they will be filled with sinners, repenting of their sins and doing penance." And contributing to the cause, he thought to himself.

At the four corners of the area, trees were cut off about eight feet high and rough puncheon platforms built on top of them. These were covered with a layer of dirt and with fires built on them, would serve as light for the services, which the good Doctor predicted would be protracted.

Soon several committees had been organized. The ladies had made plans for dinner on the grounds after the first Sunday meeting, which was scheduled for the 24th of August.

Dr. Mercer, in the meantime, gave each of the participating families the pleasure of giving him a place to sleep and always blessed the bountiful meals the ladies lavished on him as they so eagerly served this man of God.

His plump belly and full cheeks, which were only partially covered by curly strands of less than a full beard, gave testimony to the fact that he had conducted many revival meetings and had fared very well from the efforts of devotion to the word.

"Late summer is not the best time for a meeting," he told his committee on fire building." He paused to let them wonder about the vastness of his knowledge of such things.

"For one thing," he continued, "Fresh vegetables are at a premium and the fresh pork of late fall has not yet been butchered.

The small band of supporters of his cause soon became aware that food for the body was almost as important to their new-found preacher as food for the soul.

Mary Lee was excited. Just to have a diversion from the boredom of life in camp was enough to lift her spirits. She was also tired of hearing of all the daring exploits of the men on their raids into Missouri.

And silently, she prayed that Aaron would be touched by the words of the evangelist and come to Christ.

CHAPTER 9

Secreting themselves in the woods south of Fredericktown, Sam, along with Aaron and Tom, rode the next night to the Big River Mills area. There they went to the home of an old friend of Sam's and let him know they were in the area. Then they went to the bluff and hid in a cave Sam had played in as a boy.

Soon his old friend joined them and Sam learned of the death of his brother, Henry.

Once again, Sam went into a rage, vowing to kill Judge Murphy even if it cost him his own life.

"Wait Sam," cried Tom as Sam started to saddle his horse.

"Revenge!" screamed Sam.

Tom and Aaron ran after him and managed to grab the bridle of the horse and held on.

"If I go back without you," Tom pleaded, "What will I tell your wife and children?"

"Tell them I died killing Judge Murphy," Sam growled as he tried to pull the horse loose from Tom's grip.

Sam began to calm down a little and finally got off the horse.

"I will kill him," he said, "Sooner or later, I will kill him."

Tom stood before Sam, who sat on an outcropping of gray rock, his head in his hands.

"I do not believe Judge Murphy sanctioned the killing of your brother," he said, "He could not rescue him from the mob or stop an army from carrying out their dastardly deeds and the burning of your home, but the Judge happens to be a member of an order that dates back for centuries, and they are sworn to protect each other's interest and to shield each other from danger."

Tom was so serious, Sam promised never to harm a member of that order, except in self-defense. And except Judge Murphy.

The next night, they started on the trip back to Arkansas and as they rode through Madison County, still wearing the Federal uniforms, Sam spotted a fine horse in a corral by a farm house. He dismounted and decided to free this fine animal from the Yankee sympathizer who obviously lived there.

He was trying to get the rope halter around the mare's neck when a huge woman came out on the porch.

"See here! What are you trying to do?"

"I'm trying to catch this horse," Sam answered.

"Let her alone, you good for nothing scamp! Don't you look pretty, trying to steal my only horse."

"Yes, maam, but I fear you are a Rebel"

"I am a Rebel, sir, and proud of it! I have two sons in the Rebel army and if I had six more they would all be Rebels, you white livered, insignificant scum of creation! You had better let my horse alone. Why you are worse than Sam Hildebrand. He would not take the last horse from a poor widow woman."

As Sam took the halter off the horse, Tom fell to the ground laughing and Aaron put his head on the saddle horn and shook with laughter.

The rest of the ride home, Tom and Aaron would snicker every so often and Sam would scowl at them. They camped out just south of the St. Francis and Sam brought out a black bottle of burst-head.

They passed it around and were soon very drunk, including Aaron.

*   *   *

When Aaron rode back into camp with Sam and Tom, he was not greeted with the respect he felt due him as a returning hero. He had supper with the Lemley's that night and since the Lemley table was known to be the best in camp, Dr. Mercer was there, too.

Aaron decided he did not like him, even before he saw the gravy running down the front of the Reverend's shirt and the piece of yam hanging from his scrawny beard.

"You a Christian, boy?" the preacher asked Aaron in between mouthfuls of fried chicken.

"My Maw and Paw always took me to Sunday School at the Methodist Church when I was growin' up," said Aaron.

"That is not the question," the preacher pushed on, "You got to be washed in the blood of the Lamb. You got to repent of your hell bound ways. You got to give your life to Jasus!"

Mary Lee looked down at her plate. Religion was something she and Aaron had not discussed in private, and she felt the supper table, in front of her parents, was not the place she would have chosen to ask him about his faith.

Aaron's face turned red but he tried to ignore the preacher and eat his meal.

But it didn't work. "Let me put it this way, boy, if you were to die today, do you know where you would spend eternity?"

Aaron looked up directly into the Dr. Mercer's eyes. He could see little images of the lantern light dancing in them.

"No," he said, half rising from his chair, "I can only hope it will someplace where you are not!"

He turned to Anna while the preacher's huge mouth gaped open.

"I hope you will forgive me and excuse me," he said, and left the cabin.

He heard the door close behind him and without looking back, knew that Mary Lee had followed him out of the cabin.

He hurried up the trail toward his hut but felt her hand on his arm and stopped and turned to face her.

He did not see anger in her face as he had expected. Only love and concern.

"I'm sorry, Aaron," she said, "He shouldn't have pushed you like that, especially in front of everyone."

Aaron was full and could not speak. He was embarrassed for what he had said as a guest in the Lemley home.

"The meetings start tomorrow night," Mary Lee said, "Will you go with me?"

Again there was silence.

"I don't believe so," said Aaron, "Sam, Tom, John and I are riding north on Monday and I got a lot to do to get ready."

She let go of his arm. "You just got back!"

"Well, winter will be here before you know it and we need to get some things done before it gets cold," he said, looking down at the ground.

"Winter is months away!" said Mary Lee.

Now her eyes were full of tears and she could not speak. Finally she managed to touch her lips to his cheek and whispered, "I'll be praying and waiting for you."

She turned and ran toward the cabin, but this time she did not look back.

Aaron watched until she had disappeared and then went to his cabin, flopped on his cot, pulled the cork from a black bottle he had "confiscated" from a Dutch store owner in Caledonia on their last raid, and took a long drink from it.

*   *   *

He did not sleep much that night and spent most of Sunday in bed, partially to sleep off the effects of the contents of the black bottle, and partially so he would not see anyone, especially Mary Lee.

Looking out the small window in his hut, he could see the glow of the fires on the platforms where they were holding the services. He could even hear hymns being sung, and when the good Reverend Melclair began to preach, you could have heard him half way to Missouri.

Aaron shut the window, turned up the empty bottle, threw it against the wall, and buried his head under his blanket.

An eternity of tossing and turning later, while the dancing flames in Reverend Melclair's eyes chased him, he finally saw the first rays of the sun penetrating the cracks in the door.

He leaped to his feet and suddenly found out why they called it burst-head. Throwing some cold water in his face, he staggered outside and soon had his bedroll packed, his horse saddled, and hurried to meet the others at the corral.

On the way, he had to pass the area where the church services had been held. There was a small, lone figure kneeling at the mourner's bench. It was Mary Lee.

          ✶   ✶   ✶

Not even Tom Haile was in a good mood as the foursome rode north toward the Missouri state line. The trip was mostly uneventful and silent except for the creaking of their saddles.

They reached Madison County and stopped at a friend's home about eight miles south of Fredericktown just as daylight caught them.

"Good to see you again," James Norwood, the owner of the house said, "Come on in, Mr. Hildebrand, and Sarah will fix you some breakfast."

Sam nodded as he dismounted and led his horse to the watering trough. Tom, John, and Aaron followed and soon they were inside, while the smell of bacon frying filled the room.

"Seen any Federals around?" asked Sam.

"Ain't seed none in a long time," Norwood answered, "And I was in Fredericktown just day before yesterday and there were nary soldiers at all."

Sam looked at his boys. "Well, then perhaps we can ride on today instead of holing up and reach Big River Mills sooner than we planned. Eat up, boys, and we'll ride on."

After breakfast, they thanked Sarah for the meal and rode off. On each trip, Sam had followed the same route but since it was daylight, he varied it just a little and reached the gravel road that ran from Fredericktown to Pilot Knob about two hundred yards from his usual crossing place.

The crackling of rifle fire filled the air, and looking down the road, Sam saw that an ambush had been set up.

Sam's horse took a ball in the chest and went down and Sam felt a burning sensation as a bullet pierced his pants leg.

"Scatter, boys!" he yelled, "You know where to meet!"

Aaron rode up beside Sam and they rode double through the woods for about a mile where they tethered their horses in a small ravine and made their way back toward the ambush in a circular pathway.

"I thought I told you boys to split," Sam said.

"I don't see you running," said Tom.

"All right then, we is were we are at," Sam said,"Let's see what we can do. Tom, you and Aaron go to the left, Cato and I will move right."

Sam and Cato crossed the gravel road around a bend. They doubled back and soon reached a knoll where they could observe the soldiers.

There were six or seven of them. Sam raised Killdevil and drew a bead on the one wearing shoulder straps.

As the officer crumpled to the ground, the other Federals made a charge toward Sam's position and Aaron and Tom fled deeper into the woods.

"All heck gonna break loose now," said Tom.

Sam stopped and smiled as he looked back and saw the soldiers following him into the woods. Moving from cover to cover behind fallen trees and rocks, the Bushwhackers fired on the soldiers from hiding, only to move to another point of concealment and fire again.

Aaron and Tom took cover in a clump of rock outcropping and watched as several of the soldiers moved cautiously toward their position.

Suddenly Aaron stood straight up! The leader of the group was a fat, dumpy Sergeant with an unkempt beard and handlebar mustache. He was so close Aaron could even make out the flattened nose.

"Git down!" whispered Tom, "You tryin' to get us both kilt?"

"It's the one who killed my Paw," Aaron said as he raised his rifle to his shoulder.

He was in his front yard. The blood from his Paw's chest had turned his white shirt red and a small stream was running over the porch and down the steps. He looked up and saw the face of the Sergeant clearly. He felt the rush of hate that possessed his body.

His entire body was shaking as he fired the rifle. The bullet slammed into a tree just over the Sergeant's head and he fell to the ground and fired his pistol at Aaron, who was standing in plain view.

Aaron heard the shot career off the rocks in front of him and ducked back into cover.

"Now you done it!" said Tom, "We got a fight on our hands now. If'n you had kept down, we could have picked them off one by one."

Peeking over the edge of the rocks, Aaron and Tom saw four of the Federal charging toward their position, running in a squat and staying behind trees as much as possible.

The Sergeant was still on the ground, keeping up a covering fire.

Aaron and Tom lay behind the rocks. "When I give the word," said Tom, "We jump up and fire. They will be close. We got to get at least two of them the first volley. You ready?"

Aaron nodded. He cocked his pistol and waited.

"Now!" cried Tom, "Now!"

When Aaron stood the first of the Federal was not more than ten yards away, running directly toward him.

He raised the pistol and fired at precisely the same time Tom did, and two of the blue coats went tumbling forward, their momentum carrying them to the very edge of the rocks.

The other two, who had been a little behind, turned and ran in the opposite direction dodging between trees for cover.

"Let's go git 'em!" Aaron shouted.

"Let's get out of here while we can," said Tom, peeking over the rocks again to see several other soldiers coming through the woods.

"But he's still alive," Aaron cried.

"I think you better leave him that way if we want to stay in the same condition," Tom said, "Come on."

Aaron realized that afoot they had little choice but to escape, for they had no idea how many Federals were in the area and would respond to the gunfire.

When they got to the spot where the horses had been tethered, they were gone, and so were Sam and Cato.

Reluctantly Aaron followed Tom down the side of the hill and after making a couple of false turns, by nightfall they had worked their way to the spot Sam had designated earlier that they should meet if split up.

Sam and Cato were already there, and Sam was carving four new notches into Killdevil's stock.

"Cato had what you might call a water haul," Sam said, "How'd you boys do?"

"We got one a piece," said Tom.

Aaron had been so intent on killing the Sergeant, it had not sunk in until that moment that he had killed a man. A faceless, nameless man he did not know or hate. He had not seen anything but a blue uniform coming at him and he had fired directly into the man's face. How old was he? Did he have a family? Where was he from?

There were no answers to the questions.

He walked off into the woods a few yards and tried to throw up, but it was only the dry heaves.

He thought about his Maw and Mary Lee and wondered how he could ever face them again. Finally, he rejoined the others and there was silence for a long time.

At last, Sam spoke. "You boys remember seein' Norwood's son ride off while we was eatin' breakfast?"

"I sure do," said Tom, "He seemed in a mighty hurry."

"I think we need to visit Mr. Norwood again on our way home," Sam said, "This little ruckus is going to have Federal swarmin' all over these hills. Probably best we cut our trip short and head south."

"We gonna walk all the way?" Cato asked.

Sam smiled. "Nope, just to Fredericktown."

"Fredericktown?" Aaron and Cato said almost as one.

"Yep," said Sam, "We got to git us some horses. We'll hole up here and rest up all day. By the time we get to town, it will be very dark and very wet."

As Sam had predicted, the rains came in torrents as the four of them walked the muddy street of the little town, entered a livery stable, and helped themselves to fresh horses.

In the dark, they were unable to locate any saddles, and rode out of town bareback, with only halters on the horses. No one seemed to even notice the dark little band of men trudging through the muddy street.

By morning, they were thirty miles south of Fredericktown. A stop at Mr. Norwood's farm had proved fruitless as the provider of their breakfast on the way into the ambush the day before had found fit to leave the country for a spell.

"Probably got Hildebrand fever," Tom laughed, "And went north for his health."

Detouring from their usual routed home by a good twenty miles, the little band stopped at a store at a crossroads that was owned by a Union man who had been known to report on Rebels, but was also very well stocked with provisions, to which the boys helped themselves generously.

"Charge it to Uncle Sam," said Sam, "And put the Big River mob down as security for the loan."

Aaron didn't notice when they rode off that Tom had stayed behind, but when he looked around for him, flames were leaping from the front door of the store.

*   *   *

Aaron wondered if he should call on Mary Lee as soon as he got back to Crowley's Ridge, wait a while, or just not go at all.

Girls were sure hard to understand. If you made a pledge to revenge your Paw's death, it was something that had to be done and he didn't need religion or queasy hearted females talking him out of it.

But still, they had become close and her family had been a big help to him and her mother was the best cook on Crowley's Ridge and it probably would not be polite not to go to the Lemley home and let them know he was safe.

He dreaded it, because he knew he could not be dishonest with Mary Lee and had a pretty good idea how she would feel about him killing a man and the store burning down.

He had barely slid from the saddle when the door to the Lemley home burst open and Mary Lee came running out and almost took him off his feet as she flew into his arms.

He returned the embrace and it felt good until he heard Bill clear his throat from the doorway and Aaron let go of Mary Lee and stepped forward to shake her father's hand.

"Good to see you back," Bill said, "We been praying for you since you rode off. Come on in, Anna's got supper almost ready."

Once again Aaron felt the warmth and love of the Lemley home and the evening meal went by swiftly with pleasant chatter and Aaron's and Mary Lee's eyes met in stolen moments.

Finally the Lemley's were properly thanked and Aaron and Mary Lee walked up the trail toward his hut.

"Aaron," she said, "I was wrong to try to force you to go to the religious services. As it turned out, the good Reverend turned out to be more glutton than preacher and the meetings were less than what I had hoped they would be."

They walked on for about fifty yards.

"I killed a man," Aaron said softly.

Mary Lee stopped short and her hand went over her mouth and Aaron thought for a moment she was going to pass out.

"Who was he?" she asked.

"I don't know, just some Federal soldier. But Mary Lee, if I hadn't shot him, he would have shot me."

"I know men are being killed every day in this awful war," Mary Lee said, "But it's different when someone you know does the killing or is killed."

"It's different when you are doing the killing," Aaron said as he looked at the ground. He had been dreading this moment all the way home and had rehearsed telling her a thousand times as he lay awake at night or rode the trails.

"Something else happened," he said.

"What?"

"I saw the Sergeant who killed Paw, even got a shot at him."

Mary Lee was silent.

"You're going back, aren't you?"

Aaron eyes filled with tears.

"I got to go, Mary Lee, I got to go."

"I won't quote the Bible to you," she said, "I was wrong to try and force my religion on you before, but I want you to know two things."

"What are they?"

"I believe killing is wrong," Mary Lee said, "Even in war. But I believe God can even forgive killing if you come to him with a repentant heart and confess your sins."

"Was it all right for him to kill Paw?"

"No, of course not," she said, "But what is really standing between you and God is the hate you have for a man you don't even know. It's doing more damage to you than it is to him, even if you do someday succeed in killing him."

They were almost to his hut and he stopped once again and faced her.

"Mary Lee, I am going to find the Sergeant who killed Paw and I am going to kill him and neither you or your God can stop me."

There was silence as they stood and looked at each other through tear filled eyes.

She could hardly speak but finally took Aaron by the hand. "Aaron, I love you and I will continue to do so, for my feelings for you are not based on how you act. I will love you no matter what you do, not only as a girl loves a boy, but as Jesus loves us all."

She let go of his hand and started back down the trail. After a few steps, she stopped and turned to face him again.

"I promised not to quote the Bible to you," she said, "But remember that Jesus even forgave those who killed him as he died on the cross. I will continue to pray that you will discover that kind of love to replace the hate that is consuming you."

Aaron stood until she was out of sight, then went into his cabin and opened a fresh bottle of burst-head he had gotten from the store they had burned in Missouri.

*   *   *

The cooler nights of September settled on the ridge but failed to lessen the heat of hate that surrounded the evening campfires.

The same old stories were repeated over and over as each man related the misfortunes that had befallen him and his family.

Aaron idled the first two weeks away. Sam had gone on a raid into southwest Missouri with three of Quantrill's men and Aaron couldn't figure out why.

Quantrill's men were different. They seemed to enjoy killing, even without a cause.

"I owe them a favor," Sam had said, but didn't explain.

Aaron and the others mostly played cards and drank and bragged about their exploits, but Aaron felt an uneasiness he could not explain.

He had started toward the Lemley cabin several times but just couldn't face Mary Lee. For one thing, he usually had hard liquor on his breath and he knew she would not be happy about that.

And so he went to his hut and finished his last bottle of burst-head and fell asleep. But it was not a peaceful sleep, when the face of the soldier he had killed was not before him, it was the Sergeant.

"Get up," he heard a voice in the darkness, an angry voice.

Someone kicked his cot, and he tumbled into awareness as his eyes accustomed to the dark.

He looked up through reddened eyes into the face of Sam Hildebrand.

"I leave camp for a few days and look what happens to you," Sam said, "Get up, boy, we got a long ride ahead of us."

Aaron got up and staggered to the metal wash pan where he splash tepid water onto his face. He dried on a dirty towel and tried to mash his hair into some sort of order, but finally gave up and just put his hat on.

Quickly he slipped on his shirt and pants. As he was pulling on his boots, Sam held the door open. He was obviously in a hurry.

Sam had already saddled Aaron's horse and they rode down the trail as Aaron swayed in the saddle and could hardly hold his head up. Burst-head was again taking its toll.

Finally, as the cool morning air cleared his head a little, he spoke.

"Where we goin'?"

"These folks are goin' to need supplies for the winter," said Sam, "Captain Bolin and myself and you boys are aimin' to relieve those supplies from the army wagons being run into Bloomfield from Cape Girardeau."

"Bloomfield?" said Aaron, "Ain't that where your wife is?"

Sam never answered.

At the bottom of the ridge, they met Captain Bolin and the rest of the group, which included the entire clan, Haile, Cato, and Burlap.

"Sam has assured me you boys can carry your weight," Bolin said, "But all I've seen you do lately is carry your booze, and some of you have not done that very well."

Aaron and the others glanced at each other, and averted eye contact with Sam or Bolin.

"Well, you're riding with me now, and I don't intend to get shot by some Federal because some boy who can't hold his liquor is suppose to be watching my back side. There will be no drinking on this excursion, and if you have any with you, get rid of it now."

Four bottles of burst-head flew into the brush.

"Good," said Bolin, "Now let's ride."

Aaron looked around at the rest of the group. He was glad to ride with old friends and was relieved to see that none of Quantrill's cutthroats had returned with Sam.

He recognized Bill Banks, an older man who was from Bollinger's Mill and Jeff Stanwood, a young man from Sedalia, like Mary Lee and her family.

The rest of the ten riders he knew by face and had seen them around camp, but did not know their names.

They arrived on the banks of the White River, which along with Castor Creek, forms the eastern fork of the St. Francis.

"We'll camp here," Bolin said, "Until we can get some information on when the wagons are due and how many guards they have with them. I need someone to do some scouting."

"I'll go," said Sam, "Just give me a little time to get ready."

Bolin started to object, but Sam, he knew, was hard to change once his mind was set.

Sam put on civilian clothes, leaned Killdevil up against a tree, and started walking up the road, carrying only a halter.

"Where you goin'?" Bolin asked.

"Up the road to look for the mule I lost yesterday," said Sam, and kept on walking.

Hiding in the brush beside the road about a mile from camp, Sam waited.

A man driving a cart and oxen came along, but he did not like the looks of things and let him pass.

In about an hour, he saw a boy coming down the road. Sam stepped out of the brush and walked toward him. The boy was whistling parts of "John Brown".

"You seen a mule?" Sam asked.

"No sir," said the young man.

"Well, I think I will give up looking," said Sam, "I have walked about all I can tolerate."

"Them government wagons will be comin' down the road tomorrow," the boy said, "Maybe you could catch a ride with them."

"Naw, I don't think so," said Sam, "The rebels might jump those wagons and I don't want to be caught in a fracas."

"No need to worry," said the boy, "They got twenty soldiers guarding each one of them wagons."

"Well, thanks son, I might just do that."

After the boy had disappeared, Sam hurried back to Bolins' camp and gave his report.

"Sleep tight," Bolin said to the men, "We're gonna have a little action in the morning. But remember, our mission is to get supplies, not to kill Yankees."

They made a cold camp and sat in the darkness of the woods, well hidden from the road.

"How was that raid you made with Quantrill's men?" Aaron asked Sam as they leaned up against a boulder and chewed on the beef jerky that had become a staple in their diet.

"Not well," said Sam, "I do not wish to ride with them again. They are reckless and almost cost me my life."

Sam paused as he washed the rest of the jerky down with a draw from his canteen.

"The four of us attacked a bunch of Federal up in Madison County. One of Quantrill's men had reported there were only thirty of them, so naturally, we charged them. Turned out they must have been a hundred. Two of our horse's was kilt and one man wounded. On our way home, a citizen told us it had been reported we kilt five of the Yankees and wounded several others. But we barely got out alive."

"How'd you get away?" asked Cato.

"Got into the woods and ran as fast as I could," said Sam, "I've noticed the blue bellies have stopped following me into the woods."

Aaron couldn't see Sam's face in the dark, but he knew there was a little smile on it.

"Had a strange thing happen then, "Sam continued, " I went on to Big River and got a bead on James Craig, but Kill-Devil misfired."

"Kill-Devil?" asked Aaron in amazement.

"Yeh, so I decided it was time to skedaddle out of there and headed for home but a large detachment struck our trail between Pilot Knob and Fredericktown and they chased us for about ten miles."

"Anything good happen on that trip?" Haile asked.

"Several profitable events took place," said Sam, and again Aaron could sense the smile on his face, "We went shopping at Bean's Store on Flat River and got some good supplies, all on account. On the way up, we hung that rascal Skaggs down at Fredericktown who had been reportin' on our activities, and on the way home, we found Mr. Slater at home down in Madison County and he will not be spying for the Feds any more."

*   *   *

Aaron rolled out of his bed roll the next morning into grass covered with dew. He pulled on his hat so he wouldn't have to comb his hair, and sat chewing on a piece of jerky and stared at the gray ashes of the small fire they had built the night before. Captain Bolin walked up, strapping on his saber.

"Soon's you finish that scrumptious breakfast, you and your friends cross the road and hide in the timber, just around the bend and deep enough so no one can see you."

"Yes sir," said Aaron as he picked up his gun and went to kick the others out of their sleep.

The morning warmed, gnats flew around them in droves, and it was almost high sun before the wagons came down the road, just as the boy had said, each guarded by twenty men.

They certainly looked military in their blue jackets and the buttons glistened in the sun.

A very good target.

The Rebels opened fire from the woods and then charged, yelling at the top of their voices as they entered the road just in front of the front wagon.

The driver dove from the seat and crawled under the wagon. Two blue jackets fell hard off their horses into the dust while the others turned tail and fled back down the road.

Packing all they could from the wagons onto their horses, the Rebs began immediately the trip back to Crowley's Ridge.

Winding their way through Mingo Swamp just in case there were pursuers, they soon arrived at the St.Francis River and found it running bank full, with much debris floating on the turbulent water.

"Only way to get across is to get across," said Sam and plunged his horse into the muddy, swirling spray. One by one, the others followed, until only Aaron and Banks remained. Banks went first but half way across, a tree limb wrapped in grapevines caught his horse and Banks plunged into the water, entangled in the twirling vines.

Aaron tried to work his horse toward Banks, who kept going under the tree and coming up on the other side as it rolled in the river.

For a brief moment, stretching out as far as he could, their fingers touched but were pulled apart by the current.

Banks eyes bugged out and his mouth was open in a silent scream as the water pulled him away and under for the final time.

Aaron closed his eyes, trying to blot out the image, the face of fear and death written on Bank's face.

When he opened his eyes, Banks was gone, and he turned to his own salvation, finally reaching shore as his frightened steed fought for life himself.

Finally reaching the safety of Crowley's Ridge two days later, they divided up the supplies from the wagons among the little band of settlers and Aaron went to his cabin.

Pulling the black bottle from beneath his cot, he took a long draw and tried to forget Bank's death mask.

*   *   *

With the harsh north Arkansas winter approaching, the men of Crowley's Ridge joined together to prepare. Existing cabins were re-chinked with mud, stoves and chimneys were checked. Some of the newcomers living in tents or make-shift shanties, had help in constructing more permanent homes of logs.

The men spent time hunting and trapping in the woods, salting away meat for the expected long, hard winter. Already the women had canned the vegetables from their summer gardens.

Sam and Aaron volunteered to do the hunting, and almost anything that moved was a target, from raccoon to possum to rabbits.

"When it really gets cold, probably in late November," said Sam, "I'll teach ya how to butcher a hog. That's something I really know how to do."

Aaron didn't tell him that he had helped his Paw butcher many times.

In the evenings, with the first nip of fall in the air, the men huddled around the camp fires and shared again their stories of barbarities that had been committed on their families by the Federals.

It was here Aaron learned something about Sam he did not know.

"My own brother, William," said Sam, "jined up with the Federal and is somewhere right now, wearing a blue uniform."

He stared at the fire and the light flickered across his reddened face, his eyes half closed as if he could see his brother in the fire.

Then for a moment, Aaron thought he smiled a little.

"Come to think of it," he said, "I wear a blue uniform most of the time, too."

Several chuckled but soon it grew silent.

"They took an old man out and shot him," said one of the newer pilgrims who had just arrived from St. Francois County, "Just because he took Sam Hildebrand in on one of his trips."

Sam had been stirring the coals of the fire with a stick but when he heard that, he swirled the fire so violently, sparks and hot coals landed on the men.

Several cursed as they jumped up and brushed the fire off, but grew quiet quickly as they feared Sam's wrath.

But Sam kept his eyes on the flames.

"Did I ever punish a man for feeding a Federal?" he asked no one in particular.

The men stared at the fire and grew deathly still. They could feel the rage boiling up in Sam.

"Have I ever taken from a needy widow, or punished children because their father was a Union man?"

No one answered.

Sam's neck grew redder and finally he stood up. He brushed the dirt from the seat of his pants and seemed to shudder from head to toe.

"A rabbit ran over his grave," thought Aaron, that's what Maw used to say when that happened.

"I'm riding north in the morning," Sam said his voice calm and quiet. "Who wants to go with me?"

Aaron didn't look around to see if anyone else was going, he just got up and started toward his cabin. He soon found Tom, John, and Cato walking fast to catch up with him.

"Better get some sleep," he said, "You know Sam likes to leave early."

*   *   *

It was still very dark when Aaron got to the corrals and began to saddle his horse. Only Sam was already there, but in a few minutes the other straggled in. Burlap, as usual, was last, running as he tried to put on his shirt and rub the sleep from his eyes at the same time.

Captain Bolin and six others had joined the little group.

The brush were heavy with dew and there was a fall chill in the air, but the sun promised to rise as they headed out of camp.

Their trip up the eastern side of the St. Francis was uneventful, for the Federals did not want to tangle with Rebs that far south and they did not want to go into Mingo Swamp, Rebs or no Rebs.

"One of these days," said Haile, "I'm gonna have to show them Feds where the water moccasins are so they can cross the swamp stepping on their backs."

They crossed the river and deviated from the usual route and soon reached West Prairie. Cato, scouting ahead, came back to report there were about thirty Federal camped out just on the edge of the town.

Sam reached into his bed roll and pulled out an extra pistol, stuck both his hand guns in his belt, checked Kill-devil and cradled it in his right arm.

He placed the reins in his mouth, looked at the boys, and said, "Come on, let's get us some blue bellies!", and without waiting to see if they were going to follow, charged down the road.

To a man, the Rebels drew their revolvers and follow Sam's charge toward the enemy camp.

Directly into the center of the Federal they rode, firing their pistols at close range. Four soldiers in blue fell at once, while the other scrambled to reach cover or ran in panic.

Only a few had the courage to stand and fire back at the screaming Rebels.

Aaron felt the minie ball slam into his thigh. He almost fell from his horse but managed to hang on, dropping his pistol as he clasped his mount around the neck and rode until they were well beyond the Federal camp.

Then he fell and writhed in agony as the pain in his leg hit full force.

"Grab him and hold him still, boys," yelled Sam. "He'll pump all his blood out rolling around like that. Git that leg up in the air!"

Bolin and the others rode back down the trail to be certain the soldiers had not followed, but decided they wanted no part of this little reckless band of Rebels.

Aaron found himself pinned to the ground by Haile and Burlap while Cato held his leg up.

Sam slit Aaron's pants leg all the way up. Blood was spurting from the ragged hole.

Sam pressed his hand on the hole and pressured the flow until it eased. With his other hand, he felt around on Aaron's leg.

"It went in and turned up," he said when his fingers found the hard lump on the back side of the leg, "But I think it missed the bone."

He handed his knife to Cato and whispered so Aaron couldn't hear, "Build a fire and heat the blade until it is red hot, then bring it to me. We're gonna have to cut it out from the other side."

Sam went to his horse and produced a black bottle and poured the brew down Aaron's throat.

"Kinda breakin' the Captain's no drinking rule, ain't ya?" Tom Haile joked, but nobody laughed.

Cato handed Sam the red-hot knife and as the blade touched Aaron's flesh the stench made even Tom turn away as Aaron's body arched in pain.

He took another swallow of the burst-head.

"Put a stick in his mouth," said Sam, "So's he won't bite his tongue off."

Aaron spit the stick out and screamed as Sam made the incision, then thankfully, he passed out.

*   *   *

Mary Lee was taking the cone pone off the fireplace as she and her mother prepared lunch.

"Oh!" she screamed, clutching her stomach. The hot skillet with the bread crashed to the floor.

"What is it?" her mother said as she caught Mary Lee and eased her into a chair.

"I don't know," said Mary Lee, "A sudden burning, stabbing pain just hit me all at once."

"I'll get your father."

"No, its easing now, Mother. The pain is almost gone, but I feel a deep, deep fear within."

*   *   *

Sam eased the ball out of Aaron's leg and held the bloody missile for the others to see. Tearing the end off of his own blanket, he wrapped it around Aaron's leg and tied it with thinner strips of the cloth.

"Don't never tie it too tight," he told the others, "You'll shut off the flow of blood and the poison will set in."

Then he poured a generous dose of the burst-head on the bandage. Even in his unconscious state, Aaron writhed in pain.

"Too bad we ain't got no coal oil, " he said, "It sure burns, but it'll stop the infection."

Tom made a resolve never to get himself shot when Sam was around. "The dying can't be any worse than the cure," he said to himself.

"Some folks put a spider web on a wound," said Sam as he cleaned his hands and wiped off the blade of his knife, "But I think that's an old wive's tale."

When Aaron woke up, he was riding in the back of a spring board wagon, just like the one Sam was in when they first met, and ironically enough, for the same reason.

He raised up and peeked over the side. Cato and Burlap were riding in front of the wagon, while Haile sat on the driver's seat.

"Where we goin'?" Aaron asked.

"Well, look who is back among the living," said Haile, "You must be feeling better. We're on our way back to deliver the injured hero to his girl friend at Crowley's Ridge."

Aaron tried to move and the pain from his leg forced him back down. "Well, I ain't feeling any better," he said, "And I don't have a girl friend."

Haile laughed. "You got to look on the bright side, Aaron. You got hit in your gimpy leg, you still got one good one." He laughed again but when no one else joined in, he fell silent and flipped the reins on the rumps of the mules.

Soon the little caravan arrived at Crowley's Ridge and they took Aaron to his hut and making him as comfortable as they could, left him in the still darkness.

His leg throbbed with pain and when he tried to put weight on it, he collapse back on the bed, exhausted.

His head still hurt from the burst-head, and so he laid as still as possible to avoid the pain.

He had almost dozed off when the door to the shack opened slowly and Bill Lemley stuck his head in.

"All right to come in?" he asked.

"I guess so," mumbled Aaron.

Bill opened the door wider and before he realized what had happened, Mary Lee was at Aaron's side, her eyes full of fresh tears.

Aaron turned his head from her to hide his own tears and perhaps, he realized, in shame.

"I'm so glad you were just wounded," Mary Lee said, "When we heard you had been shot, I was afraid you had been killed."

She took his hand in both of her's and squeezed so tightly, he almost forgot the pain in his leg.

Anna Lemley was right behind her husband with something that smelled an awful lot like chicken soup. Aaron had not eaten for two days and the smell was irresistible.

Propped up on the cot on his elbows, Mary Lee shoveled the soup into his mouth almost faster than he could swallow. When it was gone, he lay back and just looked at her.

"You are going to come live with us 'til you get well," Bill said, "I know you don't think too much of my wood shed, but we have raised the roof and cut an opening into the cabin. You can stay there where Anna and Mary Lee can nurse you properly."

Aaron tried to object but was filled and could not speak. He also realized he needed help and the thought of spending so much time with Mary Lee was certainly appealing.

Finally he regained his voice. "I don't know why you folks are so nice to me," he said, "I ain't brought you nothing but trouble."

"I saw something of value in you the first time we met," Bill said, "Sometimes a good person has to go through a lot of trouble before the goodness pops out. Besides, we love you because Jesus loves you, regardless of how good or bad you are."

That seemed strange to Aaron. He had always thought that God loved good people and hated bad people.

He looked into the eyes of Mary Lee.

Maybe, he thought, Tom was right. He was pretty lucky and he did still have one good leg.

*   *   *

Later that day, Cato and Burlap showed up to help move Aaron into the Lemley's newly remodeled wood shed.

"Haile was gonna help," Cato told Aaron, "But he is kinda under the weather, if you know what I mean."

"Yeh," chimed in Burlap, "And he don't think Mary Lee would be glad to see him cause she thinks he has ruined your morals."

The wood shed was, indeed, greatly enlarged, and there was room for Aaron's cot and he could almost stand up straight in the center of the room. This is, he could stand up with the help of Burlap, who hardly fit into the room at all.

An opening had been cut into the cabin wall and a blanket hung over it so he could have privacy.

"It'll be great," said Burlap, "Just look at the advantages. Just go out the back door, and you can be the first one to the outhouse every morning."

"Why don't you leave the jokes to Tom," Aaron said.

He spent the next few days, for the most part, propped up on his cot with the blanket pulled to one side so Mary Lee and he could talk.

Burlap and Cato showed up everyday to check on him, usually at mealtime, Aaron noticed.

One morning there was a rap on the door, and when Anna opened it, Sam was there.

"How's the boy?" he asked.

"Come in and see for yourself," Anna said, "Would you like a cup of coffee?"

"Yes, I would, thank you," said Sam as he removed his cap and entered the cabin. He was dressed in a Federal uniform. "Just got back last night and thought I ought to check on him."

Mary Lee barely acknowledged Sam's greeting and went to her room, pulling closed the curtain that served as a door.

Sam accepted the hot cup of coffee from Anna and sat on a stool beside Aaron's cot.

"Got somethin' for you," he said and from under his coat produced a pistol. "Heard you lost yours."

"Looks almost new," said Aaron.

"It's a Leech and Rigdon," said Sam, "One of the finest made, although it was copied from a Colt. Shoots six times without reloading and takes a .36 caliber bullet. You'll notice the frame is made of brass."

"Wher'd you get it?"

"That's a funny thing," said Sam, "Them guns was made for Southerners and I don't know how a Yankee got holt of one, but it don't matter, cause he will have no further use for it."

Aaron did not have to ask why.

Sam got up.

"Got to go," he said, "I'm heading north and would like to get as far up the way as I can before dark."

"Who's goin' with you?" asked Aaron.

"Making this trip alone," Sam answered, "Got some private scores to settle and I want to be able to move fast."

"Good luck," said Aaron, "And thanks for the pistol."

He thanked Anna for the coffee, ducked out the front door, and was soon gone. Only then did Mary Lee come out of her room.

"I didn't mean to be rude," she said, "But I felt it was better to leave."

"It's all right, I think Sam knows how you feel, but remember, he saved both our necks out on the trail that day."

She looked at the floor. "What did he want?"

"Just to see how I was and to tell me he was going on another raid, and oh yeh, he gave me this."

Mary Lee looked at the pistol.

"Someone had to die," she said softly, "So that you could have a gun that will probably kill someone else. When will it end?"

"Sam has had a lot of people do him and his family wrong," said Aaron, "I have only one and I promise you that when my Paw's death has been avenged, I will never kill another man."

"Its not the killing that is destroying you," Mary Lee said,"It's the hate."

CHAPTER 10

It was now late in January and although the winter was not as harsh as the past two had been, it was still bone chilling in the saddle as Sam rode alone into Missouri.

He followed the usual trail up the St. Francis, his plan was simple: kill some of the Vigilantes, and on the way back, move his family from Bloomfield to Crowley's Ridge.

Once into territory controlled by the Feds, Sam rode at night and while crossing a brushy ridge, was challenged.

"Who comes there?" asked a shaky voice in the dark.

Sam halted and realized he had almost ridden right into a Yankee camp! His mind had been on Margaret and the children and he had not been his usual cautious self.

Wheeling his horse into the woods to his right, he dashed down a steep hill for a short distance. In a moment, horse and rider were airborne as they plunged over a precipice about ten feet high. Sam flew over the horse's head and landed in a deep hole of black water.

Dazed, he checked his horse and knew at once it was dead. Trying to keep his wits about him, Sam waded out into the stream as far as he could. The cold water not only shocked him back into reality, but hid him, he hoped, from the Federal soldiers who were making their way down the embankment. Movement was slow motion, as the black water soaked into the woolen Federal jacket.

Eternity seemed to crawl as he inched his way across the stream, finally reaching the far bank, but not able to pull himself out of the water. Exhausted, he dragged his body up on the ground and back into some brush where he stole a few seconds to regain his strength and breath, and then he started to make his escape complete when he realized he did not have Kill-Devil! Somewhere, back in the cold black hole of water, which was now surrounded by Feds, was his prized gun, and his record of his conquests.

There was a lot of yelling and cursing but none of the Yankees seemed to have any desire to track the mystery rider in the dark.

Soon they headed back toward camp and as the lantern lights faded, Sam made his way back to the hole and waded out into the water up to his chin. The near frozen water bit at his bare skin and he found himself making a little whining sound, in spite of the danger of being heard by the Feds. He knew where he had hit the water and it didn't take long for his feet to feel something that moved on the bottom of the pool.

He tried, and tried, to lift the gun with his foot so he could grab it, but each time it slipped back to the bottom. He realized there was only one way, as he forced himself under the water until his hand finally grasped the rifle and he popped to the top, his lungs hungry for air.

There he stood, holding his water logged gun in his hand, when some of the Federal came back, jabbering to each other and holding a lantern high in the air.

Sam shivered in the cold water as they found his dead horse and walked around for about ten minutes with the lantern casting shimmering, golden light across the surface of the water.

One of the soldiers checked the far side of the stream as Sam slowly worked himself beneath some vines hanging from the bank. He bite hard to keep his teeth from chattering, for he knew that even the slightest sound would be amplified across the water.

"Here's his trail!" the soldier yelled and immediately they all crossed down stream a little where it was shallow, and headed up the hill, following the short trail Sam had left before he remembered that Kill-Devil was missing.

As soon as they were out of sight, Sam climbed out on the other side, circled around their encampment, and made his way through the woods, freezing and carrying his precious weapon. "I got to keep going," he said to himself, "If'n I stop walking, I will surely freeze to death."

He could barely put one foot in front of the other when just before daybreak, he reached the home of a member of the Knights of the Golden Circle and was taken in, dried out, and well fed.

Exhausted, Sam soon fell asleep in the loft of his benefactor's barn. It was morning of the next day when he woke up, had a good breakfast, thanked his host who had cleaned Kill-Devil for him, and again started on the quest of death for the Vigilantes, riding a work horse he promised to return, or provide a more than adequate substitute on his return trip.

Riding in the direction of Federicktown Sam was once more his usual alert traveler, his ears attuned to the woods from any sound that did not belong there, his eyes scanning from side to side and even behind him. Even the snap of the smallest branch, the click of metal on a tiny stone, the breath of a horse, or the slightest creak of leather, and he would disappear into the shadows of the woods.

That was why he saw the riders before they saw him.

Secreting himself in a gully, he waited until they were close enough to identify for sure, for sometimes it was not easy to tell if Rebels were Rebels dressed as Federals, or real Federals.

"All ya gotta do is look fer bullet holes in the jacket," Tom Haile always said, "If'n you see any, they's Rebels."

And these indeed, were real Rebels. Sam saw no bullet holes, but the very fact that none of the uniforms seemed to fit very good was another sure sign. Most Rebels rode better horses than the Federal rode, too. Most of the Rebel horses used to belong to Feds.

And besides, he spotted Cato in the group.

The leader was a Lieutenant Childs, of Bolin's command. Besides the Lieutenant and Cato, Sam also recognized a man by the name of Henry Resinger, a sincere man Sam had spent many hours at the campfire with, sharing their woes.

"Sam," said Childs, "You're getting a little reckless, riding alone by daylight, ain't you?"

"Well, I found out a couple of nights ago that riding alone in the dark ain't too safe, either. Where you boys headed?"

"Up to Bollinger Mills," answered Childs, "Got word there is a whole passel of Yanks up there been givin' some of our folks a hard way to go, and we intend to give them a lesson in manners."

"I'll ride with you, if you don't mind," said Sam.

"Be glad to have you," said Childs, "As a matter of fact, I would be obliged if you would just take command and lead us, after all, I'm just a Lieutenant and you are a Major."

"Them titles don't mean a thing when the lead starts flying," said Sam, "But I will be glad to assist you if you want. I only got one request."

"What's that?"

"I like to ride with men I can trust," said Sam, "I want each of your men to take a vow they will never surrender. If we all pledge to fight to the end, we will all be safer."

"What do you say, men?" asked Childs.

To a man they agreed to ride with Sam and took the oath to fight to the death, if necessary, rather than surrender.

The one hundred and fifty Federal soldiers camped out at Bollinger Mills thought there were a thousand Rebs charging them as Sam and his new command swept into the camp with pistols firing in all directions.

Riding directly through the camp and out the other side, the little band killed twenty-two soldiers in a matter of five minutes, leaving Henry Resinger behind with a bullet hole in his forehead.

Several of the Rebels were wounded and stopping to rest, Sam and Childs decided it was best to head back south. The little incident would be bringing Feds from all over the area.

As they prepared to leave, Sam took the time to carve three new notches on Kill-Devil's stock.

"They's coming from the right!" Sam heard someone yell after they had been on the trail south for several hours.

"And on the left!" cried another panicky voice.

Hit from both sides by the Federals who had circled around and overtaken the little band, mostly because they had been slowed by the wounded, the Rebels were split in two.

Sam rode to the top of a ridge and prepared to take a stand to protect the rear of his charges. He looked back just in time to see seven of this boys, including Cato, being taken prisoner and roughly shoved to the ground.

His first thought was to charge down the hill, but Childs came up beside him and seemed to read his mind.

"No use, Sam, " he said, "You can't help them now, let's take care of what we got left."

Sam had to reluctantly agree it was the only course to take, but he dreaded going back to Arkansas and telling Aaron his friend was in a Yankee prison, or dead.

He soon learned another of the Rebels had been killed in the attack, but when they crossed the swollen St. Francis, he knew they were safe and made camp to care for the wounded and rest the horses.

"Bring me a horse!"

Sam grabbed Kill-Devil and ran to the river band.

"I said bring me a horse," the voice yelled again, "Do you think I can walk on water?"

It was Cato.

Sam's facial features cracked just a little as he watched one of the men cross the river and bring the lad over, his hands still tied together with Yankee hemp.

CHAPTER 11

In the thick blackness of his tiny room, Aaron woke. He could feel the heat of his body as he kicked off the blanket. On the blanket that covered the opening, amber shadows danced, as the glowing embers in the fireplace responded to the updraft.

To Aaron, they became demons and he began to scream and thrash about. The pain in his leg and the nightmares in his mind became unbearable.

Bill Lemley was at his side almost at once, as Anna leaned over his shoulder and Mary Lee stood behind her mother, her hands over her ears to shut out the horror of his pain, a pain she could feel within her own body.

"He's got the fever," said Bill, "The wound must be poisoned."

Anna took charge at once.

"You go wake up that newcomer who says he is a doctor," she said as she pulled back the blanket and started to remove the bandages from Aaron's leg. "Mary Lee, you put some sassafras tea on and get some bacon fat out of the storm cellar."

Mary Lee went to the hearth and stirred up the dying embers and began to add wood.

"You sure you want that so called doctor?" asked Bill,"I heard a couple of folks say they doubted he even was a man of medicine."

"He's all we got," said Anna.

"All right," Bill said, "But I never heard of sassafras tea to cure the fevers."

"That's just something to keep Mary Lee busy," whispered Anna, "This is going to be a long and probably very difficult night for her, and for Aaron."

Bill pulled on his pants over his nightshirt, slipped into his shoes and draped his coat over his shoulders as he went to find the doctor in the coldness of the early morning hours.

Mary Lee followed him into the front yard. "Is he gonna be all right?" she asked.

"He'll be fine, " Bill said and hoped he sounded surer than he felt. "Your mother has handled this sort of thing before and probably knows more than our new found doctor. Now you get back inside before you get sick, too."

Back inside the cabin, Mary Lee eased over to the opening to Aaron's room. She had no tears now, just a ball of fear that hung in her throat and painful compassion for her young love.

"The tea is on, Mama," she said, "What else can I do?"

"Pray, honey," said Anna, "Pray."

Bill found the cabin of Elisha Bronton in the dark with very little difficulty. Rousing the good doctor from a drunken stupor took a little longer and much more patience.

Elisha Bronton had only arrived in camp two weeks earlier, and told everyone he had been a doctor in Rolla before the war, but left when his practice had been closed down by some drunken Dutch soldiers who claimed he had killed one of their men on purpose, which he neither denied or admitted.

Some of the Crowley Ridge settlers, however, had already questioned not only his story, but his credentials. No one had seen any kind of paper which attested to the claims of Elisha that he had been to a school of medicine.

At Aaron's bedside, Elisha peered in the semi-darkness at the reddened wound, now even black at the core and swollen with puss. He put his hand on the boy's leg for a moment and stepped back.

"It'll have to come off," he said.

"What will have to come off?" asked a shocked Anna.

"His leg," said Elisha, "His leg."

"You'll do no such thing," cried Anna, "At least not until we try to draw the poison out and get his fever down."

"The wound has got the poison," said the doctor, "It will only spread and if it is not cut off, it will kill him. As for the fever, every medical man knows that body temperature has nothing to do with a person's health."

Anna looked at Bill and he nodded.

"Doctor," he said, "I'm sorry to have awakened you at this time of the morning. Please feel free to return to your cabin. we will call you tomorrow if we have need of your services."

"You don't want me to operate?" asked Elisha.

"We certainly do not," answered Anna, "At least not until we have tried to get the poison out."

"Very well," Elisha said, perhaps with a little indignation, or perhaps it was relief. He snapped his black bag shut and headed toward the door.

"Bring me that bacon fat, Mary Lee," Anna said after the doctor was gone, "And rip up some of my dish towels, the white ones, into strips about three inches wide."

Soon Mary Lee was back with the strips. "What should I do now, Mama?"

"We don't have any alcohol or turpentine, but your Dad's horse liniment may do just as well," said Anna, "Get it and put a little on a rag and clean around the wound. It is going to burn and hurt him, but we must do it."

Aaron gritted his teeth as Mary Lee applied the horse liniment. Mary Lee could hardly bear it, but she managed to do what her mother had said.

Anna came with the bacon fat poultice, warm and with the grease dripping from it as she applied it to the wound and wrapped another of the cloth strips around the leg to hold it in place.

"Bring me a pan of cool water," she told Bill, "We will take turns bathing him until the fever breaks."

"What should I do?' asked a frightened Mary Lee.

"Go to your room and pray," said Anna, "We are gong to need divine intervention."

The rest of the night was spent bathing Aaron's hot body and changing the bacon poultice every hour or so.

Mary Lee, in her bedroom on her knees, continued to seek God's help.

When daylight came, she went to Aaron's little room. Her mother was asleep by his bed, her head propped up on the side of his cot. Bill was laid back in a chair, his mouth open and snoring.

"Mama," Mary Lee said softly as she gently shook her mother's shoulder. "Is he all right?"

Anna woke with a start and a little embarrassed that she had dozed off.

She placed her hand on Aaron's head. It was damp, very damp. His cot was soaked with sweat. He was asleep, breathing normally and evenly.

Anna pulled off the last poultice and looked at the wound. It was pink around the edges and the swollen center had gone down considerably.

She looked at Mary Lee and smiled as she wrapped her weary arms around her daughter. "There will be no amputations in this house today," she said.

Mary Lee burst into tears of joy and relief as Bill awoke and joined the happy couple.

The three of them stood looking down at Aaron for a long time.

To their surprise, his eyes opened and after blinking a couple of times he said, "I'm kinda hungry."

The Lemley family shed tears of happiness as Anna went to the kitchen and began to make potato soup.

"Mama did it, Daddy," said Mary Lee.

"I learned many years ago that your Mama and God can do anything," said Bill, "And your prayers had just as much to do with healing Aaron as her poultices."

*   *   *

"You will leave Bloomfield at once," Colonel McNeal of the Federal army told Margaret Hildebrand as she stood outside the home of a friend, surrounded by her few belongings and five children.

"The wife of that desperado, Sam Hildebrand, will not be allowed to remain within one hundred miles of my headquarters."

And so, in a borrowed wagon pulled by borrowed oxen, Margaret began her lonely journey south.

About twenty miles out of Bloomfield, she saw a lone Federal soldier riding up the road, too late for her to pull off in the woods and hide the children.

As he neared there was something familiar about the way he rode a horse, the torso straight and stiff and the arms sticking out to the side.

"Sam," she cried, "Is that really you?"

Sam could not believe his ears. He had started north for the expressed purpose of bringing his family back to Arkansas with him, but to find his wife and children on the road, out of enemy clutches, was more than he dared hope for.

There had been other activity on his trip north. He and the three men with him had encountered a company of McNeal's men just after crossing the St. Francis, and for once, Sam had deemed it necessary to retreat in the face of overwhelming odds.

One of his companions had been wounded and as the others had crossed back over the river and headed for Crowley's Ridge, Sam had ridden on alone, with more hope than plan, that he could at least contact his wife and family.

And now, here they were, on the road and headed in the right direction.

There was little time for reunion, just a simple embrace of Margaret, tousling the hair of the older boys, and hugging the girls, Sam revealed about all the emotion he was capable of, or willing to show.

"The roads are filled with soldiers," Margaret said.

"We will ride in the open," Sam told her, "For Providence has been with us so far, and I believe will continue to guide and keep us safe."

After camping out for the night in the woods, Sam's faith in their providentially provided protection was tested early the next morning.

Six Union soldiers met them on the road.

Sam, dressed in Federal blue, hailed them.

"How's it goin' men?"

"Going fine," a sergeant replied, "But what are you doing out here? What command are you from?"

"Captain McNeal's command," Sam answered, "Stationed in Bloomfield."

"And your purpose for being this far south?" the sergeant asked.

"I was assigned to escort this lady and her children south, she is the wife of Sam Hildebrand and has been expelled from south Missouri."

"Sam Hildebrand!" the sergeant said, "By all means, carry out your assignment with haste, we want nothing to do with that rascal."

Sam had to chuckle to himself as they rode off. Margaret, for once, did not see any humor in the situation and told Sam so in very clear words.

"Perhaps it would be safer for you," Sam said, "If I followed you in the woods, concealed from the traffic of the road."

No sooner had he reached the concealment of the timber than an entire regiment of Feds came up the road.

Sam watched in fear as they stopped his wife's wagon, talked with her for a few minutes, then turned the wagon around and headed north.

"I'll kill them all!" Sam said, fighting the urge to attack the entire regiment single handed.

He watched in agony as his family, so miraculously delivered yesterday, headed back toward her imprisonment.

Not two miles from his position was the home of Milas Stanton, a member of the Knights of the Golden Circle who had befriended Sam on other occasions.

Riding to the Stanton home, Sam learned that Cato and Wash Nabors, another resident of Crowley's Ridge, were sleeping in the barn.

Quickly he told them of his family's plight.

"I plan to make them pay dearly for their ride north," he said, "You boys up to a little bushwhacking?"

Cato grinned. "You bet, Sam, let's see if we can thin their ranks a mite."

"My plan, Sam said, "Is to make the detention of my family so costly, they will release them to my custody."

About sundown, the trio secreted themselves on a hill overlooking the road and waited for the soldiers to make camp.

As Sam directed, Cato and Nabors went in different directions and during the night, fired into the camp, then moved at once to a new location. Just before dawn, they met on a designated hilltop.

"How'd you do, boys?" asked Sam.

"We must have picked off five apiece," Cato said, "Kinda hard to tell for sure in the dark."

"That's about the number I counted, " said Sam, as he sat and carved notches on the stock of Kill-Devil.

"Now, let's follow them on toward Bloomfield at long distance, take what shots you can and remember to keep moving. We want them to think there are more than three of us."

Again they split up and as Sam had instructed, fired into the ranks of the Federals for most of the morning, almost to the outskirts of Bloomfield.

They met again on a hilltop.

"Guess we better head back," Sam said, "Too many blue bellies in town for just the three of us. We'll see if we can pick up some stragglers on the way back down the road. McNeal is sure gonna be sore when them soldiers bring my family back."

Rounding a curve, Sam and his companions were surprised to find Margaret and the children, minus wagon and oxen, standing beside the road.

"It worked!" Sam cried, "The Yanks decided a woman and five children were not worth so many of their men."

Cato and Nabors were whoopin' and hollerin' and waving their hats in the air.

"Calm down," Sam said, "It ain't over yet. Them Feds have reported to McNeal and you can rest assured, an entire army will be on our trail by morning."

Making camp for the night, Sam fed his hungry brood and gave Margaret instructions on how to find Stanton's farm.

"We will ride on ahead and tell him to meet you with a wagon," he told her, "When it settles down and the Federal know we are back across the St. Francis, Stanton will bring you and the children to Crowley's Ridge."

The next morning the Hildebrand family was split again as Sam, Cato, and Nabors rode in a circular fashion to Stanton's farm, then headed south for the river and the safely of Mingo Swamp.

As Sam had predicted, a large force rode out of Bloomfield under orders from Colonel McNeal and under the command of Captain Hicks, whose regiment had suffered so many losses from the Rebel sniping.

But when they reached the St. Francis, the Union soldiers balked at following the Rebels across.

Captain Hicks seemed to be upset with the attitude of his men, but after careful consideration, decided the river was the end of his jurisdiction, and besides, they had lost the trail. At least that would be his report to McNeal.

Sam had only been back at Crowley's Ridge for one day when Stanton arrived with Margaret and the children.

"Margaret," said Sam, "I have decided to become a gentleman farmer, at least for a while, and enjoy the family life."

She knew he could only be content for a short time, but was delighted as Sam, with the help of the settlers of Crowley's Ridge, repaired a log cabin vacated by a Rebel who had become a galvanized Yankee.

It was the spring of 1863. By April, Sam had a few pigs, some chickens, and even a milk cow. In May he planted corn while Margaret put in a vegetable garden of turnips, corn, potatoes, and okra.

As the temperature rose, Margaret could see the tranquility coming to a close as Sam would return from the camp fires each evening, knowing that he was being stirred to renew his crusade of vengeance.

The young corn was not a foot high when Sam, along with six others, rode north again.

＊　　　　　　＊　　　　　　＊

The winter of 1863 passed slowly for Aaron. The first couple of weeks, when he was confined to his cot and waited on by Anna and Mary Lee went fast enough, but when the wound began to heal, he felt uncomfortable staying in the Lemley home and with the help of Cato and Burlap, moved back to his little cabin.

By the time the really cold weather arrived and the little community settled down into winter quarter and contented themselves to staying warm and well fed, Aaron was getting restless.

He knew that Sam was continuing to make raids in spite of the weather, until he had gotten his family moved to Crowley's Ridge, and after that, it seemed that even old Sam had mellowed.

When the thaw came and brought spring to northern Arkansas Aaron helped Bill Lemley with his garden and even pitched in to help

Sam on several occasions, figuring he would probably be getting some free meals there, too.

"I don't know why I'm doing this, " he told Margaret one day. "I hated working in the field when I was home and Paw was alive."

Margaret was sitting on a stump, watching with a smile on her face and the baby on her hip as Sam tilled hard soil that had never been broken.

It was good to see her husband with a plow in his hand instead of Kill-Devil.

"I would be content to stay right here for the rest of my life," she said to Aaron, but he got the feeling she was really not speaking to him. "I fear we will never be able to live in Missouri in peace again, even if the war ends."

Aaron hadn't really thought about the war ending. He had heard reports from folks passing through that the St. Louis Times newspaper was reporting victories for the Yankees in the east in places like Chancellorsville, and even closer to home, Ulysses S. Grant had Vicksburg, Mississippi, under siege.

"That the same General who was at Ironton?" Aaron asked a tinker who passed through camp.

"Yep, the man said, "After he left Ironton, he got whupped at Belmont, just a few miles from here, but since then he has been on the winning side of every battle he had been engaged in, including two forts in Kentucky."

Other things were changing. General Thompson had joined Van Dorn's command the year before and apparently decided to fight in a "real" army.

And now, leaning on a hoe as he had been doing the day his Paw was killed, Aaron still wondered what it was all about as he watched the vicious and merciless killer, his friend and protector, Sam Hildebrand, gently pulling weeds from around the spinach and onions in his garden.

Visiting the Hildebrand cabin, Aaron saw the other side of Sam as he played with his children and tucked them in at night. The rough hands and powerful arms that could break a man's neck and the heart that could, in clear conscious, hang a man in a tree with the bark off a hickory tree, belonged to a gentle and loving father.

The peaceful scene was about to change rapidly, as Sam met around the camp fires and listened to the reports coming back from Missouri. He was soon worked up enough and on the 10th of May, gathered six men, including Aaron, and started for Castor Creek.

Except for Sam, Aaron did not know the men he was riding with and felt a little uncomfortable without Cato, Burlap, and Haile.

Skirting Bloomfield, the little band of raiders rode into Madison County in search of some friends of the North who had been reporting on Southern sympathizers.

But as Tom Haile had once said, the informers had all been taken down with "Hildebrand fever", and apparently gone north for their health.

"Let's hole up at the Stanton place," said Sam, "I need to properly thank him for helping my family. Perhaps we could see what his needs might be and fill them at the local Yankee store."

Milas Stanton was at home, but was ill and his wife advised the group that they would be welcome to stay in an old tobacco barn on the farm.

It began to rain heavily and since they had not stopped for two days, Sam led his troops to the barn, posted a guard, and told the others to get some sleep.

The next morning, Sam woke early. There was a heavy grayish dawn and fog clung to the ground. He found his vidette asleep by the door.

Sam kicked the man awake and called for the others to get up and be alert. Peeking out the door, he was greeted by a bullet slamming into a board, less than a foot from his head!

"We got blue bellies", he shouted "Looks like they got us surrounded."

Aaron and the others grabbed their weapons, pulled on their boots, and waited for Sam's orders.

"About thirty of 'em, I 'spect," he said, "Best for us and for Stanton if we get out as fast as we can."

As he always did, Sam already had a plan for escaping from the barn he had worked out in his mind the night before.

"Everybody to the back, " he said, "Pull some of those old boards off and crawl outside. And keep low and quiet."

Soon the Rebels were all outside and laying on the ground in back of the barn.

"Their line is thin," said Sam, "I'll go first, you boys follow, but stay thirty yards apart. Head for the hollow where we left the horses."

Sam ran from the cover of the barn and into the open as bullets whizzed about him. He felt the sting as one grazed his shoulder, while another spent minie ball bounced off his belt.

When he reached the hollow, there were only two Federal soldiers between him and the horses. Sam did not pause, but simply ran straight toward them, pulled his pistols, and shot them both.

One by one the Rebels ran the gauntlet and miraculously escaped the hail of balls that fell around them. Except for Sam's shoulder, there were no injuries.

They mounted and on reaching the edge of the woods, Sam and his men felt the safety of their habitat, knowing that if nothing else would save them, the Yankee's fear of following Sam into the woods would probably turn the trick.

"Let's go back and give them a little surprise," Sam said.

Several of the men looked surprised themselves, but before they could object, Sam and Aaron were riding at a gallop back toward the barn.

The other four decided they would rather die charging the Yankees than face Sam later if they didn't.

But it was an empty charge. The Federal had gone, leaving behind Milas Stanton's dead body and his widow, who lay prone across his body in their front yard, sobbing softly.

"The informer was a man name Wammack," she told Sam when she was finally able to compose herself, "They rode off toward Fredericktown."

"Aaron," Sam said, "You take a couple of the boys and all our horses. Head toward Fredericktown and travel on open ground as much as possible, so as to be certain you leave a plain trail even a Yankee could follow. Any more Feds come along, I want them to think we went that way."

"You gonna walk?" asked Aaron.

"Just for a spell," answered Sam, "About eight miles from here, you will come to a creek. Follow it for some distance until you come to the home of Jason Honn. Wait there for us."

"You got hit, Sam," said Aaron, "Are you all right?"

"Just a graze," said Sam, "You understand the plan."

"Yessir." Aaron wished that just once Sam would let him know how the "plan" was going to work out, and not just the beginning.

But he had learned not to question Sam. Taking the two men and all the horses, he rode off on the trail to find the creek and Honn's house.

Sam and the others started on foot, keeping in the woods, just off the road. Soon they saw three men, two in Federal uniforms and one civilian, coming down the road and leaving their rifles in the woods, stepped out and hailed them.

"Can you tell us how to get to Cape Girardeau?" Sam asked

"What outfit you with," one of the soldiers asked.

"We just got furloughs at Ironton day before yesterday," Sam said, "And are headed for Illinois to see our families."

"You better be more careful wherever you are going," the soldier said, "We had a skirmish with a bunch of bushwhackers a while ago up this road and they are probably still in the area. Them blue uniforms of yours make a pretty good target for old Sam Hildebrand and his gang."

"We will keep close watch," said Sam, "How'd you do against the bushwhackers?"

"Well, sir, we killed four of them, and the rascal who was harboring them, a rebel named Stanton. "We're headed back now to see if the bushwhackers come back to bury him."

Sam felt he had all the information he needed. He looked squarely at the civilian, who had remained very quiet. "And your name, sir?"

"Wammack, Simon Wammack. You don't have to worry about me, I am a Yankee through and through."

"Well, Mr. Simon Wammack," said Sam, pulling out a pistol, "My name is Sam Hildebrand, and as you may have heard, I am not too fond of any kind of Yankee."

As Wammack's manhood melted, he fell to his knees while the soldiers stood like statues. Sam gave one of the Knights of the Golden Circle signs, and to his surprise, the two men with Wammack gave the proper response.

"You two are free to go," Sam said, "But only after you go back to the Stanton farm and bury Silas."

They gladly agreed but as they started down the road, Wammack jerked out a pistol, fired once at Sam, and ran after them. He made about forty yards before Sam was able to bring him down with a bullet between the shoulder blades.

"You can bury him, too," he yelled at the soldiers, "Let's go meet Aaron and the others, boys."

At Honn's farm, Aaron and Sam's men spent the night, leaving as soon as the sun was up.

Riding into Wayne County, Sam spotted some Federals entering a barn. Knocking on the door of the farmhouse, he learned there were five soldiers sleeping in the barn..

"Let's give 'em a hot time," Sam said, "Pile some hay up against the barn, boys."

Soon flames licked at the sides of the barn and the Federal, aroused from their sleep, began to make their way out, coughing on the smoke from the wet hay and rotten wood.

"I'm Sam Hildebrand," Sam yelled, "I have twenty men and you are surrounded. Come out and lay down your arms and we will be easy on you."

The Feds all came out and dropped their guns in the barnyard.

"Where are you men stationed?" asked Sam.

The Federal soldiers, hoping all they had heard about Hildebrand was not true, stood trembling.

"Ironton," said one of the soldiers.

"Here's the plan," Sam told them, "Two of our boys are being held prisoner at Ironton."

Aaron and the others had been trying to put out the fire, but when he heard the word Ironton, he stopped and listened closely.

"We will release you if you will vow to see that our men are allowed to escape when you get back," Sam was saying.

"How can we do that?" said the boldest of the Feds.

"That's your problem," said Sam, "Mine will be finding you and killing you if they do not escape."

"We might not even get back," said the soldier, "This country is crawling with Rebs like you. Give us a pass so we can get through safely."

"I will guarantee your safety." said Sam, "If you agree to see that our men are freed."

"Agreed," said the Fed, "But can't you give us a written pass?"

"My word will be your pass," answered Sam and it was obvious he was getting irritated.

Aaron stepped forward.

"I'll write out a pass for them, Sam," he said, "If'n you want me to."

"That will be fine, private," said Sam. It was the only time he had ever called Aaron anything but "boy" or "Aaron".

Aaron wrote the pass and the Federal soldiers, minus their horses and rifles, headed north.

"Where we going now, Sam?" asked Aaron.

"Back to Greene County."

"If its all right with you, I think I will go to Shepherd Mountain."

"Just be careful, boy," said Sam, "No one knows who you are but if they find out you are riding with me, they could take vengeance on your mother, like they did on my family."

"I'll be careful," said Aaron.

They had been through a lot in the last couple of years and the boy had become like a son to him.

"Let's get some grub and you can leave in the morning," Sam said, "You sure you know the way."

"I can find Shepherd Mountain in a snow storm with my eyes closed," said Aaron.

After their bellies were filled, they bedded down in the soft hay of Honn's barn. The rancid smell of burnt wood still lingered heavily but their sleeping place was up wind and bearable.

There was a hole in the wood shingle roof of the barn and Aaron lay on his back and looked through it at the stars.

He knew Sam never went to sleep until all his men had.

"You believe in God?" Aaron asked.

"I ain't sure what I believe in anymore except KillDevil and my wife," Sam said, "But my dear mother does, and I believe in her, so maybe I do."

Aaron stared at the stars until he could not keep his eyes open. When they opened again, dusty shafts of sunlight were winnowing through the cracks in the barn.

CHAPTER 12

Alma Bloom looked out the kitchen window at the field that was once filled with fresh corn at this time of year, like dark ranks of tasseled soldiers protecting the farm, and promising a bountiful harvest.

Now the field was a tangle of rotting corn stalks and weeds. A plow or a hoe had not touched it in two years.

She didn't have to go outside to see what the house looked like. The paint was peeling off in great chunks and several window screens hung at odd angles, while the gutter on the front porch drooped from the weight of dead leaves that had not been removed.

The first year had not been so bad. Her brother had seen that the cellar was filled with salted meat and had given her the excess from his garden of vegetables for her to can.

She had survived, clinging to the hope that she would see her son again.

But at the end of the 1862, her brother and his family had moved to St. Louis where he took a job in a mill, and to escape the oppressive Federal rule of southeast Missouri.

Alma had relied on the kindness of neighbors, although many of them had packed up and headed for Arkansas, and some even to the territory of Idaho, where there was no war.

She had put in a small garden, just enough to keep food on her table, and along with a few chickens and a milk cow left by her brother, was determined to stay on the farm. Aaron would be home.

The house was as clean as it had always been, perhaps even cleaner. Fresh curtains hung in Aaron's room and Henry's clothes still hung in the armoire, his socks and underwear were neatly folded in drawers, as though she expected him to come home at any moment and resume their life together.

She finished rinsing out her plate in the dish pan and placed it on a towel to dry. As she wiped her hands on her apron, she glanced out the window.

Someone was coming up the road!

Since Henry's death and her son's disappearance, the Federal soldiers at Camp Blood, now known as Fort Davidson, had left her alone, but now a soldier, dressed in Union blue, was turning in the gate.

She took the shotgun off its rack. She had no idea how to load it, much less fire the thing.

The soldier rode right into the yard, right where the Sergeant had been when he killed Henry.

Alma peeked out the door and saw a small figure dismount. He started toward the porch and she raised the shotgun, hoping it would scare him off.

Then she saw the limp! It was unmistakable.

The shotgun dropped to the floor as the screen door flew open so hard it banged against the porch.

Alma ran down the steps and wrapped her arms around her son. He was dirty and did not smell so good, but it didn't matter.

There was no need for words, not at this moment. Her tears ran as she held him in his arms and swayed back and forth.

Finally she released the embrace and placed her hands on Aaron's wet cheeks. Then she embraced him again.

Aaron regained his composure. "Maybe we better git inside, Maw."

A wave of fear rolled over her as she noticed he was looking back down the road.

"Of course," she said, "Let's get inside."

It took a while for Aaron to explain the Federal uniform, and he tried to make it sound like nothing much had happened.

Alma, in her domain of the kitchen, was soon bustling about, stuffing wood into the stove and rattling pots and pans.

"You've lost weight," she said, "But we'll soon take care of that. You stay right where you are while I go to the cellar and get a ham."

"I can get it," said Aaron.

She looked out the window down the road. She wasn't sure what she was supposed to look for, but it was clear all the way back to the ford.

"No," she said, "I'll get it. You look tired and you have lost a lot of weight, haven't you?"

"You said that once already, Maw," said Aaron, "But I don't think so. As a matter of fact, I been eating pretty good."

She didn't hear him. "I have been planning this meal since the night you left," she said, "And now my prayers have been answered. I'll soon have you fattened up."

Aaron decided it was best to sit back and enjoy his Maw enjoying him, and doing what she did best: cook.

The meal was just as he had imagined it would be. Fresh salty ham with sweet yams and hot home made bread. There was warm fresh milk, straight from the cow, and as he ate, he could smell the apple cobbler baking in the Dutch oven.

That's when he knew he was home.

After the meal, they sat at the kitchen table and by the light of the coal oil lamp, he told her all he had done, well, almost everything.

"I'm so glad you found a family like the Lemley's to help you," she said, her eyes running over again as Aaron told her about his wound and recovery.

"Is Mrs. Lemley a good cook? Tell me more about Mary Lee. Is she pretty?"

"Yes maam, she is a good cook, but not as good as you. And yes, Mary Lee is very pretty."

Then he told her about Sam Hildebrand.

"Sam Hildebrand! I've heard that he is a cold blooded killer and thief!"

"Sam is a gentle man, turned into killer by the injustices done his family," Aaron said, and he told her all about Sam's family and how his mother had been evicted from her home.

"I think I understand," she said, "This war has turned a lot of good men into vile persons."

"That sounds like something Mary Lee would say."

"Tell me about her," said Alma.

Aaron did his best, but found describing Mary Lee and their relationship very difficult.

"She's very religious," he said in summing it up.

"And of what faith?"

"I ain't sure," said Aaron, "It never came up."

Alma began to clear the table and place the dishes with the food dried on them into the dish pan to soak.

"I saw him once, Maw," said Aaron, "Even got a shot at him."

She rattled the dishes in the pan and pretended not to hear.

"Aaron, have you killed anyone?"

He looked down at the table and didn't answer.

It must have been after midnight when Aaron crawled between the fresh clean sheets, although they did smell a little of musty. In his own bed, he was exhausted and felt warm and secure for the first time in two years.

In a few moments his Maw came in as she had done that night after his Paw had been killed.

She touched his disfigured cheek, tucked the quilt around his neck tightly, and kissed him gently on the forehead.

"It's good to have you home," she said.

She started back toward the kitchen

"Maw," he said in almost a whisper.

"Yes, Aaron, what is it?"

"Maw," he swallowed hard, "I got to leave again in the morning."

"Why?"

"'Cause I still ain't done what I left home to do."

As she had done nearly two years earlier, Alma Bloom stared through the lace curtains into the black Missouri night and wept.

*   *   *

It had not been easy to say goodbye to his Maw. He hated to leave his real bed behind, too. His saddlebags were bulging with food as he rode down the lane, turned left, and followed the west branch of Knob Creek before it ran into Stout Creek, and worked his way around the perimeter of Shepherd Mountain.

Across the valley, on the very top of Pilot Knob, he could see where the top of the peak had been chopped off on one side as the precious iron ore had been removed.

He was dressed in his Federal uniform but somehow felt he would have a harder time than Sam passing himself off as a Union soldier. He also lacked Sam's boldness. Or was it recklessness?

Across the way he could just see a point of light at Fort Davidson, which was being transformed into a six-sided earthwork with walls built up to five feet in height, and outside was a moat, twelve feet wide and about eight feet deep. Someone had told his Maw it was bristling with cannon.

It was time for the soldiers to be stirring, and Aaron could just make out shadowy figures as they moved between him and the lantern.

Sam had taught him well. As he rode north he passed the giant granite boulders where he had gone on Sunday School trips. There he
turned to follow the east fork of the Knob Creek, and soon was following, from inside the woods, the road to Farmington.

It was the longer way to go, but the road to and from Fredericktown
was always filled with troops, supply wagons, and scouting parties.

He could see the chimneys of Farmington when he turned south and
headed toward Fredericktown.

Early summer in the foothills of the Ozarks was a beautiful time and
Aaron moved slowly through the trees, staying far enough off the road
to be hidden from traffic, but he had seen none all day.

The woods were filled with a variety of trees, from hickory to elm
and maple, to fruit trees such as mulberry and persimmon.

A mockingbird sang its many songs from the top of an evergreen and
Aaron remembered what Sam had told him once.

"You're all right when the mockingbird is singing," he had said, "Just
watch out for yourself if he shuts up."

Stopping just outside Fredericktown after riding a hill on the edge of
town in a semi-circle as Sam had taught him, he made a cold camp at a
spot where he could watch the road and also see anyone who might be
tracking him. He ate a couple of the biscuits his Maw had packed for
him, along with some more of her ham, which only made him thirsty.
Taking a long drink from his canteen, he wiped his mouth on his sleeve,
and waited for dark.

Only a few miles down the road, he and Sam and the others had had
the running fight where he killed the man, and saw the Sergeant. Aaron
was certain the Sergeant was stationed in Fredericktown, but he was
uncertain what he should do about it.

He remembered that almost two years previously, Thompson had
fought a big battle at Fredericktown.

When the fullness of darkness was come, he rode down the hill and
into the little community.

"What would Sam do?" he asked himself, and answered the question by riding boldly up the street toward the center of town.

But this night, Fredericktown was far from being a sleepy little village. The streets were filled with Federal soldiers, some of them obviously drunk even though the hour was not that late.

"Must be payday," Aaron thought as he kept moving at a slow pace past one of the saloons. "Just ride slow and don't draw any attention to yourself."

A small group of soldiers walked right in front of him and his horse reared!

"Watch where you're goin' boy," said a gruff voice.

One of the men grabbed his reins on the left side and settled his horse down.

"Sorry," said Aaron.

"Well you sure ought to be sorry," the man said, "If'n you wasn't so small, I'd give you a quick lesson in manners. But ain't nobody gonna admire me for beating up a runt."

Aaron looked directly into the eyes of the Sergeant. Their eyes met and fixed. Aaron thought he saw a moment of recognition in the beady eyes that peered at him from under bushy eyebrows.

The Sergeant released his grip on the rein and started to catch up with the others. Then he stopped and looked back at Aaron.

Pulling the Leech and Rigdon and killing him right here would be easy, but it would mean his own death, too. In that moment of indecision, he recalled Tom Haile's advice to Sam when he had seen his home burning. Better to bide your time and live to kill more Yankees that to sacrifice yourself.

The Sergeant started walking back toward him!

Aaron could only see a blue blur moving toward him out of the corner of his eye. He fought the urge to look around. One part of him cried "Run as fast as you can," while the other screamed for him to draw the Leech and Rigdon and put a ball between his tormenter's eyes. He spurred his horse a little harder than he intended and had to pull back on the reins to keep the confused mount from panicking. With a great deal of self control, he began to ride slowly down the street. He could feel his heart pounding and his breathing was in short and rapid gasps.

He rode on for more than a block before he finally found the courage to look back. With all the soldiers milling around, he couldn't see him at first, but then there he was, still standing in the middle of the street, looking after Aaron.

Aaron continued to ride slowly until he had cleared the outskirts of town, then broke his horse into a gallop and made for the woods.

Reaching the heavily foliaged forest, he stopped and rested for a few moments, his hands on his knees and he breathed deeply.

He felt the urge to ride back and shoot the Sergeant, but a picture of Mary Lee dashed through his mind and he mounted and headed for Greene County. Knowing that sleep would be impossible, he rode all night through the woods.

The next day, he crossed the St. Francis south of Greenville and camped in an area he and Sam had used several times.

Eating some more of the food he had brought from home, he slept a disturbed sleep, rising before sunup to continue his trek toward Crowley's Ridge.

Traveling in daylight this far south was considered perfectly safe and so Aaron stuck to the roads.

He thought he must be somewhere near the Arkansas state line when he saw a number of riders coming toward him and as they neared, he could see the Federal uniforms and knew at once they must be some of the boys from Crowley's Ridge.

But his recent adventures had made him cautious, so he rode off the road and into the brush and waited.

He waited a long time. They did not come.

Just as he was about to edge back into the open, he found himself surrounded by six men, their weapons all pointed at him!

"Got you this time, Yank," one of the men said.

Aaron recognized Tom Haile's voice. He looked around and Cato and Burlap were there too, and they were all having a good laugh at his expense.

They stopped laughing when Sam rode up.

"Get yourself caught, boy?"

"Yessir, I guess so."

"I guess it would be funny, if it wasn't for the fact that in the Bushwhacking department, it only takes one mistake," said Sam.

"Yessir."

"What if you had been on sentry duty," Sam went on, "You could have cost all our scalps."

"Yessir."

Sam headed for the road. "And quit calling me sir!"

"Yessir," said Aaron, and he turned his horse and fell in with the others. "If I went back to Crowley's Ridge," he said to Cato, "I'd probably just end up chopping weeds in Bill Lemley's garden."

"Or making hay with his daughter," chimed in Haile.

"One of these days, Tom," said Aaron, "I'm gonna shut up that smart mouth of yours."

"Why not right now?" Haile answered.

"Because right now we got Yankees to fight," Sam said without even looking around, "No need to fight with each other. But remember, if you two boys get in a scrape, the winner will have to fight me next."

Aaron and Tom thought about that and decided to be friends.

*   *   *

Just south of Bloomfield, Sam halted and held up his hand. The others waited and watched as he raised Kill-Devil, took more than usual careful aim, and fired.

A hundred and fifty yards ahead, a Union soldier fell from his horse as the other fifteen or twenty whirled and headed back toward Bloomfield.

"After 'em, boys!" yelled Sam, "They's headed to Bloomfield, keep 'em moving in that direction. Aaron, you come with me."

His commands were obeyed immediately and without question.

Aaron found himself trying to catch up with Sam as they rode through the woods and brush, splashed across a small stream, and finally hit the road several miles ahead, just as the retreating Yankees came around a bend and in front of their position.

Sam and Aaron fired at the same time, but only one of the Feds fell, but from the way he flew off his horse, Aaron knew he had not shot the man, for only Kill-Devil had that kind of force.

The other Yankees veered off the road into the woods and disappeared in a dozen different directions.

Soon the rest of Sam's little band rode up.

"Hadn't we better git outta here?" Tom asked Sam, "Them boys will git to Bloomfield and be back with a passel of troops."

"And they will expect us to head back into Negro Wool Swamp," Sam said, "Which is exactly why we will ride toward Bloomfield."

"Toward Bloomfield?" Tom cried.

"Maybe just a little south of Bloomfield," said Sam, ignoring the urgent tone of Tom's voice. "Toward Wayne County. I got a Dutch friend up that was I think we ought to pay a visit."

They had hardly skirted Bloomfield on the south side when they met a lone rider on his way to town.

"Howdy, boys," he said, "Everything quiet in town?"

"Some of our boys had a little skirmish up the road with some Rebs, but they high tailed it back south."

"Good," said the rider, "I really ain't in the mood for any trouble today."

"And your name, sir?" asked Sam.

"Crane," the man said, "Tom Crane."

"Name sounds familiar," said Sam, "You from Wayne County?"

"Yes, I am," Crane said, a little nervously.

"I thought so," Sam said, "Heard your name around a camp fire one night. You remember a man named John Resinger?"

Fear filled the man's eyes. He glanced around at the other Rebels, and the fit of the Federal uniforms told him these were not Union soldiers.

"Never heard of him," he said.

"That is strange, said Sam, "His son Henry, has ridden with me and told me you had turned his father in as a Confederate."

The fear in Crane's eyes turned to panic for only a brief moment, for Sam raised Kill-Devil and shot him in the gut.

"Henry's hunted him for over a year," Sam said, "To bad he wasn't here to do the killing. He would have enjoyed it.

Come on, I know where we can get some food and shelter for the night."

Riding the east bank of the Black River, Sam led his men to a farm house and hailed the occupants.

"Goot to see you agin," the man said as he came out on the porch, "My woman vill get some vittles goin' if der boys want to wash up at the well und store der gear in dat old abandoned house over yonder."

Sam tipped his cap and turned his horse toward the well.

"Sam," Tom asked softly, "Ain't he German?"

"Yes, but I have stayed here before and not had any problem," Sam answered as he shook his hands dry and finished the job on his dirty uniform, "Besides, he knows the signs of the Knights of the Golden Circle."

The meal was pleasant enough, with the short little woman of the house serving up bowls of boiled corn on the cob, ham hocks, and butter beans, along with the usual corn pone and home made butter, washed down with butter milk.

"You boys get some rest," their host said after the meal, "I'll keep watch and let you know if der is any trouble comin.'"

Aaron spread his bedroll on the floor of what used to be a living room in the old house and before long had dozed off, but it was not a deep sleep and after several hours, he was jolted to his feet by the thundering of horse's hoofs.

Sam was already peeking through a crack in the wall.

"Looks like we are surrounded," he said, "And that German is right in the middle of the line."

"What we gonna do?" asked Aaron.

"It's only about a hundred and fifty yards to the woods," Sam said, "We're gonna make a run for it."

"Maybe we should just give up," said one of the new men.

Haile looked at him in disbelief. "This your first time to ride with Sam?"

"Yes," the man said, "But I don't want it to be my last."

"It won't be," yelled Sam, "Just follow me!"

Without hesitation, he leaped out the door with pistols blazing and ran crouched toward the woods, followed by Aaron, Cato, Burlap and Haile, and close on their heels the new men. The man who wanted to surrender followed, making a little whimpering noise and he ran out into the light and a fusillade of bullets.

It was like being caught in a swarm of bumblebees. Sam felt a tug at his arm as one bullet nicked him, and before he reached the woods, three others had brought blood, one clipping his leg, another just stinging the lobe of his ear. Another ball went through his cap without even taking it off.

Stopping in the woods and taking cover behind a fallen tree, he was joined almost at once by Aaron, Cato, Haile and Burlap. Two more tumbled into the shelter of the woods, but as they looked back, the man who had objected to trying to escape lay in the middle of the field, his right arm pointing strangely upward and his left leg bent up behind his head.

The only other injuries was an arm wound in one of the new men, and in a few moments, after reloading, they scrambled through the brush woods behind them and up a bluff.

Taking cover among some rock outcroppings, Sam ordered the men to keep their heads down and wait.

It seemed forever, but finally the Federals came, walking toward their position like they were on the parade field.

"Fire in the order you lay," Sam said to his men, "That way we will all shoot a different man. But wait until I give the order."

Aaron sighted down his rifle and waited. The blue uniforms came closer and closer. It seemed Sam was going to let them walk right up to their position!

He counted down to the fifth man. He could actually see the man's face, the fear filled eyes, and he was biting his lower lip.

"Close enough, Sam," he said to himself, "Close enough."

Still there was no order to fire.

They were less than twenty feet away!

"Is he going to let them step on us!" whispered Haile, who lay next to Aaron.

Fifteen yards.

"Fire!" yelled Sam, and as one, the Rebel rifles spoke.

Four blue uniforms crumpled to the ground, while the others dropped their guns and slid and scrambled down the slope as best they could, chased by the second round of fire from the Rebels.

"Come on, boys," cried Sam, "Let's go git 'em!"

But by the time they reached the edge of the woods at the bottom of the hill, the boys in blue were already mounting their horses in the front yard of the Dutchman.

"Watch this," said Sam, as he raised KillDevil to his shoulder.

"You can't hit nothin' from this distance," said Tom.

Sam continued to look down KillDevil's long barrel.

"KillDevil and I believe we can," said Sam, "These boys is about to be without leadership."

KillDevil roared and the soldier with the shoulder straps slumped in the saddle.

The rest of the Federals ran in the opposite direction.

Sam took out his knife and nodded toward the running Yankees.

"That's a new Yankee military maneuver, called bringing up your own rear and advance."

CHAPTER 13

Making their way back down the Black River, the little band of raiders camped out for the night and the next morning went to the home of a friend of Sam's.

"Let's don't trust no more Dutchmen," Tom said, "Even if'n they do know the right signs."

Sam fixed on him with his obviously not very happy icy blue eyes. He maintained the stare until Tom dropped back to the rear of the pack and kept his head down.

The road was soon abandoned as they entered an area where there seemed to not be even trails, but Sam wove his way through the brush and tangled grape vines and scrub oaks for several miles before entering a small clearing and calling for a halt.

"You can make camp here," he said, "Best I go in alone. My friend is not too fond of company and is very particular who he associates with."

Tom thought about asking if his friend was part monkey, but decided it was not a good idea after the Dutchman incident.

"Can we build a fire?" asked Aaron.

"A small one," said Sam, "But don't fix breakfast yet. When I get back, I will have plenty of provisions."

Sam rode off and had not gone more than ten feet into the brush when he disappeared completely.

About an hour later, he reappeared just as suddenly out of the tangled growth.

"Here's not only breakfast," he said, handing down a couple of sacks to Burlap and Cato, "But enough food to get us back to Arkansas with plenty left over."

Soon the smell of bacon permeated the air and hot coffee was being poured into tin cups while they enjoyed the sour dough biscuits and milk gravy.

Aaron ate so much he propped up against a tree and could have taken a nap if Sam hadn't mounted his horse and started back into the maze they had come through the night before.

"Let's ride," he said, "Them Yankees hightailed it to Patterson after out little squabble and left word for some local citizens to bury their dead and take their horses to Patterson today."

"How'd your friend know all that?" Cato asked, "It only happened yesterday and he's been stuck out here in the boondocks."

"I don't ask why or how," Sam said, "But believe me, he knows, for his information has always been correct. I would bet my life on it."

"Come to think of it, boys, I'm betting all our lives on it."

Reaching the Patterson road, they hid in the woods and waited. It didn't take long, for soon an old man with two young boys came up the road, leading not only the Yankee's horses, but also those lost by the Bushwhackers. Aaron counted seventeen mounts in all.

Sam rode out to meet them.

"Howdy," he said, "Mighty fine looking horses."

Obviously the boys were scared but the old man seemed calm.

He reached up and took the corn cob pipe out of his mouth.

"Yessir," he said, "Several of them are good horse flesh."

"We aim to find out for ourselves," Sam said, "For we are taking these horses with us and plan to make Rebels of them all."

The old man fringed fear, but Sam could see a twinkle in his eye.

"It would be against my orders to turn these horses over to Sam Hildebrand," he said, glancing back at the boys with him, "But I guess I have no choice."

"You do not," said Sam, "And if I hear that anyone has blamed you for their loss, I will return to see that they are rewarded for their treachery."

The old man released the reins to the horses he was leading and turned slowly to head down the road. His two companions had already left, at a gallop.

"Take the horses back to Crowley's Ridge," Sam said, "Except you, boy," as he nodded at Aaron.

Sam dismounted and handed the reins of his horse to Cato.

"We gonna walk?" asked Aaron.

"Yep," said Sam, "The job we got to do can best be done afoot. Besides, you been eatin' so much of your Maw's food and at the Lemley's table so many times, your gitten a little fat. The walk will be good for you."

"Yeh, but he spends so much time chasing after Mary Lee," said Tom, "The food don't hardly have time to stick to his bones."

Aaron's red face kept the laughter of the others down. But it was again Sam's penetrating stare that made Tom turn his horse and head down the trail.

Sam and Aaron walked up the side of a low hill in their usual semi-circle pattern, and rested for the remainder of the day, taking turns watching the trail that led to the road.

When dusk was just beginning to set in, they left their hiding place and headed for the home of the Dutchman who had turned them in to the Yankees. The gray skies hinted of rain but none fell as night began to close in and they reached the Dutchman's home just about the time darkness was fully come.

They hid in the corner of the fence and waited, but there was no sign of their intended victim, although his family was home and seemed to be conducting their normal evening chores without concern.

Aaron backed off and found a place in the woods to sleep. The clouds of morning were even more ominous and Sam and Aaron retreated to Honn's home, where they ate a hearty breakfast.

"All I had to eat since yesterday morning was that old corn pone," Aaron said, If we keep this up long, I won't have to walk to lose weight."

"Leave the fun making to Haile," said Sam.

"Yessir."

After sleeping most of the day in Honn's barn, they returned to the Dutchman's house in the early afternoon and again hid in the fence row, covered on two sides by the split rails.

It was quiet for about two hours, then three men rode up to the house and talked with the Dutchman's wife on the front porch.

After just a few minutes, they rode off but it was after dark when Aaron and Sam heard the plodding of a single horse on the road.

"Stay down," whispered Sam, "I'm gonna work my way up to the woodpile."

The Dutchman rode up carefully to the house, stopping by the woodpile. He tied his horse to a tree limb, and started up the porch.

Sam stepped from behind the woodpile and leveled Kill-Devil at him.

"Get ready to meet your maker," said Sam, "And I hope you get exactly what you deserve."

The Dutchman crumbled to his knees and began begging for mercy.

"If I could call my good men, who died because of your treachery, back from the dead, how much mercy do you think you would get?"

The Dutchman sprawled on the porch, crying and moaning when his wife came out the door.

"Get a horse out of the barn," Sam told Aaron.

Aaron ran to the barn and hollered back to Sam.

"Ain't nothin' in here but a mule."

"That'll havta do," said Sam, "Bring it here." He looked at the Dutchman's wife. "We will need a saddle for the mule."

"All I got is my saddle," she said.

"Your's will do," said Sam, "Fetch it."

They tied the Dutchman's hands behind him and loaded him on the mule, who immediately began to kick his hind legs in the air and bray as only a Missouri mule can bray.

"Watch out!" cried Aaron as he backed away from the beast, who obviously was not going to move until he had finished his song.

When the mule finally settled down, they led him, with the Dutchman still on board, down into the woods.

Sam stopped and handed his knife to Aaron.

"Careful boy, it's real sharp."

"What you want me to do?" asked Aaron.

"Strip several long strips off that hickory tree over yonder," said Sam, "And twist them together."

Aaron did as he was told, although his hands were shaking, for he suspected what was about to happen.

The Dutchman had resorted to a moaning sound, interrupted by gasping for breath spells, and whispered pleas for mercy.

When the makeshift hickory bark rope was finished, Sam tied a slip knot in one end and placed it over the Dutchman's head, then he threw the other end over a low limb on the hickory tree.

The Dutchman was crying and begging for his life but Sam did not hesitate, but slapped the mule on the rump, who promptly bucked the Dutchman off and began to bray again, drowning any last words the hanged man might have been able to say.

Aaron looked at the face of the dying man, whose eyes were bugged out of his head, the sharp edges of the bark had cut into his throat and blood ran down his shirt.

He swung in oblong circles, dangling at the end of the bark rope. For a few minutes, his feet kicked wildly and his body twisted in the air.

Aaron was glad he had not had anything to eat since breakfast, for his stomach was dry heaving.

It was several minutes before he stopped struggling and hung limp.

"Just like they did my brother Frank," Sam said.

"How come you didn't just shoot him back at the house?" asked Aaron.

"Don't seem right," Sam said, "To kill a man in front of his wife and children, no matter how much he deserves it."

As the Dutchman swung gently in the breeze, Sam mounted his horse, and motioned toward the mule.

"Mount up," he said to Aaron, "And let's head for Crowley's Ridge. But first we'll stop by Honn's place for something to eat."

Aaron was not exactly elated about mounting the mule or getting something to eat, but he climbed on the back of the beast, hung on while it bucked a few times, then waited patiently for it to quit braying. Sam seemed to be enjoying the event.

Finally they were on their way to Honn's and arrived just before mealtime.

With fried chicken, corn on the cob, and slaw, along with some fresh tomatoes from Honn's garden, they were enjoying the repast, although Aaron had to force himself to forget the face of the Dutchmen as he was hanged.

Sam was of little help. "We swung the Dutchman from a tree," he told Honn, "He didn't die easy, but neither did my men he betrayed."

"And his wife?" asked Honn.

"She is fine," said Sam, a little irritated that Honn might imply that he would harm a woman.

"I meant does she have the means to take care of herself and her family," Honn said, "She is a good woman. When my wife was sick, she stayed with her the whole time. All the neighbors will tell you she has done many good deeds."

Sam sat silent for several minutes.

"Take the horse and mule back to her tomorrow," he said.

"Sam, I can't do that," said Honn, "If the Federals get wind that I brought them back, they'll know I have helped you."

Sam thought a moment.

"Take them back tonight and put them in the barn after dark."

Honn nodded.

"And while you are there," Sam added, handing a purse to Honn, "Throw this over the fence into the yard where she will be sure to find it."

When they had finished their meal, Sam and Aaron started back to Arkansas…on foot.

✳   ✳   ✳

It had been a warm and wet spring at Crowley's Ridge and the gardens were producing an abundance of vegetables. The women were busy canning as much as they could and drying some, knowing that an unpredictable Arkansas winter could use up their supplies.

Aaron jumped in to help the Lemleys as soon as he returned. He was busy doing his favorite job, chopping weeds, while Mary Lee thinned the beans in the next row.

Somehow chopping weeds was not as terrible as it had been at home.

The warm summer days soon set in and Aaron spent most of his time at the Lemley's, avoiding the nightly camp fires as the men gathered to work themselves up for another raid and drank burst-head or home made beer.

He had only been back a few weeks and was in the Lemley garden plot with Mary Lee when Sam walked up, dressed in Federal blue.

"Goin' on a raid," he said, "You wantta go?"

Aaron quickly glanced at Mary Lee. Her face was clouded up.

"I reckon not," he said, "Mr. Lemley shore needs a lot of help gittin' the vegetables in, and tomorrow we plan to pick some wild berries we found back over the ridge."

Sam nodded and without another word, walked away toward the corrals.

Aaron looked at Mary Lee. "He ain't a bad man, you know."

"No worse than most of them, I suppose, " she said, "But I am beginning to wonder if he is really out to avenge his family, or if he has found he just enjoys hunting and killing."

Aaron didn't say anything. He was beginning to wonder the same thing about himself. It would be good to stay in camp for a while.

The next morning early, he and Mary Lee headed for the berry patch, excited about the prospect of hot berry cobbler, and of being alone.

As soon as they were out of sight of the Lemley cabin, they joined hands.

Aaron had always enjoyed picking berries, but with Mary Lee along it was more than fun, it was exciting!

Their fingers stained blue by the soft berries, they tossed unripe fruit at each other.

When finally their pails were full, Mary Lee spread a table cloth she had brought on the ground and they ate cold fried chicken and homemade bread.

Laying back on the table cloth, Aaron felt a peace he had not known for over two years. The warm sun and nearness of Mary Lee beside him wiped away the fears and hate, at least for a short time.

Time! He jumped up.

"Mary Lee, the sun is going down," he said, "Your folks will be wondering where we are."

She stood and folded the table cloth and place it on top of her berry pail. They were very close and Aaron decided he didn't need another kissing lesson.

He took Mary Lee in his arms and pulled her to him, a little surprised at how easily she came.

He tried to kiss her straight on but their noses bumped and she giggled. The second try he made it and she stopped giggling.

*   *   *

"Sure takes a long time to pick a pail of berries," Bill Lemley said as they came in the door of the cabin.

"Now Bill, you leave the young ones alone," Anna said, "With all Aaron has been through, a day in the sun without war to think about is a good thing. You kids hungry?"

Mary Lee and Aaron looked at each other.

"We ate our picnic late," Mary Lee said, "And Aaron ate more berries than he picked, so I think we can just skip supper."

Aaron felt awkward and soon excused himself and headed for his shanty. It was one of the first nights in the past two years the Sergeant did not chase him through his dreams.

The days passed quickly as Aaron and Mary Lee spent many hours together. She wanted to know everything about him. He felt he knew all he needed to know about her.

She seemed to avoid the question of his religion and he was glad for he found the best thing to do with God was not to think about him.

Aaron walked into the Lemley home one July morning and found Bill reading a newspaper. He was obviously upset.

"Bad news?" asked Aaron.

"Very bad news," Bill said as he continued to stare at the paper.

"Where'd you get it?"

A tinker passing through gave it to me," said Bill, "It's the St. Louis Times, only two weeks old."

"What's the bad news?" asked Aaron, who gathered he was going to have to ask to find out.

"There has been a very big battle in the east," Bill said, "At a little town called Gettysburg in Pennsylvania. Lee's army was defeated and is retreating to Virginia. On top of that, Vicksburg has fallen after a long siege by General Grant."

"Grant! Ain't he the one that used to be at Ironton?"

"I reckon it's the same one," said Bill, "It looks like the beginning of the end for the Confederacy. All this killing may soon be over and we can go home."

Aaron thought about that. He wanted to go home, of course, but he hadn't killed the Sergeant yet. And what about Mary Lee?

If she went home with her folks to Sedalia, would he ever see her again?

Things were changing and Aaron was not sure he was ready for the change. Even Sam had come back from his last raid and seemed to settle down. You could see him and Margaret and the kids walking in the woods in the evening when it had cooled down and he seemed to be spending less time around the camp fires at night.

Things were sure changing.

Cato, Burlap, and Haile had been in and out of camp on missions of their own. Aaron was spending so much time at the Lemley's he hardly saw them anymore.

That night, he and Mary Lee walked down by the place where the revival with the Reverend Mercer had been held.

"Daddy thinks the war may soon be over," Mary Lee said.

"Yeh, he told me that, too," Aaron said, "But there's still a lot of wrongs need to be righted."

"Why don't you let God take care of that?"

"Because he ain't done nothin' about any of it yet," Aaron snapped. He could feel his anger rising. She knew he didn't like to talk about religion.

"He will in his own time," she said, "You have to learn to trust him."

"I trust my Leech and Rigdon, I trust Cato and Burlap, I trust Sam." His voice was rising and he could feel the redness of the back of his neck. "I have seen what they can do. I ain't never seen God do nothin'"

Mary Lee decided she had picked a bad time, but it was too late now. "God takes care of us," she said.

"Did God have my Paw killed? Did God give me this scar? Did God make my leg crooked?"

Mary Lee said nothing, but Aaron was not through.

"Did your God allow all of Sam's family to be killed" And what about Tom's father? What about your paw and his brother?"

"Let's not talk about it any more," said Mary Lee.

"That's fine with me," said Aaron, "As a matter of fact, let's not talk about anything else tonight. I'll walk you home."

They walked back to the cabin in silence and at her door, she turned to face him.

"Good night," Aaron said, and turned and walked away.

*   *   *

But Aaron never made it to his cabin that evening. Instead, he headed for the corrals and joined Cato, Haile, Burlap and several others around the camp fire.

The more burst-head he drank, the madder he got. He was sick of hearing about that religion stuff from Mary Lee. There was a war going on and he had a job to do.

Tom Haile was not even in a good mood. The lanky Cato was unusually quiet and Burlap, as was normal for the big guy, said nothing at all.

"I'm ready to go on another raid," Aaron said, "How about you guys."

Tom got up and brushed off the seat of his pants.

"Let's see if Sam can pull himself away from the wife and kids to go with us," Aaron said.

Sam was working in his garden when they walked up to the fence.

"What's up, boys?" he said, tossing a weed he had pulled over the fence.

"We're ready for some action," Aaron said.

Sam looked around at Margaret who stood just outside the door to the cabin with the baby in her arms.

"Reckon I am, too," Sam said, "Anything beats pulling weeds. Be at the corrals at dawn."

As he always did when he was going on a raid, Aaron could not fall asleep. The burst-head had worn off by midnight and he tossed and turned the rest of the night, except just before dawn when he must have dozed off, for in his dream he remembered the look on Mary Lee's face when he left her and the Sergeant grabbed her and carried her away.

He sat up in bed, sweat running down his face and he was breathing in short, small gasps.

It must be close to dawn.

As they rode out of camp, the morning light was sifting through the woods and he looked back toward the Lemley's and wished he wasn't going. Or a least that he had told Mary Lee.

The mosquitoes were huge in Mingo Swamp this time of year.

Counting Sam, there were eight men in the group, as three others who had been at the camp fire the night before decided to join up.

They camped out on Castor Creek for two days, waiting for news of Federal movements and a couple of friends had agreed to let them know the whereabouts of several informers Sam had wanted to find.

Finally, one of the scouts came into camp with a report.

"They's Feds camped out just south of Bollinger's Mill," he said.

"How many are there?" asked Sam.

"Don't rightly know," the scout said, "I got as close as I care to get, and then skedaddled back here."

Aaron and the others got up and started saddling their horses.

"Not so quick, boys," said Sam, "Lets wait until dark and we can use surprise to our favor."

About ten that night, Sam gave the signal and they headed for the Federal camp.

Just before they reached the spot the scout had reported, they ran into pickets and drove them back toward the camp.

"Let's go get 'em!" yelled Sam as he placed the reins to his horse in his mouth and with pistols in hand, rode at a gallop toward the camp, with his men close behind.

Firing on each side, Sam rode right into the camp, only to find the Federal had made camp at a narrow place in the road and blocked the exit on the other side with wagons.

Sam's horse reared. "Get out as best you can, boys!" he yelled, "It's a trap!"

For a few moments, the little band whirled in confusion as the Union soldiers opened fire at close range. Two of the Rebels fell from their horses and right beside Aaron, Cato took a ball in the shoulder.

Aaron could hear the bullets whizzing around him, as thick as the mosquitoes in Mingo Swamp! Somehow he got his horse turned around and headed back down the road, his head down against the horse's mane and at full gallop.

Nor did he slow down until he reached the camp site on Castor Creek. Then he slid off the horse and collapsed.

One by one the others drifted in, except for the two who had fallen. Cato had his right hand held tightly about his left shoulder to stem the bleeding. His shirt was stained a dark red.

"Just a flesh wound," Sam said after he had torn open the shirt and looked at it, "Best he go back to Arkansas, through."

"Best we all go back," said Tom, "We could all git kilt pulling stunts like that."

"You don't like the way I lead a raid?" asked Sam.

"Well, we have charged Federal troops who outnumbered us before," Aaron said, "But we ain't never rode into a beehive like that in the dark, and not even knowing how many there were."

"Yeh," chimed in Cato, "And on the last raid, we nearly got wiped out because we trusted a Dutchman, just because he knew a silly Golden Knight's sign."

Sam unsaddled his horse, spread his blanket on the ground and used the saddle for a pillow.

"Come sunrise," he said, "You younguns better head back to Crowley's Ridge and get Cato's wound taken care of proper. I'll finish this raid by myself."

When they got up the next morning, Sam was already gone.

CHAPTER 14

Making his way toward St. Francois County, Sam had only one objective, to kill Judge R. M. Cole, who had shirked his duty by not taking Frank away from the Vigilantes when he had the opportunity.

Cole, Sam had heard, was a Southern man, but still Frank could have been saved if the Judge had done his duty.

Sam reached the Cole farm on the Flat River and found the Judge plowing, softly singing to himself.

Sam rode to the back side of the farm, hitched his horse to a tree, and waited near the field until about sunset.

Finding some oats for the horse and a watermelon patch for his own supper, Sam settled down at a corner of the field, and waited for morning.

Judge Cole resumed his plowing early and Sam was ready. As the Judge made a round, Sam lifted Kill-Devil and took aim.

The Judge was singing again. Sam began to tremble and could not pull the trigger!

Sam bit his fingers to stop "buck ague" and waited for another round.

Once again he lifted Kill-Devil and took aim, but as before, he began to shake.

"Could it be the man is innocent?" he asked himself, "Perhaps he could have done nothing to save Frank."

Again he took aim, then slowly lowered the rifle.

Judge Cole continued to follow the mule and the plow, never knowing how close he had come to the end of his life.

Sam mounted and decided to ride back by way of Bloomfield and the home of Captain Hicks, commander of the company which had followed he and Margaret all the way to the St. Francis.

Captain Hicks, Sam had heard, had boasted that he was the one who shot Sam at Flat Woods.

He camped out in the woods for four days, dining in splendor from the Captain's well stocked smokehouse.

On the evening of the fourth day, Hicks walked out into his garden with his wife. He picked up a hoe and chopped a few weeds.

"Howdy," Sam said as he walked up to the garden fence.

Hicks froze, disturbed to see a stranger with a rifle just on the other side of his garden fence. Especially a stranger who resembled the descriptions he had heard of Sam Hildebrand.

"What do you want?"

"Well, I hear you been looking for me," said Sam, climbing the fence and walking closer to Hicks. "Name's Hildebrand, Sam Hildebrand."

Hicks swung the hoe at Sam and nearly took his head off. Kill-Devil spoke and as Hick's wife screamed, the good captain fell to the ground.

Sam climbed into the saddle and headed on back to Arkansas.

*   *   *

The ride back to Crowley's Ridge had been uneventful, and very quiet. Tom rode ahead of the others, with Cato and Burlap in the middle, and Aaron bringing up the rear.

They skirted Mingo Swamp to avoid the mosquitoes. "I'd just as soon face a swarm of Yankees and them bugs," said Tom.

The summer sun of southeast Missouri beat down on them and they were all thinking about their conflict with Sam.

Finally back at camp, Aaron went straight to his cabin after unsaddling his horse, wiping her down and making sure she had hay and what little oats he could find in the corral.

He flopped on his cot and exhausted, soon fell asleep. The sun hung low in the west, reddened by a hazy sky. It was about supper time at the Lemley's, he thought when he woke up.

"Come in, "said Bill, a little coolly, Aaron thought.

"Just got back," he said, "And thought I better come see if you folks are all right."

"We're fine," said Bill, "You're just in time for supper, come and sit down. It ain't much, just some left overs, but it'll stick to your ribs."

"Mrs. Lemley's leftovers is better than any of the food I have had for several days," said Aaron as he seated himself across the table from Mary Lee.

"Howdy," he said.

"I'm glad you got back safe," she said, "Are you all right?"

"I'm fine, but Cato got nicked on the shoulder. It bled a lot but he is fine."

"Let's not talk about such things at the table," Anna said.

"Yes'm," said Aaron, as he helped himself to some beans and corn bread.

The meal was finished in silence.

"You want to go for a walk?" Aaron asked Mary Lee after the dishes were put away and Bill had lit his pipe.

"Yes," she said, "I think I would like that."

"Don't stay out after dark," Bill said as they went out the door.

"Yessir," said Aaron as they stepped outside.

The walk was a lot like the meal had been, mostly in silence for a long time.

Finally Aaron spoke the words he had been choking on.

"I'm sorry."

"Me too," said Mary Lee, "And I promise not to force religion on you again."

"Maybe it wouldn't hurt me none. I didn't tell your folks everything. We had two men killed on this trip and I still don't know how I got out of it alive."

She reached out and took his hand.

"I pray for you every day, Aaron," she said, "And I believe you have a Guardian Angel looking over you."

Aaron broke her grip on his hand.

"There you go again! Can't say two sentences without preaching at me."

"But you just said it wouldn't hurt you."

"But it does hurt me! Sometimes I lay awake all night thinking about God and the devil."

"You're under conviction," Mary Lee said.

"What's that?" he asked, remembering how Sam had told him how Frank and he were convicted of killing the wrong hogs.

"When the Holy Ghost begins to deal with a person, they are under conviction because of their sins," she said, "God is dealing with you even now."

"I don't believe that stuff," said Aaron, angry that she would assume she knew what was happening inside him, even though he couldn't explain that funny feeling he had in the pit of his stomach every time he even thought about God.

"Someday you will," she said, taking his hand again, "Someday you will."

"And in the meanwhile, if I git kilt?"

"I believe God has a plan for you life," she said, "And he won't let that happen, at least not until you are ready."

When they got back to the cabin, just as the last hint of daylight faded into the darkened woods, she let him kiss her goodnight, but he walked home with a troubled mind.

When he got to his cabin, Burlap and Haile were there.

"We got an idea," said Tom, "We're gonna spend the winter in Texas. You want to come with us?"

"Texas!"

"Yeh, Texas," said the usually silent Burlap. It was the most excited he had ever seen his big friend, and for Burlap to say more than one word at a time was strange.

"Lots of warm sunshine all winter long and pretty women and lots of real whiskey instead of burst-head," Cato beamed.

"All of Quantrill's men go there for the winter," said Tom.

"From what I've seen and heard of his men, I'm not sure I want to go where they are," said Aaron.

"Well, think about it," Tom said, "We ain't planning on going for a couple of months. We need to go on another raid with Sam to get the supplies we will need."

"Are you sure Sam will let us go on another raid with him? He was pretty upset."

"Aw, you know Sam," said Tom, "He thinks he's responsible for us. We're his "boys", ain't we?"

"I'll think about it," said Aaron, "Let me sleep on it."

But there was to be little sleep for him again that night as the Sergeant, the Devil, and Quantrill chased him through his nightmares.

When morning finally came. he woke up early but didn't move. It was hot and he was worn out from tossing and turning, but more importantly, he could hear hushed movement outside his door.

He jumped when someone banged on the door. He pulled his pants on halfway and hopped to the door.

It was Burlap, Cato, and Haile.

"Well?" asked Tom.

"Well what?"

"Are you going with us or not?"

"I told you I'd have to sleep on it."

"What did you do last night?"

"It could hardly pass for sleep," said Aaron, "I ain't gonna made a decision 'til I talk to Sam. He's ridden with some of Quantrill's men and wasn't too happy afterward. I want to see what he thinks."

"We ain't gonna ride with them," said Tom, Only spend the winter in Texas and have a good time."

"Yeah," said Cato, its at a place called Mineral Creek, near a city called Sherman."

"I'll think about it," Aaron said.

"Gotta ask Mary Lee if you can go?" asked Tom.

Aaron only glared at him and slammed the door. In a few minutes he slept a sleep of exhaustion and it was mid-afternoon before he woke up.

CHAPTER 15

"How about it, Sam, will you help us out?"

The embers in the camp fire had almost grown cold before Tom got up enough courage to ask Sam to take them on a raid.

"Cato and Burlap both got family up near Hamburg and they's being treated miserably by the Federal. Cato's folks had their home burnt and Burlap's cousins were thrown in a Yankee prison, all because they is riding with you."

"I'll go," said Sam, "As long as you boys promise to obey my orders without question."

"We will," said Tom, "Won't we fellars?"

Cato and Burlap both nodded.

"Lot's of Dutchmen in that area, and plenty of Union troops," said Sam, "We'll need some more men, about fifteen, I reckon."

"We'll get 'em," said Tom, "Don't worry 'bout that."

"Then you may have to wake some of the boys up," Sam said,"Cause we ride at dawn."

It was after midnight when Cato and Haile knocked on Aaron's door.

Aaron only cracked the door open and stuck his head out.

"We ride with Sam at dawn," Tom said, "Will you be ready?"

Aaron squinted into the darkness, trying to shake the sleep from his head and let the words sink in.

"Dawn!" he said, "It must be practically that now."

"Naw," said Tom, "Only a little past midnight, you got plenty of time for some more sleep and still get packed."

"Come back by and get me," said Aaron, "I ain't sure I'll wake up again if I go back to sleep."

"I'll be here," Tom said, "Don't worry 'bout that. Ifn there's one thing we've learned, its not to keep Sam waiting."

Aaron flopped back on the cot and wondered why he had told them he would go. He had decided not to go on any more raids, especially with Tom.

"Oh, Tom is all right," he said to himself, "Sometimes he's just a smart mouth."

It was well before dawn when Tom rode up to Aaron's cabin, but Aaron already had his horse saddled and packed.

"Ready?" asked Tom.

"Just about," Aaron answered, "Just got to get my weapons."

They rode down the trail to the corrals and Sam was already mounted, along with about a dozen others, ready to ride.

"What kept you boys?" asked Sam.

"Sleepy head here," said Tom, nodding at Aaron, "Had a hard time shaking the cobwebs out of what he calls a brain."

Aaron glared at him and Sam only turned his horse and started down the trail out of camp.

They followed their usual route up the east side of the St. Francis, and camped just on the edge of Mingo Swamp and waited for darkness.

Barely had the sun disappeared through the trees, shooting bright golden beams in all directions at once, when Sam stepped into his stirrup.

"Let's ride, boys," he said, "Let's go huntin' Dutch."

Soon they were in unfamiliar territory, at least for Aaron. Riding into Butler County they crossed into Stoddard County south of Bloomfield, crossed the Little River above Buffington, and entered Scott County.

About ten o'clock the next morning, they rode up to the home of one of the men who had turned Cato's family in to the Federals.

The Dutchman came out of the house, glad to see so many men dressed in Federal blue. He began talking in German.

"I am not of that persuasion," Sam said.

"Vell, its goot to see you," the Dutchman said in broken English, "Vot can ve do for you?" He walked over to Aaron and stuck out his hand.

"You can tell us why you had some of our friend's home burnt down, for one thing," Sam said.

The Dutchman realized his mistake and began yelling in Dutch back toward the house. Soon his wife and children came out and gathered around him, speaking German but obviously pleading for his life. They began to wail and cry until Sam could hardly bear it.

"Take him, boys," he said, "I know its not easy, but war is war and justice must be done."

Burlap and Haile took the Dutchman by the arms and dragged him away from his family.

About a mile down the road, they hung him and rode on toward their next victim.

But this one saw them coming and ran out the back door of his house so fast that only a volley of fire from the Rebels brought him down.

"That's two of them," said Sam, "Only two more to go."

In a short time, they rode into the little village of Hamburg.

The street exploded from every side with rifle and pistol fire, punctuated by shotgun blasts. Two of the Rebels fell from their horses at once.

"Charge 'em, boys!" yelled Sam, as he spurred toward the puffs of smoke.

The Federal and civilians broke and ran, not even firing back at the charging Rebels, and took shelter in an old house at the edge of town. Sam counted twelve men.

"You boys," he said, pointing at Cato and Burlap, "Go around to the south side. Haile, you and Aaron go to the north. The rest of you come with me. Don't let any of them get out."

After his boys were in position, Sam led the others to the very front of the house, and Sam walked up on the porch, calmly lighting the bundle of dry hay he had brought, and placed it against the front door.

As the smoke rose slowly from the porch, Sam and his men waited for the Federals to try to escape.

"Ride, boys,!" yelled Sam as he leaped from the porch and into his saddle, "Ride!"

Aaron heeded no more encouragement. He didn't even look back, but he could hear the crack of rifle fire and the pounding of many hooves.

Coming from three directions, Union troops were bearing down on them!

"This way!" hollered Sam as he passed Aaron.

Sam spotted an opening in their lines and they made a dash for it. Another Rebel fell from his horse, his foot hung in the stirrup and he was dragged through the brush.

The bullets whizzed around them. Aaron finally looked back. It looked like it must be a hundred soldiers. He saw three more of his comrades fall from the saddle.

Finally they reached Little River and swam their horses to Coon Island, taking cover in the tangled woods to repel the Yankees.

But they did not come, not anxious to be open targets in the water of the stream.

Aaron checked around to see who had made it. Cato, Burlap and Tom were there. Aaron laid back on the grass and looked up at the sky, his chest heaving.

"Maybe Mary Lee was right," he said out loud, "Maybe I do have a Guardian Angel."

"What'd you say?" asked Sam.

"I said that looked an awful lot like a defeat."

"Just a strategic movement," Sam said, "Merely a change of base."

When Sam had moved on, checking on the others and counting the losses, Haile moved over near Aaron. He was joined by Cato and Burlap.

"Strategic movement, my foot," said Haile, "This is the third time that old man has led us into certain death. I think he wants to die and don't care who he takes with him."

"Yeh," said Cato, "I ain't anxious to ride with him anymore. If'n he wants to kill hisself, that his business, but I aim to keep my self alive best I can, and riding with Sam Hildebrand ain't the way to do it."

"Soon as we can get back to Arkansas" said Tom, "We're headed for Texas. You comin' with us, Aaron?"

"I reckon so," said Aaron.

*   *   *

Aaron was flat on his back on the bank of Coon Island, looking up at the western sky, and as he watched, it slowly turned from cerise to orange. He closed his eyes for a few moments and looked back over the events of the day and his near death.

When he opened his eyes again, the sky was changing to a deep purple, tinged with a thin line of burnt orange at the horizon.

He looked behind him and in the eastern shy, the cumulus clouds were tinted with a reflected pink. It was something his Paw had taught him long ago. "Sometimes the prettiest sunsets are just a reflection of the real thing," Paw would say.

Aaron wondered what he had just agreed to do and why he had done it. Going to Texas for the winter had not been his plan. But then, he thought, he really didn't have a plan, anyway.

"Load up, boys," Sam said, "Let's get off this island and into familiar territory."

"It's almost dark," complained Tom, "Why don't we just stay here tonight?"

Sam turned to face him, his eyes riveted to Tom's until you could see Tom's resistance melt.

"You boys promised to obey my orders without question! Now mount up!"

"Yessir," said Tom as he tossed his saddle up on his horse.

They rode south until they reached the St. Francis sometime before dawn and weary from the fight and the ride, plopped on the ground and slept until the sun was high.

"C'mon," yelled Tom as he kicked the feet of his companions, who were still rolled up in their blankets, "Let's take a swim!"

Aaron, Cato and Burlap begrudgingly rolled out and headed for the outcropping of gray rock that jutted over a bend in the St. Francis. They had swum here before and at the very turn of the river, there was a deep pool that was always cool water. Huge oaks overhung the banks and there were grapevines to swing on.

Aaron finally shook the sleepiness out of his head and was soon naked and running toward the rocks, prepared to jump over the edge and into the live-reviving water.

Tom had already reached the rocks and stood looking over the edge.

"Stop, Aaron!" he shouted.

But Aaron had up a head of steam and could not stop. Tom threw himself in front of him and they both rolled over on the rocks.

Aaron got up and rubbed his skinned elbow. "What's th' matter with you?" he asked, "You tryin' to kill me?"

"If I hadn't of stopped you, that's just what would have happened," said Tom as he stood with his hands on his knees and fought to regain his breath, "Look over the edge."

By this time Cato and Burlap had arrived and the four of them peeked cautiously over the edge of the rocks.

Barely sticking out of the water were the sharpened ends of cedar poles. They had been driven into the bottom of the river and placed so that anyone diving off the bluff would be impaled on them.

"Look at that," said Tom, pointing to the opposite bank of the river, "The water level had dropped some or you wouldn't have even been able to see them."

Aaron sat down on the rock, his knees weak and trembling. But for Tom Haile, he might be dead right now. Or was it Mary Lee's Guardian Angel again?

Sam came over to see what the to-do was all about. He took in the scene and walked back to camp where his horse was already saddled and ready to travel.

"You boys stay here 'til I get back," he said, and without an explanation, rode out of camp, headed north.

Before nightfall, he was not far from Bloomfield, riding boldly down the road. He stopped at a farm house and drew a bucket of water from the well.

A Dutch lady came out on the porch.

"Goot evening," she said, "A loyal Union soldier is alvays velcom to drink at der vell."

"Thank you, ma'am," said Sam, "Perhaps you can help me. I am looking for a Mr. George Oller. I was told he lived near here. My commanding officer has sent me to commend him for his attempts to catch the bushwhacker, Sam Hildebrand."

"Da, da," she answered, "Mr. Oller's place is just two miles down the road. My husband was der yesterday and Mr. Oller told him about a trap he had set for der Rebels at der swimming hole."

"I see," said Sam, "And I heard he had been drawing outlines of Sam Hildebrand on trees and practicing shooting the monster, should he ever see him."

"Da, dat he has, " said the Dutch lady.

"Thank you for the information," Sam said as he turned in the direction of Oller's home, "I aim to see that Mr. Oller is rewarded for his efforts."

It was already dark when Sam reached the Oller farm. He secreted himself in the bend of a split-rail fence and waited for dawn. But the next day passed without Oller making an appearance. Sam took shelter that night with a friend nearby, and obtaining two days rations, went back to Oller's.

It didn't take two days. The next morning Oller walked out, his rifle over his shoulder, and went to the pig pen where he laid the rifle down and began marking a shoat.

Sam stood straight up and just as Oller saw him, Kill-Devil spoke and Oller fell into the mud of the pig pen.

About a hundred yards away, Sam stopped and listened. There was an unearthly squealing sound coming from the pig pen. Sam rode back slowly. Could it be that he had missed from such a short range?

When he got there, he discovered the reason for the squealing. Oller had fallen right on top of a young pig and it could not escape his deathly embrace.

Back at camp, Sam sent all his men back to Arkansas except Aaron, Cato, Burlap, Tom, and a new recruit named Rucker.

"Got one more stop to make," he told them, "Bring a couple of them horses our boys got shot off of, gonna need some pack horses."

Several days later, they rode openly into Irondale just after dark, and seeing no Union soldiers around, stopped at the home of Dr. Poston and compelled him to go to Bean's store and ask to be admitted.

Dr. Poston rapped on the door and in a few moments, Bean appeared from his living quarters in the rear carrying a lantern.

Before either of them could speak, Sam forced his way into the store, and with a pistol pointed at Bean, waved for the rest to come in.

"My boys and I just came by to pick up a few supplies," Sam said to Bean, "You mind if we fill up our gunny sacks?"

"I most certainly do," said Bean, "This ain't nothin' but thievery!"

Sam walked behind the counter and threw a receipt pad at Bean.

"You got us wrong," he said, "Why we aim to just charge our purchases. You keep a record of everything the boys take, and I'll sign it."

When the horses were loaded, Sam made a great deal out of putting his "X" on Bean's pad. "Now," he said to Dr. Poston, "Let's go back by your office and pick up some medical supplies."

After cleaning out the doctor's office, the little band mounted and rode out of town, disappearing like ghosts into the black of the Ozarks.

"Couldn't have worked out better," Tom whispered to Aaron, "Our share of these supplies will get us to Texas."

Aaron looked straight ahead at Sam's back. He was confused as he had never been before. He hadn't joined the army to become a thief, but he owed his life to Sam, and maybe Mary Lee's too, and he wasn't altogether certain he wanted to go to Texas, especially with Tom Haile. But come to think of it, he owed his life to Tom, too.

It was sure a mess. He wished he could go back home to Shepherd Mountain and Maw. Or did he want to go to Sedalia with the Lemleys?

He reached into his saddlebag and took out a bottle of corn-mash whiskey that Mr. Bean had donated to the southern cause.

Turning the bottle up and letting the liquid roll down his throat, he soon forgot his confusion and by the time they reached Crowley's Ridge, he could hardly stay in the saddle.

*   *   *

Aaron was exhausted and spent a couple of day sleeping off the effects of the raid, as well as the sour mash whiskey. He knew he did not want to see Mary Lee until he was completely sober. He certainly didn't need to give her anything else to preach to him about.

But in his haunted sleep, the old fears danced through his mind at a tortured pace. The Sergeant, laughing as he shot Aaron's Paw over and over again. The Dutchman Sam had hung, swinging from the hickory tree in that oblong circle, his eyes bulged out of his head. Over and over Aaron looked over the rock again and saw the Federal soldier, his eyes wide with astonishment as Aaron's bullet slammed into his body. The face of Banks as he disappeared into the swirling waters.

And even when he dreamed of Mary Lee, the words kept coming over and over, "God won't let anything happen to you until you are ready." Ready for what? This religion stuff tormented his sleep almost as much as the killings.

The mornings in northern Arkansas were cool now as the first taste of fall nipped the leaves and the woods began to turn into a fantasy of color.

Sam had ridden out of camp alone, headed on a trip to the Springfield area in southwest Missouri with some of Quantrill's men. Aaron couldn't figure out why Sam wanted to ride with them.

After about a week, Aaron determined he had to see Mary Lee and after splashing cold water on his face and matting down his hair as best he could. he started down the trail to the Lemley cabin.

"One more won't hurt," he said, as he lifted the bottle and held it up to the sunlight so the content level would show through the dark glass.

He tilted the bottle to his lips and downed what was left, tossing the empty bottle into a gully filled with fallen leaves.

He tapped lightly on the Lemley's door and waited. Mary Lee opened the door about half way and said, "Hello, Aaron."

His expectations had been that she would fling open the door and throw herself into his arms.

"Howdy, " he said, "You want to go for a walk?"

"Just a minute," she said as she turned her head back into the cabin. "Is it alright if I go for a walk with Aaron?"

Apparently the answer Aaron could not hear was yes, for Mary Lee stepped out the door. She was dressed in a white dress with a wide belt that made her waist look unreasonably tiny.

He had never seen her looking so pretty. Until he looked into her eyes. Something was wrong! He stepped in front of her and tried to put his arms around her waist.

She recoiled from him!

"What's th' matter?" he asked.

"You've been drinking, havn't you?"

He tried to back up so she couldn't smell the whiskey on his breath. He couldn't bear the hurt he saw in those dark eyes.

"Just a little," he said, looking down at the ground to avoid those pained eyes.

"I heard you have been drinking a lot."

The anger swelled up inside him. "Who told you that?"

"What difference does it make. Is it true?"

He realized he was angry with her.

"Sure, it's true, but I've had a lot on my mind and been through a lot of things you don't even know about. The whiskey helps me forget."

"Does it help you forget me?"

"I could never do that," he said as he reached for her again, but withdrew when he felt the resistance without even touching her.

Those deep black eyes were beginning to shed tears, which ran in little rivulets down her cheeks. She wiped them away with her sleeve.

"Oh, Aaron," she cried, "I love you so much, but I can't stand to see you destroy yourself with the whiskey and the killing and the hate. It's got to end sometime."

Aaron was sober now. Or at least he thought he was.

"It will end when I finish the job I have to do," he said, "When the Sergeant is dead, I'll stop it all, but I have to do it. He killed my Paw and he's got to pay for it!"

"You're not doing this for your Paw anymore," she said, "I think you have reached the point where you enjoy killing and looting and the excitement of the chase. Revenging your Paw's death has become an excuse. Hanging out with Tom Haile and Sam Hildebrand has turned a wonderful young man into a demon."

Again, Aaron felt the anger well up inside him.

"I'm sorry, Aaron," she continued, "I care for you so much I can't bear to see you destroying yourself. And I fear a Federal bullet will end your life before you are ready to meet the Lord."

Aaron slammed the palms of his hands over his ears.

"I don't want to hear that!" he yelled, "I heard it all night long and I don't want to hear it again! I will not be ready to die until I kill the Sergeant."

Mary Lee's eyes were dry as she looked at him.

"Then I think we should not see each other again until you are ready," she said.

She turned and began to walk slowly toward her cabin. Aaron watched and wanted to run after her. Words stuck in his throat and died there. His legs felt like they would collapse under him.

As soon as she was out of sight, they did, and he fell to his knees, his hands over his face as he wept uncontrollably.

He must have been there for more than an hour. When he finally stumbled back to his shack, Haile and Cato were there.

"Sam's going on a raid tomorrow," Tom said, "You want to go?"

"I thought he was riding with Quantrill now?"

Haile snickered. "He was, but they got in a fight and he lost his horse and had to walk home, almost from Springfield. You gonna go with us or not?"

"Why not," Aaron said.

"What's wrong with your eyes?" Cato asked.

Aaron shot him a sharp glare.

"Got some dirt in them, if'n its any of your business," Aaron snapped.

Cato held up both hands, palms outward, and said no more.

"See you at sunrise," Haile said.

"Yeh, sunrise," Aaron said.

As soon as they left, he dug around in the gully where he had thrown the bottle and again lifted it between him and the sun.

There was only a spider left. He let the sip run out on his lips, threw the bottle back into the gully, and went into his shack and collapse on his cot.

CHAPTER 16

The first part of November, 1863, was marked by mild weather in northeast Arkansas. Aaron, Cato, and Burlap spent their days hunting and trapping, and making beef jerky, which they figured would be their main food supply on the way to Texas.

Their nights were spent playing cards in Aaron's shack, or sitting around the camp fires listening to the stories, which seemed to grow with each telling, and drinking whatever was available.

Aaron stayed away from the Lemley home, even taking the long path to his cabin to avoid seeing Mary Lee. He had backed out of going on another raid with Sam, as had Cato, and only Tom had gone.

By the last week of November, the weather had dropped into the teens, spiced by sharp winds out of the northwest and even some snow flurries.

Not long after Tom had gotten back from the raid with Sam, they had their supplies all ready to load on a pack mule and headed southwest.

"Shortest way is straight through Little Rock," said Tom.

"You been gone too long," Cato said, "Word around camp is that the Yankees took over Little Rock in September."

Some pilgrim gave us a map with a route marked north of Little Rock, over the Boston Mountains almost to Fort Smith, and then through Indian territory to Texas."

"That sounds like the long way, and ain't we likely to have bad weather in the mountains?"

"We done decided," Aaron said with finality, "It may be the longest and coldest, but it's the safest."

Tom shrugged his shoulders and pulled his coat collar up to fend off the biting wind they were facing.

Figuring it was all right to travel during daylight, they only made thirty miles the first day, and camped out in a ravine to block the wind.

"Let's go ahead and build a fire and cook a hot meal," Aaron said, "It may be our last for a while."

After they had eaten fried rabbit and potatoes hash-browned in a skillet, they huddled as close to the fire as they could, stretching out their hands to absorb the heat. The Arkansas night was deathly black, broken only by the trilling whistle of a screech owl somewhere in the woods.

"You ain't said nothin' 'bout your trip with Sam," Cato said to Tom.

Tom squatted by the fire and held his hands almost to the flames.

"About the same old thing," he said, "We got in a squabble on that same road between Fredericktown and Pilot Knob. Sam hid in the woods and must have picked off six or seven riders."

"He's gonna run out of gun stock before the war ends," said Aaron.

"Or people to ride with him," Tom mused, "Them two new boys got kilt. I swear they must have had every Fed in the area out chasing us."

Aaron poked a stick into the fire and thought that if he had gone, he might have been one of those killed. Maybe Mary Lee's Guardian Angel was working again.

"Where'd you go then?" Cato asked.

"Rode up to Farmington. As a matter of fact, we captured the whole durn town without firing a shot! They was people all over the streets when we rode in, but they sure disappeared fast. I told Sam I bet cellar rent was going for a high price in old Farmington that day!"

He paused so everyone could appreciate his humor, and then continued.

"Later, we rode right down the main street in broad daylight, helped ourselves at the store, and I even played barkeep for Sam in one of the saloons."

"How'd them boys get kilt?" asked Burlap.

"You remember Bill Coots?" Tom asked, "Well, we had breakfast at his house on the way back. I mean a good breakfast with ham and eggs and they had some kind of spices in them."

"Them boys died from eating Bill Coot's food?" asked Aaron.

Tom frowned at him.

"Of course not," he said, "When we went in old Coots said we could put our weapons on the bed, but Sam and I kept ours. About the time we was finishing the meal, I remember 'cause I had just sopped some gravy on a piece of bread and was headed toward my mouth with it, the door opened and a Federal officer stepped in."

"What'd you do?" Aaron asked.

"Sam shot Coots first, and he and I made a dash out the back door and for the woods. Them two other boys didn't make it."

"Sounds like Sam trusted the wrong man again," Aaron said, "Just because he knew some silly secret sign."

"Like I said before," Tom added, "I think he don't care if he lives or not. I sure ain't riding with him again."

"You said that last time," Aaron said.

They sat and stared at the fire until it was only glowing embers, then rolled up in their blanket cocoons and were soon asleep.

After a cold breakfast of beef jerky and cornbread, they put the rising sun to their backs, believing that a warm and friendly Texas lay ahead where they could forget the war, at least for the winter.

The days turned into a week before they rode into the Boston Mountains. Most of the trip had been in silence, each of them hidden in their own thoughts, doubts, and fears.

Aaron rode mechanically, slumping and almost going to sleep in the saddle. The cold had eased up some, but in the mountains, the valley's saw very little of the sun and they had to break ice on streams for the horses to drink.

The hot pot-bellied stove at the Lemley's kept going through Aaron's mind, along with the warm smile of Mary Lee. And then the vision would fade into her troubled and tear-stained face.

All of them would have turned back at the slightest indication that one of the others wanted to, but somehow they pressed on, turning south after they got out of the mountains.

Four days later they were again in the mountains, the Kiamichis, but when these were crossed, they rode into the red clay plains of the Red River and knew that Texas, warm and friendly, Texas, was just ahead.

Their food was almost exhausted and they had run out of whiskey somewhere in the Boston Mountains.

The brown-red waters of the flat Red River were forded easily near Colbert's Crossing, mainly because they had no money for the ferry fee, or at least Cato, Burlap, and Aaron thought they had none. They camped on the Texas side and ate the last of the jerky.

"The place we was told to go is called Mineral Creek," Cato said, "Near a town called Sherman. That's where Quantrill's men will be. As close as I can figure, we still got a good full days ride ahead of us."

Aaron tried to tuck the corners of his blanket in to shut out the cold wind. He smelled so bad it was a big decision whether to stick his head down in the blanket, or leave it exposed to the biting wind.

"That guy that told you about Texas and how to get here," he said, "I thought he said it would be warm."

Besides the weather, the name Quantrill had sent a shiver up Aaron's body.

"What have I got myself into now?" he thought.

*   *   *

The Bushwhacker camp at Mineral Creek, fifteen miles from Sherman, was something less than what Aaron had hoped for. A totally disorganized clutter of makeshift huts, some log cabins, and a lot of tents, filled the flat area.

Smoke rose from dozens of campfires and there was a stench in the air of raw sewage and horse manure. As they rode in Aaron wondered if some of the men sitting around the campfires were the source of the strange odor.

Most of them were dressed in either ragged civilian clothes, or a mixture of Federal and Confederate uniforms. A number had on pants, with filthy long handled underwear exposed from the waist up.

Many had on colorful shirts, with a neckline that went almost to the belly and ended with a rosette. Every shirt had four enormous pockets.

The four new arrivals rode silently through the maze of shacks, seemingly unnoticed by the men already there, until they reached the far side of the camp.

An open area on the edge of the brush, set away from the others, seemed a likely spot and they dismounted and began to unpack the mule.

"Yo'all figurin' on sitting up homestead thar?" a gruff voice asked.

Aaron looked up into the grizzled face of an older man with no teeth. Most of his head was barren of hair, while long gray strands flowed over his ears in a tangle. He was bent and dressed in buckskin, and his bowed legs spoke of many hours in a saddle.

Before any of them could answer, there was a lot of shouting and firing of pistols as a small group of riders rode through the camp, scattering camp fires and skillets, as well as several tents.

Aaron and the others dove for cover in the brush, but the old man didn't so much as turn to look.

"Yo'als a little skitterish, hain't ya?" he asked. "Twurn't nuttin' but bloody Bill and some of his boys lettin' off some steam."

Aaron crawled out from underneath a bush.

"Does that happen often?"

The old man chuckled. "Ever' day, sometimes mor'n once, and most ever' night."

"Why do they call him Bloody Bill?" Cato asked.

The old man's face grew serious. "He's always been bloody Bill Anderson, but since the Feds put his sister in prison and the building collapsed on her, as well as some of the other Rebel's families, some say he ain't just bloody anymore." His voice dropped to a whisper. "Some say he's crazy."

"Is there a reason we can't sit up camp here?" Tom asked.

"Reckon not," the old man said, "You lads look like you might be the quietest neighbors I've had yet."

He turned and walked over to a little tent a few yards away, picked up a stick, and began to whittle.

Aaron looked around. "I think Bloody Bill ain't the only crazy person here, and I ain't too sure we ain't included."

"It'll be fine," said Tom, "Let's get that tent up and see if we can find some grub."

While Aaron and Cato unpacked the mule and set up camp, Tom and Burlap went off into the brush. In less than an hour, they were back with a deer and soon a hind quarter was roasting over the fire.

With their bellies filled, Tom was ready for a new adventure.

"Got a little surprise for you'al, " he said, "I picked up a little money at that store Sam and I visited in Farmington. Found it stuffed away in a tobacco sack under the counter."

"What makes you think Yankee money will be any good down here in Texas?" asked Aaron.

Tom grinned as he pulled some coins out of his pocket. "Ain't paper, its gold, and it's good anywhere. Let's go see what this town of Sherman looks like."

They rode the fifteen miles or so into town in good spirits, looking forward to the good times they had dreamed about on the trail, lots of pretty women, and real whiskey.

The square in Sherman was dominated by a big three-story brick building that was a store and in the middle of the block was the Iron Post Grocery, which was really a saloon, "The vilest hole in town," the old man at the camp had told them.

They tied up in front of the saloon and started in. Sitting on the front porch was the old man from camp, whittling on a stick.

Aaron looked around at the others.

"How'd he get here?" he asked, "I saw him in camp when we left."

"You lads air just in time," the old man said, "Show's just gittin' ready to start." He pointed out into the street with his knife and for emphasis, spat a stream of tobacco juice in that direction.

In the street, two men were holding the meanest looking stallion any of them had ever seen. As others gathered to watch, a short, stocky man swung into the saddle, took a firm grip on the reins, and nodded to the men holding the horse.

He lost his hat the first time the horse went up in the air, its backed bowed into a horseshoe shape and it came down with all four hoofs in a three foot circle. He swung his free arm in a wide arc and yelled.

Groups of on-lookers scrambled for safety as the stallion charged in their direction. He banged into the porch posts of the saloon in an obvious effort to strip the weight off his back, but the rider held on.

He held on until the stallion gave up and the rider spurred him into a gallop down the street and out of sight.

"Who's he?" asked Tom.

"Dick Maddox," the old man said, "Best rider in town, especially when he is drunk, which is most of the time. You boys look like you could use a guild, buy a drink and I'll show you how to stay alive in Sherman."

"We ain't got much money," Tom said.

"How about them gold coins you was flashing back at camp?"

Tom and Aaron exchanged glances. "Come on in," Tom said, "Looks like we's buyin'."

The old man threw his stick away, put his knife in its scabbard, and followed them into the saloon.

The smell inside the saloon was not entirely different from the odor of the camp at Mineral Creek, and the noise was almost unbearable.

They sat at a corner table and ordered whiskey at ten cents a shot from the scantily dressed waitress. After a couple of drinks, the old man began to talk.

"Best you keep to yourselves and keep your mouth shut," he said, "You can get kilt in this here town by just looking at the wrong person sideways."

He glanced around to see who was sitting near them.

"And stay away from Archie Clements and his gang. Gittin' crossways with them is a good way to end up dead in a hurry."

Aaron became aware that someone was standing at their table, looking at him. He looked up into the face of the bully who had attacked Mary Lee back at Crowley's Ridge.

"Thought I recognized that gimpy walk when you come in," the bully said, grinning, "Where's that thar big friend of yourn?"

Aaron said nothing as the mixture of hate and fear welled up in him. The bully was obviously drunk.

"Ain't here, is he?" the bully said, "Well, I reckon its time I got even for your ruining my fun with that pretty little gal."

He drew a huge knife from his belt and lunged at Aaron.

From beneath the table, the Leech and Rigdon exploded. The bullet blew a hole in the table and struck the bully in the chest.

For a moment he seemed to hand in space, a wild and startled look in his eyes, then he crashed face first on the table.

The noise in the saloon became total silence as everyone turned and looked in the direction of the shooting, but after a few moments, they all turned back to their cards and drinks as though nothing had happened.

"You lads git on your horses and git back to Mineral Creek," the old man said, "Ah can't believe that ah barely git the words outten my mouth 'til you go and shoot one of Archie Clement's riders!"

Aaron and the others hurried out of the saloon. Several of the men at the bar turned to look at them, but nobody seemed concerned that a man had just been killed.

Back at camp, Aaron was amazed at how calm he was. Maybe he was getting used to killing. Maybe Mary Lee's Guardian Angel was working again. Maybe this Archie Clements, whoever he was, would come and kill him tomorrow. Maybe he ought to ride out of camp tonight and head back to Arkansas.

In a little while, the old man came to their fire.

"You lads jist stay put and hope for the best," he said. "Archie is off somewheres now, but you try to run and he will be on your back quick as a rattler strikes."

Aaron rolled up in his blanket and tried to sleep, but when he closed his eyes, he saw again the bullies face as the bullet struck him. The distortion of the mouth and the sudden burst of dark red on his bushwhacker shirt, and the fear in his eyes followed Aaron even deeper into the blanket.

"Another face to chase me in my nightmares," he said to himself.

✶   ✶   ✶

Three days passed without anything happening, except Aaron and his friends did notice that several of their neighbors had moved their camps as far away from them as they could get.

"Ain't nothin' to worry 'bout," said Tom, "I'fn you hadn't a kilt him, he would have cut you in slices with that knife."

The old man came to their camp the morning of the fourth day after the killing.

"Jest got work Archie is back in Sherman," he told them, "He stayed last night at Ben Christian's Hotel. Best you just keep low and hope he's got more important things on his mind, like the fight between Anderson and Quantrill."

About an hour later there was movement at the edge of camp as men hastened to get out of the way of a couple of riders who came in fast.

"It tain't good," said the old man, "Fer sure, it don't get no worse. You not only got little Archie Clements headin' this way, but George Todd is with him.

"Who's George Todd?" asked Cato.

"Quantrill's right hand killer," said the old man, "You see them black things hanging from his saddle? Them's human scalps, and his bridle is woven from human hair."

"You mean he scalps people?" Tom asked.

"Shore does, and Clements counts his victims by jumping on their dead bodies. And Todd's not only Quantrill's boy, but some say he will soon take over if Bill keeps neglecting the command and goes back to that gal Kate he has hidden away in the Sni."

The two riders worked their way through the maze of tents and shacks toward the boy's camp. Aaron noticed the old man edged off into the brush and disappeared.

Clements and Todd rode right up to the tent. Clements got off his horse. He was dressed in a frock coat, with shiny black boots and two pistols stuck in his belt. His hat was black and wide brimmed, cocked on the right side of his head at a jaunty angle.

Shiny black hair, slicked down, stuck out from under the hat over his ears and a well trimmed mustache adorned his upper lip.

The blonde-headed Todd stayed on his horse. His steel gray eyes focused on Aaron. A crooked smile seemed to be permanently engraved on his face. He looked, Aaron thought, to be about his age.

"Which one of you killed Devers?" asked Clements.

"Reckon that would be me," Aaron said, stepping forward.

Clements also stepped forward. He pulled one of the guns from his belt and placed the end of the barrel directly in the center of Aaron's forehead.

"Then you are going to die," he said.

"If I hadn't of killed him the other night," said Aaron, "He would have killed me. So the way I figure it, if you kill me now, I ain't no worse off than if I hadn't of killed him."

Clements thought about that for a moment as he looked Aaron over carefully.

"You boys are new at Mineral Creek," he said, "Who you been riding with?"

"We been riding with Sam Hildebrand for the past three years," said Aaron, "Mostly in southeast Missouri."

Clements eyes widened.

"Sam Hildebrand, huh," he said, "Old Sam rode with me just a few weeks ago over near Springfield. You might say that if it hadn't been for Sam, somebody might be carrying my scalp on their saddle horn."

His eyes narrowed as he kept the pistol on Aaron's head.

"Since you are a friend of Sam's, I just might let you go. That boy Devers wern't nothin' but trouble anyways."

Aaron felt his muscles relax just a little and Burlap took a deep breath.

"And then again," said Clements, "I just might kill you for the fun of it."

He pulled the hammer back on the pistol. It was a chilly December day but Aaron could feel the sweat running down his face. He felt the urge to run, to lash out at his tormentor, to somehow even accept the fact that he was about to die.

Clements continued to hold the gun on Aaron's head as Todd grinned from the saddle.

"What do you think?" asked Archie, looking back at the steel eyed Todd.

"Go ahead and shoot him," said Todd.

Clements smiled at Aaron.

Then he pulled the trigger.

Click!

Aaron felt his knees buckle beneath him as Clement returned the gun to his belt. Todd was grinning even bigger. "Why, you must have forgot to load your gun, Archie," he said.

"When you see Sam again," Clement said, "Tell him Archie said howdy."

He swung into the saddle and he and Todd rode out of camp as men diverted their eyes to keep from looking at them.

Aaron could stand no longer. He crumbled to the ground in a heap.

Almost at once, the old man was there again.

"You air probably the first man Archie Clements pulled a pistol on and didn't kill," he said, "You must lead a charmed life."

A charmed life, Aaron thought, or Mary Lee's Guardian Angel again?

CHAPTER 17

Aaron spent the next two weeks in camp, recovering from his close encounter with death, while the others spent most of their nights in Sherman.

They came home excited, even Burlap was grinning from ear to ear.

"We done got invited to a dance," said Tom, "A New Year's Eve dance. Gonna be lotsa pretty girls, dancing, drinking, and gambling."

Aaron just squatted in front of the tent with his arms wrapped around his knees.

"Come on, Aaron," said Tom, "You jist been sittin' around like this for days. When you gonna go with us and have some fun."

Aaron looked up at him.

"The old man told me about all the fun you had on Christmas day at Christian's Hotel," he said, "Is it gonna be like that?"

"Aw, that twarn't nothin' at all," said Cato, Jist a little ruckus with some of the boys."

"I heard you boys got drunk on something called egg nog and rode into the hotel and shot the place up pretty bad, even shot the decorations off a ladies hat."

"Jist a little fun, " said Tom, "It'll be different at the dance."

"Durn yes," said Cato, " And everybody's been asking about you and wanting to know where you are. You're kinda famous after shooting Devers, he was a bad one."

187

Aaron saw again the bully Devers laying on the table in the saloon, his dead eyes open and staring across the room at nothing, the blood soaking into the table and running in a little stream toward Aaron. He had leaped away so none of it would get on him.

"I ain't anxious to git into another fight," he said.

"We won't, promise," Burlap pleaded, "Come on and go."

Aaron pushed his stiff legs into an upright position.

"All right," he said, "But at the first sign of trouble, we hightail it back to camp."

"Agreed," said Tom, "Let's head for Sherman!"

The party was being held at Jim Crow Chile's house, better known as a gambling den, frequented by loose women. It had been planned for about twenty of Quantrill's men and they had no intention of letting outsiders attend.

"Don't even look at that Bush Smith," the old man had told them, "Some say Bill Anderson is fixing to marry her."

When Aaron and the others reached Sherman, Haile stopped in front of the saloon where Aaron had killed Devers.

"They told us to meet them here," he said.

In a few minutes several riders rode up and dismounted. All of them, Aaron noted, were wearing the embroidered shirts that marked them as Bushwhackers. There seemed to be a mixture of Anderson's men and some of Clement's boys.

"Here's what we're gonna do," one of the men said after about twenty had gathered. "We ride over to Chile's place and join the party, just like we had an invite."

"Yeah," said another, "We'll show them they cain't have a party without us."

Tom looked at Aaron.

"Wait a minute," Tom said, "I thought you said we had an invite?"

The leader swung into his saddle. "Not exactly," he grinned, "We are about to invite ourselves. Are you boys comin' or not?"

"Sure, I guess so," said Haile, as he looked at Cato, Burlap, and Aaron.

"Well, I ain't," said Aaron as he turned his horse, "I'm goin' back to Mineral Creek."

"Guess they'll all think I was scared," he told himself on the ride back to camp. "First they think I'm a big hero of some kind for killing Devers, now they'll think I'm yellar. Maybe I should turn around and go with them, I sure don't want to be called yellar."

But he kept on toward camp. He stirred up the fire and waited, unable to sleep, his mind a jumble of thought, from what his friends thought of him to Mary Lee to Devers to the Sergeant, from Banks to the soldier he killed in the woods, and then it would all start all over again.

Sometime in the night, he must have fallen asleep rolled up in his blanket.

"Aaron! Aaron!" Someone was shaking him violently.

It was Tom.

Aaron sprung up immediately. Something was wrong, he sensed it in Tom's voice.

Cato stood behind Tom and behind him in the darkness Aaron could make out a horse with a body draped over the saddle.

"It's Burlap," said Tom, "He done got hisself kilt."

Aaron ran to the horse and looked at the big round face of his soft spoken and gentle friend. His chest heaved in spasmodic convulsions. His arm rose and fell to his side. Finally he leaned against the horse and wept bitterly.

The only one of them who never caused any trouble. The only one that liked and was liked by everybody. The boy who never said much, would never speak again.

"It happened so fast," said Tom, "We couldn't help it. Them riders got to Chile's place and there was a big fist fight. We tried to stay out of it, but the next thing we knowed, some guy came running toward us with a pistol. We couldn't tell which side he was on so we jist stood there. He ran right up to Burlap and shot him."

"You said you didn't think Sam cared whether he lived or died," said Aaron, "Well, I don't think anyone down here cares whether they live or die. Soon as we bury Burlap in the morning, I'm riding to Arkansas."

"Me too," said Cato.

"That's all right with me," said Tom, "Texas sure ain't turned out to be what we expected. But we got a problem."

"What's that?" asked Aaron.

"Them gold coins is all gone, and we ain't got enough supplies to get over the Red River, much less back to Crowley's Ridge."

"We can live off the land," said Aaron.

"Not easy to do in the dead of winter," Tom said, "Let's start gittin' stuff together and we'll leave as soon as we can."

Cato and Aaron exchanged glances.

"As soon as we can," echoed Aaron.

The next morning they dug a grave out in the brush behind their camp with a borrowed shovel in the partially frozen red soil of northeast Texas.

"Shouldn't we say a few words over him?" asked Cato.

"You know any words to say?" asked Tom.

They both looked at Aaron.

"Don't look at me," he said, "I don't even believe in that stuff. None of this would have happened if there was a God. Why don't we let his bones just rest here in Texas. If there was a God, Burlap would probably just to hell anyway, after all the things we've done."

An anger arose in him. An anger against Burlap for getting killed, and at God for letting it happen. And at himself for not going to the dance and protecting his friend, and at Tom and Cato for their stupidity.

He was also mad at Mary Lee. Where was Burlap's Guardian Angel when he needed it?

He was mad at everyone except the unknown man who had shot Burlap. For Aaron saw him as just another poor soul caught in the tangled web of fear and hate that war brought.

They left Burlap's grave site, an unmarked mound, and rode toward Sherman.

"Soon's we get enough supplies," Aaron said, "We head for Arkansas, right?"

Tom and Cato nodded, but neither had any idea where the supplies would come from.

"I ain't rode with Sam all this time and not learned something," said Aaron, "Just follow me."

They tied their horses up in front of a little store halfway to town. Aaron pulled his neckerchief up over his face, pulled the Leech and Rigdon, and kicked open the door.

Tom and Cato followed him in.

An old man stood behind the counter.

"This is a stick-up," yelled Aaron, "Fill this gunny sack with groceries!"

The old man looked bored. "Help yourselves, boys," he said, motioning toward the shelves.

They were all empty! Not even a sack of flour!

"You boys must be new around here, Quantrill's men done cleaned out every store within fifty miles of Sherman."

Tom slammed the door behind him and jumped on his horse.

"We'll just have to ride out further," he said, "Bound to be some well stocked store somewheres in Texas."

"I got a better idea," Aaron said, "Let's start riding toward Arkansas and live off the land as best we can. Got to be some game and maybe even a pilgrim along the way who will trade a meal for a little wood choppin' or something."

"It's a long way back, it's gonna be cold, and an empty belly ain't gonna make the trip any easier," said Tom.

"I'd rather starve than have to steal from innocent folks," said Aaron, "That's what the Federals did to my folks."

The next day they packed up what little they had, waved to the old man who sat whittling in front of his tent, and headed for the Red River and Indian territory.

*   *   *

After they crossed the Red River, they turned east and traveled along the river basin to avoid the higher elevations of the Kiamiches but when the river took a southerly direction, they turned north toward the Quachitas.

Staying on the southern side as best they could, they had some protection from the northwest wind that whipped the top of the pine trees. But when they topped a tall crest, the wind hit them with a fury as they stood on a rock ledge and looked below.

"We'll camp for the night down there," said Tom, "Should be some protection from the wind, anyways."

Without a word they reined their horses to the left and worked their way down what seemed to be a natural trail to the bottom.

It was farther than it had looked from up above, and the trail petered out and a new one had to be found, or made through the pines and scrub oaks.

Almost at dusk, they reached the valley. The little stream they had seen from the crest of the mountain that had been a thin ribbon of white was now a frothing, screaming torrent, agonizing as it threw itself against the huge gray rocks that tried to block its way.

Dismounting on a flat layer of rock on the stream's edge, they found an abundance of dead wood and soon had a thunderous fire leaping into the air.

They had seen no game all day which was not unusual due to the sudden cold snap, and supper consisted of beef jerky and some sour dough biscuits Cato had in his saddlebags, which in spite of their hardness, were not so bad once they had picked the green mold off the edges.

They stayed up late, mostly because of the warm fire, but when the wood they had gathered ran out, Aaron wrapped himself in his blanket and stared up at the shroud of stars that filled the clear night sky, a sure sign that the night would even get colder in the early morning hours.

The river continued its cascade in the dark, as though a thousand voices were shouting for peace. But for Aaron, like the river, there was no peace all night.

Numbed by the cold, he tried to think of good things to get his mind off the bad things, but once again, only the faces of the men he had killed, and the one he wanted to kill, crashed through his mind as the river slammed into the rocks.

Morning was as he suspected it would be: clear and colder. Cato was already up and with his rifle in hand, had left camp before dawn.

"Maybe I can get us some breakfast," he said as Aaron buried his head as deep as he could into the blanket and pinched his nose to try and get it warm.

Soon two rifle shots reverberated through the valley and bounced back again.

In a few minutes, a grinning Cato came into camp with two rabbits dangling by their feet. They looked a little scrawny, but there was bound to be some meat under their thick fur.

Aaron got up and stirred the fire to life as Cato began to skin the rabbits and Tom gathered more wood.

Within an hour, their bellies were filled and the horses saddled. They filled their canteens from the clear cold stream and headed northeast.

By noon, they had made only a few miles in the rugged terrain. There were animal trails to follow, and they ran under limbs to low for a horse and rider.

The clear sky disappeared and heavy dark curtains of clouds rolled across the mountain tops.

Aaron thought it was rain when it first hit them but he soon realized the little pellets could sting when they hit exposed skin.

The sleet, however, soon turned to graupel, half ice and half snow, and before long, great windblown flakes of snow soaked their clothes.

"We better hole up somewheres," said Tom, "We could freeze if'n we don't get dried out before the night cold sets in."

They turned down a draw that put the wind to their backs and soon found an overhanging ledge of rock. There was plenty of dead wood around and with very little effort, they had a barrier built that gave them some protection from the wind, and enough firewood to last the night.

Supper consisted of what was left of the rabbits, which wasn't much. Before dark fell, they gathered enough dry grass to feed the horses and tethered them in a sheltered dell.

Aaron cut several small saplings and made a rack to dry their clothes on.

They stood in their underwear around the fire, turning one side until it was reddened by the heat, and then turning the other. It was not possible to get all the way warm at once.

When his clothes were dry, Aaron slipped the still steaming garments back on, rolled up in his blanket, and in a few moments was peacefully asleep, dreaming of Mary Lee.

He awoke with a start when a shot rang out, very close. He grabbed his rifle and crawled out of the shelter of the overhang.

Tom squatted at the fire, seemingly unconcerned, and after a while, Cato walked into camp, a young doe draped around his neck.

"We're gonna freeze to death in these mountains," Tom said as Cato gutted and dressed the deer and Aaron poured clear river water in a little pot to make coffee.

"What ya think we oughtta do?" he asked Tom.

"Head due east," Tom said as he poked the fire with a stick.

"Won't that take up right into the worst of the Quachitas?"

"Not if we skirt them to the south a little," said Tom

"But that will take us right up the middle of Arkansas," Cato piped in, "Right toward Little Rock and that's Yankee country now."

"I'd rather face a thousand Yankees than die out here in this cold," said Tom, "How about you, Aaron?"

Aaron burned his lip on the tin cup as he tried to sip the steaming coffee. He pressed his aching mouth to the sleeve of his coat to alleviate the pain.

"Let's ride east," he said.

CHAPTER 18

Mary Lee stood where she had spent many hours the last few months, staring out the small window Bill Lemley had put in the front of their cabin. Having a real window was a luxury, but there was really not a lot to see out of it.

The winter had been harsh on the Crowley Ridge colony, and the break in the cold had only brought heavy rains instead of snow.

It was the first of April and had been pouring down for several days.

She had been able to keep her mind occupied through the winter months with quilting and the Bible study her mother had at their home every week. Privately, she spent much time reading the Bible and praying, but found it difficult to concentrate since Aaron had left for Texas.

The heavy rains had flooded rivers and reduced the number of raids made by the men of Crowley's Ridge into Missouri, and it showed no sign of abating.

Mary Lee could only stare out at the curtain of water, the muddy front yard, and the water laden trees and admit that she had a bad case of cabin fever.

A dark figure caught her eye as it moved very slowly through the woods and toward the cabin. She took her hand and rubbed the window, squinting to see better.

It was, for certain, a rider.

Who would be crazy enough to be out in this storm, she thought as the rider drew nearer. He was slumped in the saddle, his hat pulled over his face. He swayed from side to side with the movement of the horse.

He stopped right in front of the cabin and just sat there. The rider leaned to the left and suddenly fell from the horse, landing in the mud flat on his back.

He did not move.

Mary Lee watched as though in a trance. For a long several minutes, she did not move, but stared at the dark, muddy form in her front yard.

"Daddy!" she cried at last,, "Someone is hurt out front."

Bill Lemley opened the door and shielded his face from the wind blown rain that pelted him. He hesitated for a moment and then dashed out, grabbed the figure under the arms, and dragged him into the house.

"Shut the door!" he yelled at Mary Lee.

In the semi-darkness of the cabin, Bill pulled the hat off of their uninvited guest.

It was Aaron!

"Is he hurt?" Mary Lee asked, her hands covering her mouth.

"I don't think so," said Bill, "At least I don't see any signs of a wound."

He knelt at Aaron's side. "He seems to be asleep, as near as I can tell. His breathing seems to be normal and…well I'll be, listen to that!"

"Listen to what?"

"He's snoring!"

Anna's snicker got a cold stare from Mary Lee, who failed to see any humor in the situation. Anna went to the hearth, stirred up the coals, and put more wood on. She began to peel potatoes for soup.

Bill, with a little help from Mary Lee, managed to get Aaron into the little room where he had stayed when he had been shot.

"Help your mother," he told Mary Lee, "I'll get him to bed."

He pulled the curtain closed and began to remove Aaron's muddy and well-worn boots. In a little while he came out.

"I got him dried off and in bed," he said, "Acts like he's just plumb tuckered out."

From behind the curtain, Aaron's snoring sounded like the braying of a Missouri mule.

Bill, Anna, and even Mary Lee broke into laughter, although Mary Lee's was mixed with tears.

Bill pulled on his hat and coat.

"I better see to his horse," he said and he opened the door and disappeared into the rain.

The potato soup sat on the hearth all night, was warmed up the next morning, and finally eaten by the Lemley's for dinner.

Aaron finally woke up about dusk.

Bill heard him arouse and pulled back the curtain a little.

"How you feel?" he asked.

"I'm hungry," said Aaron, "Very hungry."

"I'll put on some potato soup," said Anna.

"That would be great," said Aaron, "And do you have any ham? Or beans? Or maybe some of that peach cobbler of yours?"

Soon the pans were rattling as Mary Lee and Anna prepared a full meal and the smell of peaches cooking in a Dutch oven filled the cabin.

He was too weak to walk to the table, but Bill and Mary Lee helped. Then the Lemley's, who had not had supper themselves, watched as Aaron devoured everything he could.

"Take it easy, son," said Bill, "You eat too fast, you're gonna get sick."

"Yeth thir," Aaron said through a mouthful of cornbread, which he washed down with a full glass of buttermilk.

After supper and the dishes were done, Bill lit up his pipe and they sat around the table, everyone looking at Aaron.

He felt very self-conscious.

"I guess you want to know where I been?" he asked.

No one spoke. They continued to look at him expectantly.

"Well, like you know," he started, "Me, Burlap, Cato and Tom went to Texas, but we didn't like it there, so we came home."

The Lemley's waited for him to continue.

There was a long silence. "Is that all that happened?" asked Mary Lee.

"Not exactly, " Aaron answered, then paused. "Burlap got hisself kilt."

Mary Lee reached across the table and touched his hand. He looked at her and remembered the last time he had seen her and wondered why she still cared.

There was a lump in his throat. "And I kilt that guy who attacked you the day Sam saved us."

Mary Lee said nothing, but the troubled look on her face told Aaron he should have kept his mouth shut.

"Then we almost froze to death in the mountains and Cato got sick and probably would have died if it hadn't been for the Choctaw family that took us in."

"Hold on a minute," said Bill, "This sounds like it is going to be more than a one pipe story, let me get my tobacco pouch."

"Naw, there really ain't much more to tell," said Aaron, "We stayed with them injuns for a couple of weeks 'till Cato got better, then we headed for Little Rock."

"You had no trouble with the Federals at Little Rock?" asked Bill.

"None to speak of," said Aaron, "Although all three of us almost drown crossing the Arkansas River."

"Maybe I had better get my pouch," said Bill.

"No need," said Aaron, "After that it was just riding day and night in this awful rain with the hunger in our stomachs so bad food was all we could think about."

"Well, you made it," said Anna, "And that's all that matters."

"Yessum," said Aaron, "And I sure missed your cooking, 'specially since we had to eat part of Cato's horse back in the Quachitas."

Anna took it as a compliment, while Mary Lee made a face.

"Can I sleep here tonight?" Aaron asked.

"Certainly you can, son," said Bill, "The sun will come out tomorrow and everything will seem brighter."

"I shore hope so," said Aaron, "I shore hope so."

"Get some sleep," Mary Lee said, "And tomorrow we can talk all day."

"I'd like that," said Aaron, "I shore am tired of talking to Cato and Haile."

He got up and started toward his room.

"Can you make it all right?" Bill asked.

"I'm fine," Aaron said.

At the curtain, he stopped and looked back at the little family.

"You folks have sure been nice to me, and I can't figure out why," he said.

He pulled back the curtain and then paused again.

"Can I ask one question?"

"Sure," said Bill.

"What are we having for breakfast?"

Soon the snoring was going full blast again and Anna got a box out of her cabinet and began looking through it.

"What you looking for?" asked Bill.

"My recipe for horse flesh," she said.

*   *   *

Aaron spent several days at the Lemley's. Days filled with a renewed relationship with Mary Lee, who, although curious about his trip to Texas, let him tell about it at his own pace.

He finally shared the story about Burlap's death and how he killed the bully in the saloon.

As the spring rains continued, Aaron found the confines of the Lemley cabin refreshing, especially at meal times.

Bill and Anna noticed that Mary Lee had a new glow about her and apparently her cabin fever had been cured.

One day Aaron did get out during a lull in the rain to check on Tom and Cato. Cato was fine but Tom had been drinking ever since they got back and had not even taken the saddle off his horse.

Aaron made sure the animal was fed and watered and gave it a good rubdown. It was not like Tom to neglect his horse.

When the skies finally cleared, Aaron and Mary Lee walked up the trail to his shack. The door had been blown off and part of the roof was missing.

Aaron stepped in the door and then leaped back.

"Get out! Mary Lee!" he yelled, "Get out!"

Fifty feet down the trail he caught up with her and they looked back to see a skunk coming out the door.

"Think your folks will mind if I stay with you all a few more days?" Aaron asked.

"I won't mind," she said.

As soon as it was dry enough, Bill and Aaron began putting in the spring garden. Aaron found his strength returning with every meal he ate at the Lemley's, and the fresh air soon had the color returning to his cheeks.

When the odor and dampness had left his shack, he moved back in and settled down to spend the summer in the tranquility of northeast Arkansas.

"Howdy, boy, I heered you was back."

Aaron was startled by the sudden appearance of the huge frame in his doorway and leaped to his feet.

"Sam," he said, sticking out his hand, "Good to see you."

"Heered you boys got into a little trouble down in Texas," Sam said, "Burlap got kilt?"

"Sure did, Sam," said Aaron, "Them Quantrill people are crazy. Didn't care who they killed or why."

"Yeh, I know, that's why I quit ridin' with them."

"Well, I am sure glad you rode with them the last time," Aaron said, and he told Sam about his run-in with Archie Clements.

"You must have caught Archie in a rare mood," said Sam, "I ain't never heered of him not killing someone when he had a reason. Matter of fact, he has killed a lot of folks without any reason at all."

"What you been doing?" Aaron asked.

Sam kinda grinned. "O, just the same old thing, putting more notches on Kill-Devil's stock. Getting ready for a raid in a couple of day, you want to go?"

Aaron looked down at his feet, then up into Sam's eyes.

"Reckon not," he said, "I've had about all the killing I want for a while. Besides, Mr. Lemley needs me to help in his garden."

Sam touched the brim of his forage cap and was gone.

*   *   *

Mary Lee was excited! "There's going to be a revival. With a real preacher this time, the Reverend William Polk, a Baptist minister."

Aaron almost wished he had gone with Sam.

"Good," he said, "I been to hell and God wasn't there and I been to the top of the mountains and he wasn't there. I sure don't expect to find him at Crowley's Ridge."

"You may find someday soon," Mary Lee said, "That he is even closer than that."

The next day the Reverend Polk arrived at Crowley's Ridge and began making plans for the meetings. He was an older man, seventy at least, Aaron guessed. His flowing white beard hung from a thin face. His eyes sparkled with excitement and he was tall and thin, with long skinny legs.

Bill Lemley introduced them in the garden and in spite of himself, Aaron found he liked the man.

But he would have no part of this religion thing.

The area where Dr. Melchair Mercer had held his ill-fated services was once again cleared, new rough-hewn split logs arranged for seating, and the platforms at the corners cleaned off and rebuilt for the fires.

The Lemley family was caught up in the pre-revival activities and Aaron found himself spending less time with Mary Lee and more with Tom.

Mary Lee kept her word and did not try to get him to go, but he knew she was praying for him and that was almost more pressure than he could bear.

For almost two weeks, he could see the glow of the fires from his shack and hear the soft singing. He strained his ears, but could not hear Reverend Polk shouting like Mercer had done.

As the services continued night after night, Aaron, Tom, and Cato found more and more of the men were deserting the camp fires at the corral for the fires of the revival.

They sat and drank bursthead and wished they had gone with Sam just to have something to do.

The hymns floated on the early summer breeze, penetrating even to the corrals.

"Why don't we jist go up there and tell them to shut up," said Tom.

"Take it easy," said Aaron," Bill Lemley told me this was to be the last night, it'll soon be over."

"All the more reason to go break it up," said Tom, "We still got a war to fight and if everybody starts singing hymns and prayin' all the time, they won't be anyone left to fight with, 'ceptin' Sam."

"Maybe your right," said Aaron, getting to his feet a little unsteadily, "Let's go see what's goin' on, anyway. You comin' Cato?"

"Reckon so," said Cato as he followed Tom and Aaron up the trail.

When they arrived at the clearing, Reverend Polk was leading the congregation in another hymn.

"Rock of ages, cleft for me, let me hide myself in Thee"

"Ah been in them rocks down in Texas and injun country," yelled Tom as he waved his bottle of bursthead for the preacher to see, "Ain't nothin' in them rocks but rattlesnakes and horny toads!"

Reverend Polk ignored him and continued to sing. Aaron saw Mary Lee on the second row with her parents. She turned and glanced back and he looked away quickly. Suddenly the effects of the whiskey seemed to leave him completely and he wished he had not come.

When the song ended, Reverend Polk led in a prayer, closing with "Amen."

"Amen, brother Ben," yelled Tom.

Again the Reverend ignored the intrusion and began his message.

"Tonight I am preaching from the book of Romans," he began, "And will use several passages, beginning with Romans 3:23."

"Preach on!" Tom hollered.

"For all have sinned and come short of the glory of God," Reverend Polk read.

At once, that funny feeling he had before filled Aaron's stomach. He hung on every word the preacher said as he expounded the scriptures in a soft voice.

"The wages of sin is death," he said, "But the gift of God is eternal life."

Aaron took a couple of steps away from Tom and Cato. Tom, not having received the attention he had expected, had shut up.

There were other scriptures and other words and Aaron absorbed each of them, especially when the Reverend said, "Ye must be born again."

Aaron had no idea what that meant.

The sermon ended with the congregation quoting in unison, "For God so loved the world He sent his only begotten Son, that whosoever believeth in Him should not perish, but have eternal life."

The preacher prayed again and then invited repentants to come to the makeshift mourner's benches to pray. Several went down almost at once. Bill Lemley was one of the first.

Aaron looked around. Tom and Cato had disappeared.

Slowly he made his way down between the benches toward the front. He felt compelled as though against his will.

The congregation was singing a hymn, one he had heard his Maw sing as she hung out clothes, although he couldn't remember the words.

At the second row, he looked down into the tear filled eyes of Mary Lee, then almost as though shoved, he fell on his knees beside Bill.

Bill put his arm around Aaron. "Jesus will save you," he said softly, "Just let go, son."

Aaron could hardly talk for the deep sobs.

"I've done some terrible things," he said.

"Not too terrible for God to forgive," said Bill.

Aaron believed him. A peace flowed through his body that caused a physical shudder. And then he knew.

Bill led him in a prayer but before it was finished, Aaron felt a small, soft hand wrap around his on the mourner's pole and he did not have to look, he knew Mary Lee was at his side.

After the service, the Lemley's embraced him excitedly.

"Knew there was something good in you the moment I saw you that first day in camp," said Bill, "We're proud of you, son."

Anna hugged him again and wiped her eyes with the corner of a lace hanky.

Aaron looked at Mary Lee.

"I got to go," he said.

She seemed puzzled.

"Why do you have to go? Go where?"

"I got to go tell Tom and Cato," Aaron said.

CHAPTER 19

It had to be the happiest summer Aaron had ever known! Just being with Mary Lee and enjoying the same things she did, such as Bible study, made it seem like a new world.

"I got to go home soon and tell Maw," he told Mary Lee.

"Poppa says the war will end soon, maybe we can all go home."

"Maybe we can go home together," he said, kissing her on the cheek.

The faces that had haunted his dreams were gone and the hate that had eaten at him from inside, well, he had to admit was still there, but subject to the joy of his new life.

Telling Cato and Tom about his new found happiness had not happened, for they had disappeared on a raid with Sam into Missouri the morning after his conversion, and seemed to avoid him when they did come back to camp for short periods of time.

"Remember how you used to get mad when I brought religion up?" Mary Lee asked him, "You will probably find your friends will feel the same way you did. Until the Holy Spirit moves in their lives as he did in yours, they won't want to hear what you have to say."

"But it would get rid of their hate!"

"Didn't I tell you that a long time ago?"

"But......"

"Shush," she interrupted, placing a finger over his lips, "The time will come to tell or show them what happened to you, and you will know what to say and do."

"Mary Lee?"

"Yes."

"Mary Lee......"

"What is it, Aaron?"

"Mary Lee, will you marry me?"

The glow on her face and the light in her eyes told him his answer, but he was not prepared for her response.

"I've already discussed our marriage with Momma," she said, "And before he left, the Reverend Polk agreed to come back to perform the ceremony."

"But I ain't even asked you until just now!"

"Momma and I knew you would, so we started making plans," she said, "But there's only one more thing left for you to do."

"What's that?"

"Ask Poppa."

"You mean I gotta..."

"You most certainly do, " she said curtly, "This marriage cannot take place without his approval."

"Well, I think Mr. Lemley likes me all right," said Aaron, "But it ain't gonna be easy."

"Yes it will," she said.

"How do you know?"

"Because I have already discussed it with him, and he said he would be glad to have you for a son-in-law."

"Then how come I gotta ask him?"

"Because you do," she smiled, "Just because you do."

Aaron stood with his mouth open and his hands held open in front of him.

"And by the way, Aaron," she said, "The answer to your question is yes."

"What question?"

"Why, I do believe you asked me to marry you, didn't you?"

"I forgot," grinned Aaron.

"Be at supper tonight," said Mary Lee. She embraced him and their lips met in their first real kiss. "The best time to talk to Poppa is after he gets his pipe lit."

Aaron spent the rest of the day rehearsing, and changing, his speech. It seemed silly since Bill Lemley already knew what he was going to ask, but had decided the only thing he really knew about women was that it was usually best to go ahead and do it their way.

Everybody was smiling all through supper, and although there was a knot in his stomach, Aaron managed to eat his share of Anna's cooking.

When the table was cleared, Mary Lee and Anna announced they were going for a walk as Bill reached for his pipe.

Aaron waited until Bill had stuck a match to the bowl and taken several long draws on the pipe.

Aaron cleared his throat......several times.

"Is this going to be a long speech?" asked Bill, "Perhaps I should get my tobacco pouch."

Aaron shook his head and cleared his throat again.

"Don't worry about it, son," said Bill, "I know what you want to say and the answer is yes."

Aaron let out an audible sigh.

"But when Anna and Mary Lee ask me," said Bill, as he stuck another match to his cold pipe and sucked in, "I will tell them you made beautiful speech, with elegant words."

"Won't that be a lie?"

Bill chuckled as he shook the match out. "You're right, we shouldn't lie, but in dealing with womenfolk, you will have to learn to use what we call situation ethics." Then he laughed.

Aaron had no idea what situation ethics meant, but he laughed too.

When Anna and Mary Lee returned, sure enough, Bill bragged on Aaron and welcomed him as his prospective son-in-law. The ladies were giggling the rest of the night and on several occasions went into Mary Lee's room to laugh out loud.

Bill Lemley just sat and pulled on his pipe and smiled at Aaron.

Outside the cabin door, Aaron told Mary Lee goodnight. Somehow holding her in his arms felt different. He had always been scared before, or something, but now it felt so natural to hold her.

"Just one more thing," he told her, "I want to go home and see my Maw and tell her about the marriage."

Those dark eyes of hers flashed. "You don't mean to on another raid, do you?"

"No, of course not," he said a little exasperated, "I ain't doin' that no more. But I feel like I gotta go tell her."

"I understand," she said, "When will you leave?"

"In the morning, I guess."

"How long will you be gone?"

"Not more than a week," he said, "If I can, maybe she could come back with me."

"Aaron, Momma and I been talking about when we should get married," she said, "Poppa says the war is almost over. The South is losing battle after battle in the east since Grant took over the Union Army. Poppa doesn't think they can hold out more than another six months."

"You want to wait until the war is over?"

"Momma and I think it would be nice to set the date for June of next year. That's less than a year away and surely the war will be done and we could get married in Sedalia."

"I don't want to wait that long," said Aaron, "But maybe it would be best, if you and Momma think so."

She smiled and kissed him goodnight.

There were no nightmares that night, but Aaron had a hard time falling asleep. What Mary Lee said about getting married in Sedalia had made him realize he had a decision to make: live at home with Maw on Shepherd Mountain, or live in Sedalia.

Finally, before the dawn, he got his horse packed and headed for Shepherd Mountain.

*   *   *

The trip from Crowley's Ridge to Shepherd Mountain could take as long as four days, but Aaron was certain he could make it in a little over two, since he was not going to be involved in any military operations. Being dressed in civilian clothes and his youthful appearance would allowed him to take a direct route.

The problem was, Federal activity in southeast Missouri had intensified. With the regular armies of the South retreating in most areas, more troops had been sent to fight the splintered war in the western border states.

It was August and it was hot, so he traveled mostly during the night hours, both for safety and to enjoy the coolness of the dark.

He was doing his best to look like a local young man out for a ride, but feared his horse's appearance might draw attention to him, for most horses owned by Missourians who favored the South had been stolen.

By now he knew the way easily, and found himself at dawn of the third day found himself south of Fredericktown, where he turned east, skirted the town, and rode almost to Farmington before turning southwest so that he would approach Shepherd Mountain from the north side and avoid Fort Davidson and Ironton.

When he turned up the road to his home, he was appalled at the condition of the house. The peeling paint was a lot worse than it had been on his last visit, and the front porch leaned at an odd angle on one corner.

He was a little surprised that his Maw did not come out to greet him, but hitched his horse and walked up on the porch. The screen door, with several holes in it, was hanging by one hinge.

"Maw," he said.

There was no answer.

He opened the door and walked into the kitchen. The door to his Maw's room was ajar and he peeked in. She was in bed.

"Maw?"

She turned her head on the pillow and smiled.

"Aaron! Oh Aaron, come here!"

He went to her bed and embraced her, kissing her lightly on her tear stained cheek.

"Are you sick, Maw?"

"I have been honey," she said in a weak voice, "But I'll be all right now that you are home. Sit here on the edge of the bed."

She reached up as he sat down and ran her finger down his scarred cheek. "Are you all right, honey?"

"I ain't never been better, I guess," he said and began to tell her about his religious experience. By the time he had finished, she was sitting up in bed.

"I'm so happy," she said, "I have prayed for your safety ever since the day you left, but I have also prayed you would find the Lord and empty your heart of hate."

"There's something else you need to know, Maw," he said.

"What is it?"

"Mary Lee and me are gonna get married."

The transformation in his Maw was so evident Aaron could hardly believe his eyes. When he had first come into the room his Maw looked like a sick, tired, old woman. Now, suddenly, she was sitting on the edge of the bed and almost looked like her old self.

Her eyes sparkled and she brushed her tangled hair.

"I've been praying about that, too," she said, "And from what you told me about her, she is a wonderful girl."

"Yes'm, she is."

"Will you look at this mess!" she said, glancing around the cluttered room. "You get out to the barn. I still got that old milk cow my brother gave me. You get us some warm milk and I'll get supper on the stove."

Before he could object, she was out of bed and picking up clothes from the floor. "Go on," she said, making a shooing motion, "Get out to the barn, I got a lot to do, my son has come home!"

The cow had not been milked for some time, and filling a small pail with milk was no problem and soon Aaron walked back into the kitchen.

His Maw had her apron on and already a fire was going and pots were on the stove.

"Don't have a lot," she said, "But it will be warm and good."

"Yes'm," said Aaron as he sat down at the kitchen table and watched in wonder as his Maw bustled around. Soon, as she had promised, a hearty meal was on the table. There was no meat, Aaron noticed, but plenty of vegetables and the ever present corn bread.

As they ate, Aaron shared with his Maw his and Mary Lee's plans to get married.

"Well, they's mostly Mary Lee and her mother's plans," he said, "But anyway, we're gonna wait to get married next June, if the war is over."

"And if it is not?"

"Its already over for me, Maw, I ain't goin' on any more raids."

She reached out and placed her hand on top of his.

"Just as soon as the Lemley's can go back to Sedalia, I thought I would go with them, and then come and get you," he said.

"What about the farm?" she asked.

"Maybe its time we left it behind," Aaron said, "Paw's dead and nothin' will bring him back."

Aaron spent three days at home, fixing up what he could. He cleaned out the barn and the root cellar, which smelled horrible of fermented potatoes.

When he got ready to leave, his Maw packed his saddlebags with food he was certain she needed.

"I'll be back soon," he said as he swung into the saddle, "And everything will be as good as new."

*   *   *

As he rode down the road to head back to Arkansas, he turned in his saddle. His Maw was standing on the front porch, waving her handkerchief.

Again, he retraced his trail and traveling at night, soon left Fredericktown behind him. He thought about the Sergeant and wondered if he was still stationed there. Perhaps he had been killed. Maybe one of those Sam shot from long distance had been the Sergeant.

Aaron smiled as he realized it wasn't important anymore.

Crossing the St. Francis, he felt he could relax his alertness some but the smell of wood smoke reached his nose and he became cautious again.

The fire was to the south of him, maybe not more than fifty yards, hidden in the trees and brush.

Dismounting, he pulled his pistol and circled the camp, being careful to place each step so as to not snap a twig or have a rock slip out from underneath his foot.

He counted nine men around the campfire.

He stepped out into the open.

"You boys gittin' a little careless, ain't you?" he asked.

Nine pistols were pointed at him at once.

"Aaron!" said Sam, "You trying to git yourself shot?"

"Didn't figure you could hit anything this close," said Aaron. "Been on a raid?"

"Shore have," said Sam, "And sent several Dutchmen on a long journey."

Everybody laughed but Aaron. He knew most of the men, except for a couple of new ones who didn't look to be over sixteen.

"We was jist gittin' ready to ride on home," Sam said, "Your welcome to jin us."

"Sure," said Aaron, "Been to see my Maw again."

Sam nodded and thought of how long it had been since he had seen his mother.

Aaron knew that Sam must have heard about his new found religion, but it was not mentioned.

They had only ridden maybe fifteen miles when again the air was rank with wood smoke, a lot of wood smoke.

"Brush fire?" asked Aaron.

"Don't think so," said Sam, "Pull up and listen for a spell."

The muffled sounds of voices drifted on the upwind breeze.

"We better take it easy," said Sam, "Let's skirt to the left and come in from the other side."

They soon hit a little creek and followed its gully around the source of the smoke and voices. Coming out of the creek, they were amazed to see a number of brush huts, crudely build from fallen limbs. Several small fires still smouldered in front of them, but not a soul was to be seen.

Sam and Aaron dismounted and crept closer to the strange camp.

There was a muffled sound from one of the huts and Sam threw aside the cloth that covered the entrance.

"Sam!"

"Margaret!"

Margaret crawled out of the hut, the baby tucked under one arm, and threw her other arm around Sam.

Other women began to emerge from their hiding places.

Margaret, like her husband, rarely showed emotion, but now she was sobbing uncontrollably.

Eventually, she recovered enough to tell the story. A group of Federal soldiers, under the command of a Captain John from Ironton, had descended on the Crowley Ridge community, burned all the cabins, and killed the eight men who were in camp and two as they returned from a raid.

After the soldiers left, the women had divided up and gone off in different directions to warn incoming patrols that the Feds were in the area.

"They killed all the men in camp!" Aaron screamed, "Was Bill Lemley there?"

"Yes, bless his soul, they took them out and shot them all,"

said Margaret, but before she had finished speaking, Aaron was in the saddle and riding toward Crowley's Ridge.

             *   *   *

Riding across the flat land south of the Arkansas border, he could see dark whiffs of smoke rising from the hazy blue outline of Crowley's Ridge.

His horse was covered with foam when he rode into camp and his worst fears were confirmed. Every cabin had been torched. The Lemley cabin was still smouldering.

A madness of fear overtook him. He dismounted and looked at the ruins in agony. He ran a few feet in one direction, and then turned and ran the opposite way.

There was no sign of life. Even the corrals were burned and the horses gone.

Finally, for lack of anything else he could do, he went up the trail to his shack.

It was still standing. Either it had seemed to be of no value or hidden away in the woods, it had been overlooked by the marauders.

As he approached the shack he heard a muffled sound and drew his Leech and Rigdon. The wooden hasp on the inside of the door was obviously closed so he knew someone had to be inside.

He kicked the door open and leaped to one side, peering into the darkness until his eyes adjusted.

Finally, in the far corner, he saw two crouching figures. He stepped into the frame of the doorway, his pistol ready to fire.

"Aaron!"

It was Mary Lee and Anna!

Mary Lee crawled to his waiting arms, her small body racked with convulsions. Anna also came and wrapped her arms around both of them. They just knelt there for a while.

Finally able to speak between sobs, Mary Lee told Aaron what had happened.

"It was so sudden," she said, "We had no time to run. They rode in shouting and shooting. Three Federal soldiers came to our door and walked in and grabbed Poppa and took him out."

"Where did they take him?"

"They gathered up all the men in camp and went over the ridge, toward the blackberry patch."

"How many were there?"

"I don't know, but we heard a lot of yelling and saw soldiers sitting fire to the cabins. An officer and two men rode up to our cabin and told us to take what we could carry of our belongings out before they set it on fire."

She began to cry again so hard she could not talk. Aaron held her close.

"Then…," Mary Lee couldn't finish.

"Then," said Anna, "We heard shots from the direction of the blackberry ravine."

"You stay here," said Aaron, "Sam and some of his men are on their way, you are safe now."

He headed up the ridge toward the blackberry vines.

Nothing stirred as he approached the edge of the ravine. On the upper edge, bodies were strewn about. Aaron was appalled at the various positions the men had died in. Arms and legs were twisted in unnatural directions. Blank eyes stared heavenward on several, and one man's face had been blown away.

Flies swarmed on the blood of the dead men, and already there was a smell of death.

He counted seven bodies. He began to examine each carefully, but none of them was Bill Lemley, unless of course he was the man with no face.

Then he heard a groan!

From the depth of the ravine! Aaron scampered over the side and into the edge of the thorny bushes. In a moment he found the source of the groans. It was Bill.

There was a gash across his forehead and he had been bleeding from small abrasions caused by the fall into the ravine and the berry vines.

But he was alive!

Mary Lee and Anna came running to meet them and to help Aaron as he tried to support Bill.

Inside the shack, they washed his wounds. The head wound was not deep, but like all head wounds, had bled profusely, making it appear worse than it was.

A horse was heard coming up the trail and Aaron, his gun in hand, stepped outside.

It was Sam.

"Everybody all right here?" he asked.

"No they ain't," said Aaron, "I found Mr. Lemley alive, but over the ridge, down by the blackberry patch, seven men are dead, shot down unarmed, I'd say."

Aaron had seen Sam in a fury before and he expected one now, but it did not come.

"The boys are bringing the ladies and children back, " Sam said, "I rode ahead to see if it was clear. Found two more of our boys dead down by the corrals. Mrs. Lemley and her daughter all right?"

"No they are not," said Aaron, "But they are alive and uninjured."

Sam put his hand on Aaron's shoulder.

"Sam," said Aaron, " I promised Mary Lee, my Maw, and God that I was through with this war, but the next time you ride out, I'm ready to go with you."

Sam nodded and mounted his horse. After riding a few feet, he stopped, put his hand on the rump of his horse, and looked back at Aaron.

"It won't be long," he said, "Soon as we get the ladies and children taken care of, I've been asked to lead the advanced guard for an all out invasion of Missouri, led by old Pap Price. You may get to fight in a regular army yet, boy."

Aaron returned to the shack. Bill Lemley was sitting up now, his head bandaged with a piece of Annas' petticoat.

"Was that Sam Hildebrand out there?" he asked.

"Sure was," said Aaron.

Bill sat in silence for a long time.

"When you see him again," he said, "You tell him I want to be a part of that army he was talkin' about."

CHAPTER 20

Sterling Price had become a Confederate by default. Of course, as a slave-owning tobacco planter, it would have been natural for him to oppose abolitionism, but he had, it fact, tried to keep Missouri from seceding from the Union.

As a former Governor of the state, he had considerable influence, but when Governor Francis Blair and Brigadier General Nathaniel Lyon had ordered the takeover of Camp Jackson in St. Louis, Price offered his sword and services to the Confederacy.

Price was a tall, elegant statue of a man, the very embodiment of Missouri's aristocracy. In battle, he had commanded the state troops at Wilson's Creek and Lexington, but he was to win no more major victories, rather a string of disconcerting defeats in an area of combat most thought would have no outcome on the final settlement of the dispute, namely, the western theater of operations.

After Lexington, there had been Pea Ridge, Iuka, Corinth, and Helena.

And now, he was preparing to begin his greatest campaign, at a time when in his heart he knew the effort to divert Federal troops from the eastern battlefields to the west by an all-out invasion of Missouri would have little or no effect on the final outcome of the war.

But still, it had to be done, for the alternative was to give up and go home to politics and being a country gentleman and as inviting as that seemed, he could not give up the fight that had begun so gallantly.

He was also aware that if the South lost, his future in politics or as a country gentleman were also in jeopardy and in his mind, the plan had already been formulated to go to Mexico.

His plan for Missouri was simple enough, drive from Arkansas directly to St. Louis. Even the threat of Rebels taking St. Louis was supposed to cause the Yankees to slow down their pressure on Lee in the east.

Joe Shelby, his black feather waving from his hat, would command the Iron Brigade in a calvary dash on the left flank. General's Fagan and Marmaduke would march their infantry troops at a rapid pace northward toward St. Louis.

The Bushwhacker Corp, which Price sanctioned with a great deal of apprehension, would be an advanced guard, tearing up communications lines, railroads, bridges, and garnering as much as they could of the precious metal the South needed to make bullets, Missouri lead.

The plan also called for the recruitment of thousands of men into the Rebel army, a desperate hope since most of the men of fighting age were already in the army, had left the state for Idaho and other points west, or were waging their own private war as a Bushwhacker.

There were, however, an abundance of teenage boys and old men.

Price also hoped that every member of the Knights of the Golden Circle would take up arms and fight.

But even the majestic leader with the gray hair and high forehead, mounted on his horse Bucephalus, waving his hat in response to the calls of "Pap! Pap!" from the men of Marmaduke's brigade camped out at Pocahontas, Arkansas, could not transform the rag-tag army into a fighting unit. They were a mixture of lads from thirteen on up, and gray haired grandfather's who would hardly be able to make the march, much less fight. But whitebearded patriots would march beside lads whose cheeks a razor had never touched.

There were some veterans who had never "seen the elephant", for most of the men had never been in combat except for local skirmishes or private feuds.

More than half of them did not have guns, and many of those were old cap and ball pistols, flintlocks, and shot guns.

Their uniforms were a mix of butternut and blue, with a large number of them wearing civilian clothes. Some even had no shoes.

"Pap" Price was tired, but he would not let these men know. He rode up and down the lines, encouraging.

"What's your name, soldier?" he asked of one of the older men.

"Bill Lemley, sir," was the answer.

"Have you fought before?"

"No sir."

"I see you have no weapon, do you have a rifle?"

"No sir, I left my only gun at home for the protection of my wife and daughter."

"How do you expect to fight without a weapon?"

"The sergeant told us that we would be in the second wave in a charge, and would be able to pick up just about any kind of gun we wanted," said Bill.

Price rode on, hoping the men could not see the tears that filled his eyes. It was not going to be easy to send these men into battle.

When Shelby and his veterans joined Price at Pocahontas, he led his brave army across the Missouri state line on September 19, 1864. Marmaduke's brigade, which was in reality closer to regiment strength, counting the unarmed men, fanned out on the right flank while Fagan's troops went up the middle with the supply wagons and a thousand head of beef. Shelby's calvary dashed up and down the country roads on the left.

Sam Hildebrand and his Bushwhackers were already north, mining lead and shipping it in wagons south. Aaron, Cato, and Tom spent most of their time riding the area north of Farmington, planning the destruction of communications, rails and bridges.

Price's destination may have been St. Louis, but one small obstacle stood in the way, a hole in the ground called Fort Davidson, nestled between Shepherd Mountain and Pilot Knob, and the almost nine hundred Federal troops who occupied it.

∗   ∗   ∗

General Thomas Ewing had very mixed emotions as he boarded the train in St. Louis for the return trip to Ironton and his command at Fort Davidson.

He had started for Ohio where his wife was about to deliver a baby. But when General Rosecrans had gotten word that Price was moving into Missouri with 20,000 men, he sent Ewing scampering back to Ironton on the first train out.

Certainly Ewing wanted to be with his wife, but to be in a place of importance during a real battle would be the first for his career, and a victory might offset the damage Order Number 11 had done to his hopeful political career after the war.

He had migrated to Kansas from Ohio in 1856 after graduation from Brown University and set up a law practice in Leavenworth where he fought to keep Kansas from becoming a slave state.

His biggest mistake had been letting Jim Lane help him draw up Order Number 11, which called for the complete removal of pro-confederate families in four counties in western Missouri. Homes were burned in a scorched earth campaign that was not only condemned in the south, but even in the north.

As commander of the District of the Border, he was also responsible for the imprisonment of some of the wives, girlfriends, and families of Quantrill's men in Independence.

When the building they were kept in collapsed and Bill Anderson's sister was killed, Ewing knew his political dreams were going to need some daring deed to shore them up.

Maybe at Pilot Knob redemption would come, he thought as he rode the train south. They stopped at each crossing and posted a guard. As the train sped on to Ironton, he had no way of knowing that Sam Hildebrand and his men were killing the guards, taking up track, and pulling down miles of telegraph wire behind him.

Finally at Fort Davidson he climbed up on the earthen parapet and surveyed the scene. The little town of Ironton was barely visible through his glasses as a dampness hung in the early fall air from the heavy rain that had fallen earlier.

Around the outskirts of the town, a giant living amoeba like animal moved within itself as the ragged Confederate soldiers shuffled to and fro, an ever moving, ever changing, oozing expanse of humanity. Distance and brush prevented him from getting any kind of count on their numbers.

His eight hundred and eighty six Federal troops in the little hole in the ground would be outnumbered, he guessed, twenty to one.

Of course, he had learned that estimates of enemy numbers coming from headquarters in St. Louis were always exaggerated.

General Fagan's rebs had driven Ewing's outpost garrisons back to the one-hundred and fifty six foot long rifle pits that stretched from the north and south walls of the fort.

It seemed obvious the Confederates were preparing for a frontal attack as Ewing surveyed the terrain and wondered why anyone would be stupid enough to build a fort on flat ground between two domineering mountains.

The slope of Shepherd mountain had been shaved of timber for if the rebels managed to get cannon up there, they would be able to lob shells into the fort almost at will.

Twice Price sent officers under a white flag, asking for surrender. Ewing's answer to the first was no, and his answer to the second was that he would fire on any further white flags.

The second flag had been carried by an old friend of Ewing's, Lieut. Colonel Laughlin A. McLean, who returned and reported to Price that there was not time to mount cannon on the mountain. Price decided on a frontal attack.

In the wet dawn, a single Confederate cannon had fired from the slopes of Shepherd Mountain. There were three twenty-pound howitzers, four thirty-two pound siege guns, six two-inch Woodruff field guns, and two three-inch Ordinance Rifles in the fort's armament.

In a few minutes, the Rebel gun on Shepherd was disabled and its crew killed.

The rest of the morning passed without notable incident and at 2:00 p.m., an eerie silence fell over the four hundred acres of the valley floor. It lasted for almost an hour.

Then from the rifle pits came the cry that is heard before all battles: "Here they come!"

         *   *   *

Bill Lemley had not slept all night, and now as the brigades formed, he took his place in the third rank, still without a weapon.

Finally the order was given and the only way to move was forward with the flowing mass of humanity that started across the open field toward the fort.

Rank by rank of frightened, wide eyed, dirty men moved as one in the direction of their destruction.

There was no fire yet, only the almost silent movement of the army over the wet ground, punctuated by the shouts and curses of the officers.

"You ever seed the elephant 'fore?" the man next to Bill asked in a hushed voice.

"What's the elephant?" Bill asked.

"A real battle," the man answered, "I got a feeling we air about to see it now."

"Neither one of us even has a gun," said Bill.

"Don't worry, them boys up front air goin' to be dropping plenty of guns is a few minutes, jist be sure you get the ammunition pouch, too."

Inside Fort Davidson, the Federals waited. Silk bags of powder with attached shells fused for three second bursts were piled by the cannon, along with tin containers packed with half-inch lead balls for close range. Each rifleman was issued a hundred rounds.

Three hundred long distance Springfield and Enfield rifles lay across the top of the parapet, while below, three hundred men waited to reload.

"Hold your fire until the command," Ewing shouted, "Murphy, get those cannon elevations lowered. Bring in those two from the rifle pits."

Colonel Murphy was walking the top of the earthen works, stepping over the rifle barrels as he snapped orders to his gunnery crews.

Now on the open plain in the gap between the mountains, the Confederates wheeled into columns of three rank deep and began to move slowly toward the fort.

Bill was in the third rank, on the left flank. First they were walking, then it was quick step, and then as the officers shouted out orders, the men broke into a run, screaming with raspy dry throats the Rebel yell.

"Hold your fire," yelled Ewing.

The gray, screaming undulating mass moved closer, impelled it seemed to escape a torment that lay somewhere behind them.

They were two hundred and fifty yards from the fort when the order to fire was given. Like wheat before a scythe, the front ranks was riddled with holes as men fell forward or crumpled to the ground.

The crackling of rifles rippled across the valley, cannon spoke their words of death. The second rank closed the holes and they moved forward, despite the carnage.

Bill Lemley finally found a gun and grabbed the ammo bag. He wasn't sure what kind it was or if he would know how to reload, but at least he was finally armed.

He ran with the other men, feeling a strange comfort that he was not alone, that other men who seemed perfectly sane who were running headlong into the mouths of exploding cannons and swarms of bullets.

There was, in an abstract fashion, a strange madness in the madness.

Inside the fort, a cannon was double cannistered and fired, destroying the gun and killing the crew. At another gun, a swabber forgot to wet the bore and a loader with a bag of powder had his head blown off.

Bill continued to run toward the fort, reaching the abandoned rifle pits along with a swarm of Confederates. Federals raised up over the parapet and fired point blank over the sides of the fort.

Finally Bill raised his rifle to fire just as a Federal looked over the mound of dirt. Both raised their rifles at the same time, and both almost immediately lowered them.

It was Bill's brother!

The man in blue stood up and looked directly into Bill's eyes for a moment, then several rebel bullets slammed into him and he disappeared into the fort.

For a strange moment, Bill Lemley stood transfixed by the scene. Then he turned and started walking back toward Ironton as he dropped the rifle. Bullets whizzed by him but by a miracle, he was not hit.

He was joined by a officer who was cursing.

"Shot my best horse, right in front of the moat," he said, "But don't worry, we'll take them tomorrow, we'll wipe them out in the morning, as sure as my name is William L. Cabell."

Bill looked at the officer.

"I will not be here in the morning," he said softly, "The war is over for me. I'm going to take my family home."

                  ✶   ✶   ✶

Hundreds of Confederate campfires sparkled across the valley as darkness came. A glow from a pile of charcoal at the base of Pilot Knob, ignited by the shelling, illuminated Fort Davidson in a dim glow.

Inside the tiny earthen works, Ewing and his officers met to determine their next move.

Outside the fort, over a thousand Confederate soldiers lay dead. The Federals had killed more of the enemy than there were troops in the fort.

But Ewing knew another attack could not be withstood. He had received no messages from St. Louis and assumed the lines were down. He could only guess that A. J. Smith's infantry had arrived up the Mississippi, and his continued trip to Virginia had been delayed to protect St. Louis.

"We have done our task," Ewing told his officers, "Price will not surely advance toward St. Louis tomorrow. We must evacuate the fort and save our men."

"Evacuate!" shouted Murphy, "Evacuate? Have you looked over the parapet? Camp fires are fanned out in every direction! We are surrounded."

Ewing ignored him. "We will cover the drawbridge with blankets, burlap sacks, or whatever you can find to deaden the sound of the horses hooves. Spike the cannons that are still usable."

"And then?" an officer asked.

"We will simply ride out through the Confederate camps. They will, hopefully, assume we are one of their units, moving to a new position for morning."

"And if they don't?"

Ewing breathed a sigh. "Gentlemen, we have several choices. We can surrender to the mercy of the Rebels, we can stay here and all be killed, or we can and will ride right through their lines to safety."

"And your orders?" asked Murphy.

"You just heard them," Ewing said, "Prepare to ride."

The officers broke from the circle and began to make preparations for the exodus.

"Murphy," said Ewing, "Do you have a man who is experienced in handling explosives, I mean other than ramming them down a cannon's mouth?"

"Yes, I do," said Murphy, "Sergeant H. B. Milks."

"Good. Tell him to take a detail of twenty-two men and to set a slow, long fuse to the ammunition and powder storage pit, something that will give him time to escape after he lights it."

Murphy saluted and was gone.

It was well after midnight when the preparations were completed. In columns of two, the troops crossed the draw bridge and rode into the darkness.

Riding painfully slow so as not to draw attention they moved north. The first three hundred yards were simple, but then they found themselves riding to within fifty yards of the encamped rebels and they could see the men moving around their campfires.

Sentries leaned on their rifles, but there was on alarm, no outcry. Ewing had been right, they thought they were Confederates, simply moving to a new position.

Once they had broken through the ring of campfires, they picked up the pace and headed down the Caledonia road.

Back at Fort Davidson, Sergeant Milks and his detail had broken open kegs of black powder and ran a stream of it out of the pit and over the drawbridge.

They had searched the fort for stragglers, and kicked several awake and told them to leave as best they could. Not wanting the Federal dead to fall into the Confederates hands, they stacked the bodies of the fallen next to the ammo pit.

When all was ready, Milks and his men waited on the draw bridge as he sent Sergeant W. H. Moore back to check the makeshift fuse.

Milks was getting nervous when it took Moore longer than it should.

Moore walked slowly out of the pit and mounted his horse.

"No need for fire out here," he said, "There is plenty back there."

He had accidentally set the powder on fire and flames shot from the entrance to the pit. Milk and his men spurred their horses and were only about even with the ends of rifle pits when the fort exploded.

Sometime after three in the morning, the center of the valley exploded. Flames and debris rose three hundred feet into the air, every window in Ironton was shattered, as was the sleep of the few Rebels who had been able to achieve that blessed state.

Price was outside his quarters in a moment, along with his officers, who had been planning the battle for morning.

"They have blown themselves up!" said Fagan.

Price watched the sky, which was still being assailed with exploding shells and powder. Kegs of powder rose into the air and then exploded.

"You are wrong, sir," said Price, They have escaped. Get Shelby and tell him to ride north to cut them off, and do it tonight!"

But somehow he knew inside he would not catch Ewing and that the delay had canceled any hope of a drive on St. Louis. He could not see the next few weeks as his troops would drive westward, the meaningless little skirmishes where men died uselessly, or the final defeat at Westport. He could not see the inquiry that would be held concerning his actions at Pilot Knob.

But he could see what he had felt from the very outset of the campaign. It was the beginning of the end for the South.

And at the Bloom farm, Alma had spent most of the day in the root cellar, cringing in fear as the caissons rolled up and down the road. Now in the darkness of the morning, the deafening blast drew her outside and the explosions in the sky drove her to her knees. She could only hope that her son was not down there in the valley.

CHAPTER 21

Sam sat on his horse, one leg draped around the saddle horn, talking to a lady in the small community of Cadet. He had been on a scouting trip alone, leaving the boys camped out on the bluffs near Hildebrand cave on Big River.

His promise to them that they would get to fight in a "real" army had not panned out. They had spent two weeks mining lead and more time loading it on wagons and sending it south.

Outside of that, the only thing they had done to contribute to Price's invasion was tear up railroads, cut down telegraph wires, and burn bridges. All that seemed more like work to his "boys" than fighting a war.

Price's grand invasion seemed to be sort of a failure, anyway, from what Sam could learn about the battle of Pilot Knob, so he gave the boys some days off to relax.

As he talked to the lady in Cadet, inquiring as to Federal troop movements in the area, he looked over his shoulder and realized a column of Yankees had already ridden to within a few yards of him!

He continued to carry on the conversation with the lady as though nothing was wrong, but when he noticed several of the soldiers looking at him suspiciously, he knew he had to do something.

Fortunately he was dressed in civilian clothes and still talking to the lady over his shoulder, joined the column of Federals on the road.

He tipped his hat to a Lieutenant.

"Howdy, Captain," he said, "You headed to drive them Rebels out of Big River Mills?"

The Lieutenant did not correct Sam's "mistake" about his rank.

"That's right," he said, looking Sam over good.

"I'd sure be obliged to ride with you," said Sam, "If'n you don't mind."

"We do not need men who are not drilled," The Lieutenant said curtly.

About that time, Sam's horse went lame, limping on the right front leg.

"Guess she picked up a stone," he said to one of the soldiers as the column passed him.

As soon as the Federals turned the corner and were out of sight, Sam spurred his mare off into the woods and headed toward his camp at Big River.

Aaron sat at the campfire with one of the new recruits.

"How old are you?" he asked the boy.

"Seventeen," the lad replied.

"You look more like thirteen," Aaron said, "You got a weapon?"

The boy held up an old US model from 1841. It had been converted to use caps instead of a flash pan.

"You ever fired it?" Aaron asked.

"No sir," the boy said.

"Why not?"

"Mostly 'cause ah don't know how to load it," the boy said.

Aaron took the gun from him. "I'm gonna show you jist one time," he said, "So watch and listen close."

"Yessir," said the boy.

"Don't call me sir!"

"Yessir."

Aaron looked at him with disgust. He reached into the boy's cartridge bag and took out a packet.

"Stand the gun between your legs like this," he said, "With the muzzle in your left hand. You got that?"

"Yessir."

Aaron started to say something but decided to let it go.

"Take the cartridge, that's this paper wrapped bullet and powder, and put the powder end between your teeth. You got that?"

"Yessir, " the boy said, "But don't that powder taste awful?"

Aaron breathed a sigh. "Put the cartridge to the muzzle, and pour the powder in, and put the bullet on top of it."

He started to ask if the boy understood but went on with the instructions instead.

"This here thing attached to your gun is called a ramrod, pull if off like this, see?" The boy nodded. "Put it in the barrel like this, and ram the bullet up against the powder. It's a good idea to be sure the bullet is facing the right way."

Aaron had to think what was next. "Then you bring the rifle up to waist level, reach into your cap pocket, and place a cap on the nipple, like this." He handed the gun to the lad. "Your weapon is now ready to fire, and if the cap is not defective, the nipple ain't clogged, or your hammer spring ain't weak, it just might fire."

"Thanks," said the boy as Aaron started to walk away.

"Oh sir," the boy said, "What do I do with this?"

Aaron turned and the boy was holding the ramrod in his hand.

About that time Sam rode into camp in a hurry.

"Saddle up, boys," he said, "A Yankee column is headed this way and we better skedaddle. Head toward Farmington and it might be best if we spread out some. You all know where to meet if we get split up."

Riding through the rolling country side, about six miles north of Farmington, they found themselves facing a steep, short ridge that seemed to come up out of nowhere. A small stream worked its way around the base of the ridge.

All at once, white puffs of smoke, followed by the sound of rifles cracking, came from the top of the ridge.

"Split up and go around both ends of the ridge," Sam said, "They ain't many of 'em! Aaron, take the boy to the left, Tom and Cato, ride to the right. I'm gonna find a way up the middle."

His instructions were followed without question. Aaron rode up to the base of the ridge to escape fire from above and began to follow the stream.

He checked to be sure the boy was following him and noted that the ramrod had gotten back where it belonged.

Looking up at the ridge, he could see a couple of holes in the wall, probably old Indian caves.

"Come on, boy," he said, "Don't lag behind."

Aaron could hear rifle fire ahead and assumed that Tom and Cato or Sam, had made contact with the enemy.

He slowed his mount to a cautious walk as he cleared the end of the ridge and entered the wooded flat land.

Coming up over a small mound, he caught a flash of blue in the corner of his eye, wheeled to the left, dismounted and took cover behind a log.

The boy was nowhere in sight.

Peeking over the barrier, he saw a Union soldier propped up against a tree, wrapping pieces of his torn shirt around the wound in his leg.

Aaron stood up and moved forward. Then he froze.

There was something familiar about that squatty figure, the flat nose, and the dirty beard.

It was the Sergeant!

Aaron lowered his rifle, not believing that the moment he had lived for so long was happening.

Then, as though possessed, the old hatred rose up within him as his chest heaved and every muscle in his body screamed for him to kill the man.

He saw again his Paw laying on the porch and the blood on his white shirt, his Maw crying as the blood ran down her apron.

Aaron aimed at the Sergeant's head, who only stared at the one who was about to kill him.

Then Aaron lowered the rifle.

Tom and Cato came riding up. "Got you a Yankee, did you? Go ahead and finish him off."

Aaron tried to explain but could not find the words just as his delayed companion, the boy, rode up on the scene.

"Kill him!" the boy yelled, "Kill the Yankee."

"No, don't!" cried Aaron as the boy raised his rifle. He threw himself between the boy and the Sergeant.

The bullet he had loaded for the boy struck him in the chest and he fell, almost at the Sergeant's feet.

"Get the gun from the boy!" hollered Tom as he jumped off his horse and ran to Aaron.

Cato got the trembling boy off the horse and seated on a rock.

Sam came up over the ridge, flew off his horse and to Aaron's side.

"What happened?" he screamed at Tom.

"Durndest thing ah ever saw," said the weeping Haile, "It twarn't the boys fault. Aaron jumped right in front of his gun to keep him from shooting the Yankee."

"Why'd he do that?" asked Cato, "Why'd he do that?"

Sam looked at the Yankee Sergeant and remembered the story Aaron had shared around many a camp fire.

"I think I know," he said, as he lifted Aaron's head in his big left hand and looked into his little crippled friends eyes.

"That you, Sam?" Aaron whispered.

"Yeh, its me, boy."

"Will you do me a favor, Sam?"

"Anything you want."

A smile crossed Aaron's paling lips.

"Jist tell Mary Lee I was ready," he said.

His head went limp in Sam's hand. Sam reached up and with his thumb and forefinger, closed Aaron's eyes.

Sam pressed his own face again Aaron's scarred cheek for a long time, then he got up and went to Aaron's horse and got his blanket.

Wrapping the small boy's body, he gently placed it over the saddle of Aaron's horse.

"What we gonna do?" Tom asked.

"I want Cato to take the boy home to his mother, and see that he stays there," said Sam, "Tom, you take the Sergeant into Farmington and see that he gets medical care. He will guarantee your safety, won't you, Sergeant?"

The Sergeant nodded.

"Then what we gonna do?" Cato asked.

"Go home," Sam said, "And I mean go really home. This war is over."

Tom helped the Sergeant up on his horse.

"Why did he save me?" he asked Tom.

Cato and Tom looked at Sam.

"Because love is stronger than hate," said Sam, as he mounted and took Aaron's horse by the reins.

"Where you goin', Sam?" asked Tom.

"I got a job to do up on Shepherd Mountain," he said as he rode away, "And then I think I will go home, too."

EPILOGUE:

Sam Hildebrand could not stop his private war. He continued to make raids into Missouri to avenge wrongs done to him, his family, and his friends. In October of 1864, he rode north to seek and kill the Federal soldiers who had taken the Reverend William Polk from his home and killed him.

On May 26, 1865, Sam was in Jacksonport to receive his parole, ending his career in the Army of the Confederacy, whether it be real or imagined.

But Sam's conflicts did not end with the war, he had made too many enemies and too many widows. A reward was on his head and Pinkerton detectives from St. Louis searched south Missouri for him. He farmed in Arkansas for a while, then moved his family to Sherman, Texas, where Margaret died.

Never able to return to his beautiful and loved Big River bluffs, Sam moved to Illinois.

Sitting in a bar one day, he thought a man recognized him and Sam went to get his gun. A deputy saw him climbing up on a box to shoot the man through the window of the bar, pulled Sam down, and hauled him before the Justice of the Peace where he was fined five dollars and overnight in jail.

On the way to jail, Sam pulled a knife (one of several he had on his person) and cut the deputy's leg from his knee to his thigh. The deputy took a pistol and shot Sam in the head.

Sam was buried in Illinois, but a relative saw a story about the incident in the St. Louis paper and suspected it might be Sam.

The body was exhumed and sent to Farmington, where it was displayed in the court house.

Many filed by to view the remains, but none, friend or foe, would definitely say it was Sam. Historian Henry Thompson, whose wife was a distant relative of Sam, suggested that perhaps his friends knew it was not Sam, and kept quiet so Sam could live in peace, and his enemies also knew it was not Sam, but kept quiet for their own peace.

And so Sam was buried in the cemetery behind the Methodist Church in Elvins,(now Park   Hills.)Missouri in an unmarked grave.

Thompson tried to raise some money for a marker, but found very few givers.

Sam Hildebrand was thirty-six years old when he died. There were over one hundred notches on the stock of Killdevil.

9 780595 138319